Made in Hollywood

in

Made in Hollywood

a Red Carpet Romance
Book Two

MICHELLE KEENER

AMBASSADOR INTERNATIONAL

GREENVILLE, SOUTH CAROLINA & BELFAST, NORTHERN IRELAND

www.ambassador-international.com

Made in Hollywood
A Red Carpet Romance - Book Two

© 2020 by Michelle Keener

ISBN: 978-1-62020-714-7
eISBN: 978-1-62020-738-3

This is a work of fiction. Names, characters, and incidents are all products of the author's imagination or are used for fictional purposes. Any resemblance to actual events or persons, living or dead, is entirely coincidental. Any mentioned brand names, places, and trademarks remain the property of their respective owners, bear no association with the author or the publisher, and are used for fictional purposes only.

Cover Design & Typesetting by Hannah Nichols
Ebook Conversion by Anna Riebe Raats
Edited by Daphne Self

AMBASSADOR INTERNATIONAL
Emerald House
411 University Ridge, Suite B14
Greenville, SC 29601, USA
www.ambassador-international.com

AMBASSADOR BOOKS
The Mount
2 Woodstock Link
Belfast, BT6 8DD, Northern Ireland, UK
www.ambassadormedia.co.uk

The colophon is a trademark of Ambassador, a Christian publishing company.

For Brett

I love you to infinity

Chapter One

NOAH SAT IN THE DRIVER'S seat of the empty limo, too exhausted to open the door. It had been a long, loud, ridiculous night. Rubbing his temples, he tried to silence the dull throb of a headache that lingered there, a remnant of the bachelorette party he had shuttled from nightclub to nightclub, and offered a short prayer of thanksgiving that no one had thrown up in the back of his car. Driving a limo in Hollywood sounded like a glamorous job, but no one ever talked about the cleanup that happened after the wild parties and awards shows. At twenty-eight, he was starting to feel too old for it.

With a sigh, he shoved the car door open, but he didn't get out. A late summer breeze blew through the parking lot. It was the kind of warm, muggy breath that set tempers on edge, a smog coated gust of grime and heat that did little to cool the hot July night. He sat in the dark stillness, waiting for his muscles to find the strength to move. When that strength didn't come, and his muscles claimed they would be perfectly happy to spend the night in the car, he tried bargaining with himself.

If he stood up, he negotiated, he could go home and go to sleep, and at that moment sleep sounded like the most wonderful thing in the world. A warm bed, a soft pillow, and eight hours of blissful oblivion might be enough to drown out the high-pitched giggles and squeals that had echoed from the back of the limo non-stop throughout the night.

Of course, Lily would laugh until she cried if she heard him talking like that. His little sister might be engaged to one of the biggest movie stars on the planet, but she was still the same little sister that teased him endlessly about his hair, his jokes, and his unrequited crush on her best friend. If she found out he was feeling, and acting, like an old man he'd never hear the end of it.

Motivated more by a desire to avoid his sister's wisecracks than by anything else, he climbed out of the limo and stretched in the semi-darkness of the church parking lot. It was never truly dark in Hollywood. Even in the middle of the night, the lights of the Sunset Strip burned in the distance, painting the world with a muted, multicolored haze. He was lucky his dad let him park the limo at the church. There wasn't any space outside their house a few blocks away, and even if there had been, he doubted the car would survive a night out in the open. At least the church had a covered carport and a gate that locked.

Leaning against the cold metal of the car, he looked across the empty parking lot at his dad's church. A single light in a simple iron lantern illuminated the cross that hung above the front door. It seemed so small, a single circle of white light, compared to the endless, alluring glow of Hollywood. Those flashing, blazing neon bulbs never stopped shining, never stopped beckoning the innocent, the dreamers, and the lost towards its bright lights and dark alleys. How could one small church make a difference?

If his mother was still alive, she'd shake her head at his lack of faith. His parents had planted the church and led it side by side until she died, struck down by a cancer that ravaged her body, but not her faith.

Noah had been happy to come on staff and help after her death, but he had kept up his limo business as well. It brought in good money and truthfully, he didn't know if he was ready, or even called, to full-time ministry. Having the limo business meant he always had a reason to say no to ministry, even when *no* felt like the wrong answer. Looking into that single light above the door, he tried to ignore the uncertainty that rose in his heart whenever he thought of his future. He had to make a decision, to choose a path before it was too late. But he hesitated, paralyzed by indecision, and the days kept slipping past.

He turned from the church and bent to clean out the back of the limo. Glitter, shredded bridal magazines, and a lone abandoned shoe littered the plush, carpeted floor. He tried to remember the giddy bride-to-be, but her face had already disappeared from his mind. As he picked up empty bottles and discarded bags, he hoped she and her future husband would be as happy as Lily and Ben. Tossing handfuls of crumpled papers into a trash bag, he refused to acknowledge the jealousy that gripped his heart. There was only one woman he had ever loved and she was across the country, completely oblivious to how he felt. He twisted the plastic bag in his hands as nervous anticipation clenched his stomach. Kate would be out here for Lily's wedding. There was no way she'd miss it. It didn't matter how much she hated Los Angeles, she would be here to celebrate her best friend's wedding.

Noah locked the limo and tossed the trash in the church's dumpster. Three months and he'd see her again. He had three months to pray and plan. Three months to figure out how to say all the things he'd never said. Or three months to talk himself out of it and finally move on. It was one more thing he had to decide, and one more thing he had no idea how to handle.

In the middle of the parking lot, halfway between the church and the limo, he stopped and blew out a long breath. Dropping his head back, he stared up at the stars he couldn't see. The lights of downtown hid them, drowning out their shine, but they were still there.

"God," he whispered, "Tell me what to do. I will follow where You lead."

He didn't need an answer to know God heard him. An answer would have been nice, but he was prepared to wait. He may not know where he was going or what he should do with the rest of his life, but God was real. Just like the stars he couldn't see, God was there. Even in the silence, He was there. He prayed, believing that God had a plan, and that He was in control, even if He hadn't been willing to share that plan with him yet.

Striding up the sloping, concrete ramp that led to what had been a loading dock back when the building had been a plumbing supply company, he looked at the freshly painted walls. Most of the church had been destroyed in a fire that nearly killed Lily and Ben. His sister was still in a wheelchair, but she was making progress in physical therapy. And, like Lily, the church was making progress as well. The interior rebuilding work on the sanctuary and the children's wing was already done. Lily had campaigned hard for expanding their classrooms so they could add another aftercare class for the neighborhood. The inside of the church was brand new, beauty that had risen from the ashes. There was still work to be done on the outside of the building and the landscaping had to be re-planted, but at least the soot was gone and the place didn't smell like smoke anymore.

Ben had brought in so many carpenters, roofers, and construction workers that what should have taken a year to accomplish was done in half that time. His dad called it a miracle. Noah called it a perk of being a highly paid movie star. But as much as he teased Ben, he couldn't have picked a better man for his baby sister.

Reflexively, he checked the glass door on the side of the church, pulling on the handle to make sure it was locked. They hadn't had any problems since the fire, but he had been keeping a close eye on the church just in case. He walked back down the ramp to the rear of the church and pulled on the back door as well. It was locked. Safe and secure.

A blissful fantasy of sleeping in the following day filled his head, and he flipped the keys in his hand, ready to head home when an unexpected screech of tires broke the stillness of the night. He turned and looked through the chain link fence to the neighborhood behind the church, his eyes searching the quiet streets. Gang violence wasn't common in this neighborhood, but it wasn't unheard of either. No cars, no headlights appeared in the distance, but the shrill scrape of metal on pavement echoing behind him told him a car had bottomed out. As he turned back to the church, searching for the source of the noise, a car door opened and slammed shut again. The sound was too close.

He ran through the parking lot, adrenaline pumping in his veins, wild memories of fire and vandalism rushing through his brain. Tires spun, wailing in the night, as the front of the church came into view. Brake lights flashed in the darkness as a black sedan raced through the open gate and disappeared into the Hollywood night. Dreading another attack on the church, his heart thundered as his feet pounded against the pavement. He rounded the corner, heading for the front door, the single light above the cross leading the way, and then he stumbled to a halt.

A woman was lying on the asphalt, her hands reaching for the door, her body frozen in unnatural stillness, the shadow of the church resting on her like a shroud.

Fear gripped his throat, but he forced his feet to carry him forward. She was a young woman, her eyes were closed, and her skin was a sickening, deathly gray. Her feet were bare, her legs streaked with dirt and grime, as if she had been dragged through the street. The black mini-dress that barely covered her was ripped and torn. She looked like a broken doll, discarded and forgotten.

He kept walking toward her even as his mind flipped through every crime show he had ever seen. He needed to call the police. He needed to call his dad. He—

A sound escaped her lips. It was barely a whisper on the wind, a faint moan that rose from the ground and dove straight for his soul.

She was alive.

He ran across the distance and dropped to his knees beside her. As gently as he could, he laid his fingers against her neck and felt for a pulse. It was weak and erratic, but it was there, an answering reply, a cry to be heard.

"Thank You, Lord." As he brushed her hair out of her eyes, anger flared in him, hot and fast. Someone had dumped her here. Shoved her out of the car and left her die to on the steps of the church. Scratches and cuts crisscrossed her hands and face from her fall to the hard asphalt, and a deep gash sliced down her forehead over her left eye.

He pulled his cell phone out of his back pocket and called 911.

She whimpered and his heart broke.

"Hey, it's okay." He bit his lip and cursed his stupid words. It wasn't okay. This would never be okay. "My name is Noah. I am calling an ambulance right now. You are going to be all right. You're not alone."

She opened her eyes a fraction. Deep brown peeked through long black lashes, glazed and confused. As he gave the church's address to the dispatcher, she tried to lift her head.

"Don't move. The ambulance is on the way." Disjointed prayers flew through his mind. He didn't know what he was praying, but he trusted that God understood even if he didn't.

Her hand slid across the pavement. Noah took it and shivered. It was like ice lying in his palm. He stripped off his chauffeur's jacket and laid it over her back, then took her hand again, covering it with his, absorbing the cold.

Her fingers tightened against his. She had more strength left than he thought. Her slurred voice echoed in the night, the words slow and labored. "Please don't leave me."

"I won't. I promise. I'm right here." Noah squeezed her hand, willing his own life into hers, holding on to her as if he could stop death from claiming her. "What's your name?"

Silence. Her hand began to shake and he tightened his hold. "It's okay. You don't have to tell me."

In the distance a siren began to wail. Noah whispered a prayer for them to hurry and started searching the road, hoping with every beat of his heart to see the ambulance appear, knowing they were in a race against time, a race against death itself.

"Hannah."

The word was less than a whisper, barely breathed, a final word released into the night. He looked at her and smiled, knowing she couldn't see it, but doing it anyway. "You're going to get through this,

Hannah. God is here and He loves you." If these were the last words she was going to hear, the last words she would ever hear, he would make them count.

The ambulance rolled into the parking lot, its flashing lights bouncing off the windows and drenching the asphalt in a swath of red. He looked down at Hannah as a single tear slipped down her face.

Chapter Two

NOAH SHIFTED IN THE UNCOMFORTABLE hospital room chair. He had spent the night beside her bed, keeping vigil for the woman who had been abandoned and left to die. He'd been by her side in the emergency room when the doctors pumped her stomach, purging her body of a deadly concoction of drugs, asking her over and over what she took until Noah thought his heart would break. The police had shown up not long after the doctors wheeled Hannah into the emergency room and the officers questioned her until the doctors ushered them out of the room and sedated her to let her body rest as they bandaged her wounds.

He'd spoken to the cops, and given them all the information he had, but he knew from the looks on their faces that it wasn't much to go on. He kicked himself for not thinking to get the license plate number. As the officers and the doctors huddled together, comparing notes and test results, the words *overdose* and *suicide* were whispered behind his back. And though he didn't know her, he felt protective of her, wanting to shield her from the raised eyebrows and the pitying looks of the people who were trying to save her life.

As he sat by her bed, watching the steady rise and fall of her breathing, he tried to imagine what could have driven her to suicide. Her chestnut hair was tangled and matted against the bleached cotton of the pillowcase. There was a deep cut over her left eye from where her head hit the pavement. Molten brown eyes hid beneath the bandages. He remembered them with the clarity of a painting, the way his heart had twisted as she peered up at him from the pavement.

The stark white of the bandage that covered the fresh stitches made her skin look ashen and gray. She seemed so small lying on the hospital bed, buried under a mound of scratchy blankets that smelled like industrial soap. She could have been Lily's age, though he guessed she was a little younger, but she was someone's daughter; surely there was someone who cared about her. The driver of that black sedan had tossed her away like garbage, leaving her to die alone on the steps of their church.

Renewed anger rose in him and he rubbed his eyes. Anger had been a close companion recently. Only a few months ago, he had been in a room just like this one, sitting beside Lily's bed, helpless to do anything but wait and pray. For Lily, the real battle began once she woke up and realized she couldn't move her legs. Noah couldn't help but stare at Hannah and wonder what battles she would face when she opened her eyes again. If she opened them again.

"How's she doing?"

He looked up as his dad walked into the hospital room carrying two paper cups and a bag that he fervently hoped contained some sort of breakfast food. His stomach rumbled as the scent of coffee filled the small room.

His dad smiled, tried lines etched across his face. Noah had called him in the middle of the night from the emergency room and his dad immediately began praying. His dad's gaze drifted from his face to the wounded girl lying unconscious on the bed.

As his dad stepped closer to the bed, Noah marveled again at his strength. Evan Shaw was unshakable. He'd faced gang members, cancer, and Sundays when no one showed up. But he never gave up. He poured his life into the church, he loved the people, and he loved God with everything he had. Noah knew he could never live up to that. His dad would love for him to join the ministry full-time. But how could he accept if he wasn't absolutely sure? If he wasn't certain that God had called him to it? So, he stalled, waiting and praying for some sign, some irrefutable scrap of evidence, something that would point him in the right direction.

"Still the same," Noah replied. "They're waiting for the sedative to wear off to assess the . . . damage."

Nodding, his dad handed him the bag from the hospital cafeteria and a paper cup filled with coffee. Noah gulped it down and grimaced. The hospital's coffee had not improved in the last few months. He peeked into the pastry bag and almost wept with gratitude. Tearing off a piece of the still warm blueberry muffin, he stuffed it in his mouth.

"What did the police say?"

Noah shrugged as he chewed, the word *suicide* turning the muffin to stone in his mouth. "We'll have to wait until she wakes up and can tell them what happened."

Stepping to the bed, his dad lowered his head in prayer. Noah heard the soft words he spoke entrusting this unknown girl into the hands of God.

When he finished he laid his hand on Noah's shoulder. "You should go home and get some rest."

Noah nodded, knowing his dad was right, feeling the weight of the exhaustion that settled on him. "I will." But he made no move to go. Every time he thought of going home he heard her voice drifting through his mind. *Please don't leave me.*

His dad leaned down and hugged him. "Call me if you need anything."

"Thanks, Dad." Draining the last of the awful coffee, he tossed the paper cup into the trashcan. Then he sat back in the chair and resumed his vigil, letting the rhythmic beep of the machines lull him into a fitful sleep.

*****

Sleep smothered her like a thick blanket, covering her with its weight, pressing down, making her body sluggish. She was trapped, buried under a heavy darkness that tugged her back to unconsciousness. It was a blackness that threatened to swallow her, promising to envelop her until she disappeared, gone, lost in a void she would never escape. There was no pain. She didn't feel anything. Numbness wrapped around her, a cocoon of nothingness encircling her, shutting out the world, and she longed to fall once again into the abyss, embracing the emptiness that waited for her.

Muffled whispers and footsteps echoed nearby. A sudden shard of fear broke through the hazy fog, and a shiver of terror raced through her body, shocking her back to the present, to an unforgiving awareness of the life she had tried to leave.

They'd found her.

She tried to open her eyes, forcing her way through the darkness, fighting through the wall of shadows, willing her eyes to cooperate. Her eyelids fluttered and she squinted against the brightness. White light and white walls surrounded her. Her left eye refused to open all the way, and she felt the weight and scratch of something covering it. Her hand was heavy, lethargic, as if the air itself was trying to keep her motionless, as she lifted it to her face. Her fingers brushed against something soft.

"Hey, you're awake."

The deep male voice startled her and she jumped. Sharp pain lanced through her arm and she winced. She glanced down at a needle disappearing beneath the skin of her arm with thick white tape holding it in place. She followed the line of a clear tube that wound its way from her arm to an IV stand, hypnotized by the slow drip of a clear liquid that was seeping into her veins. Machines hummed and beeped, flashing digital numbers rose and fell on the monitor by her head and she didn't understand any of it. Her heart raced and nausea twisted in her gut as confusion, fear, and disorientation assaulted her.

"It's all right . You're in the hospital. They're taking care of you, Hannah."

The voice was soothing, an island of calm in the midst of a raging storm. How did he know her name? She hadn't heard that name in over five years. No one called her Hannah — not anymore. That name belonged to a girl who didn't exist, a girl who had disappeared on the streets of Hollywood, a girl everyone had forgotten. A girl she had forgotten.

Moving her head carefully, fearing every movement would bring a fresh wave of pain, she turned to find the source of the voice. A man was standing by her bed, a weary smile on his face. His blue eyes were red-rimmed and dry, alert as he studied her, his gaze sweeping over her before returning to meet her stare. His dark blond hair was a mess and his clothes were wrinkled. Blood stains peeked through the rolled-up sleeves of his white dress shirt. The first two buttons were undone and the collar was askew, as if he'd been sleeping in his clothes and had just woken up. She blinked again, trying to figure out where she knew him from, trying to pick out his face from the jumble of memories that swam in a fog of nonsense through her mind.

"I'm going to get the nurse. I'll be right back." He was reassuring and gentle, like he was talking to a wounded animal, and she supposed that was what she was.

Instinctively, she reached for him and he took her hand. Memories tugged at the edge of her mind, dark and full of despair. And she knew.

She never should have woken up.

Chapter Three

NOAH STOOD IN THE HALLWAY while the doctor checked on Hannah. As soon as he told the nurse that she was awake, a doctor had appeared and swiftly kicked him out of the room. His head ached from too much caffeine and too little sleep, and his body was stiff and sore from trying to sleep in the hard chair beside her bed. Crossing his arms, he leaned against the cool wall, thankful it was there to keep him upright, knowing without a doubt he would have collapsed without it. He should go home. There was nothing left for him to do here.

And yet he stayed.

"Long night?"

Lily pushed her wheelchair to a stop next to him. He bent down to hug her, the sight of her sitting in the chair bringing a familiar stab of sadness that he had learned to keep from showing on his face. Why her? Why did she have to suffer because of another person's twisted ambition and rage? But Lily smiled, heedless of the emotions that churned inside him, and hugged him back, reaching up from the chair like it was old habit.

"Too long," he said as he straightened up again, feeling the truth in the words as surely as he felt the kink in his neck. "What are you doing here, Brat?"

"Dad brought me in for physical therapy." Lily lifted the edge of the blanket that was draped over her legs and wiggled her toes in her flip-flops. "Not bad, huh?"

Any progress was good and he knew he should be grateful, but he was exhausted and frustrated and he wanted his sister to have her legs back. Still, he watched the tiny movements of her pink painted toes and smiled with as much encouragement as he could muster. "Not bad at all. Where's Ben?"

"At the studio. They're doing a read through for his next film. *Beyond Time.*" She said the title dramatically, drawing it out like a voiceover in a movie trailer.

Noah furrowed his brow, certain they had told him about the movie, but unable to place it. Between the construction at the church, the film, and the endless wedding plans who could keep track of it all?

"Another action flick? Spies and battles and things blowing up?"

"Not this time. It's a love story."

Rolling his eyes, he tried to imagine Ben Prescott, star of fast-paced thrillers and action movies in a sappy chick flick. Clearly, he needed to mock his future brother-in-law for the new direction his career was taking.

He snickered. "Falling in love with you has made him soft."

Lily punched his arm, a little harder than necessary. "You're soft."

The door to Hannah's room opened and a white-coated doctor stepped out. Springing off the wall, Noah met the doctor before he could disappear down the long hallway. "How is she doing, Doc?"

The doctor took off his silver-rimmed glasses, his eyes assessing them as they waited. "Are you family?"

Noah fidgeted under his gaze, unwilling to lie, but equally unwilling to give up. He couldn't leave until he knew she would be all right, until he knew the worst was over.

"I'm the one who found her." The doctor pursed his lips, effectively silencing himself, but Noah was too tired to be patient. "Please, Doctor, I've been here all night. I just want to know if she'll be okay."

Lily slipped her hand into his as they faced the doctor and the clipboard he held against his chest like a closely guarded secret. The doctor wiped his balding head, the thin wisps of white hair that framed his head flattening under his hand, and looked at them, indecision dancing in his eyes. "She'll recover. She needs to stay here for another day, her body is still in shock from the drugs in her system and we'll need to monitor the concussion. The facial injury is deep, but it shows no sign of infection. She'll have a scar, but if all goes well, she should be able to leave tomorrow." The doctor paused, his fingers drumming against the back of the clipboard. "Do you know if she has somewhere to go?"

Noah shook his head, his brief burst of energy evaporating like the morning mist. "I don't know anything about her."

Excusing himself, the doctor walked away. Noah leaned against the wall again, his body worn out, his mind troubled. He had done everything he could. He wasn't family. He wasn't a social worker. He should go home. Go home and leave Hannah in the hands of the doctors and nurses who could help her. Now that she was awake would she even want him there? A man she'd never met. She didn't even know his name.

He squeezed his eyes shut, blocking out the harsh fluorescent light. Standing in the empty hallway, he debated what he should do next. The soft squeak of Lily's wheelchair echoed in the long corridor, and he opened his eyes in time to see the back of the chair disappear behind the door to Hannah's room.

Apparently, Lily was done waiting.

*****

As soon as the doctor left, Hannah forced herself to crawl out of the bed. She couldn't stay here. She had to run. She had to disappear. If Lincoln found her, he'd never let her go. And she wouldn't go back with him. Ever.

The floor was cold beneath her toes, and when she stood the room tilted wildly, like a merry-go-round that had been sent spinning into motion. Clutching the IV pole, she waited for the dizziness to pass, breathing deeply to keep the queasiness in her stomach from overwhelming her. It felt as though she was moving through water. The air around her was thick and heavy and her limbs felt like lead. She focused on the floor, the simple tile pattern that separated her from the freedom on the other side of the door. Her hospital gown fluttered, and tears filled her eyes as she saw the bruises and bandages that covered her legs. What had Lincoln done to her?

Panic pursued her. Sweat beaded on her forehead as she struggled to walk. She had to find her clothes. She had to get out of here.

"Going somewhere?"

She turned too quickly towards the voice and dizziness washed over her like a tidal wave. Falling backward, her legs hit the side rails of the bed and she grabbed the metal bars to keep from falling. The needle in her arm jerked and she bit her lip, silencing the cry of pain that leapt to her mouth.

"Let me help you." A young woman in a wheelchair rolled to her side. Her hands were warm and light as she guided Hannah back into bed. "It might be too soon to be planning an escape."

Though her voice was light, Hannah's heart raced and the blood drained from her face at the woman's words. Had Lincoln sent her? Did he know where she was? Don't trust anyone. It was a lesson she learned a long time ago.

The young woman must have seen her terror because her face softened. She settled her wheelchair next to the bed and smoothed a blanket over her, being careful not to hit the IV needle, tucking her in with a mother's gentleness.

"You're going to be all right, Hannah. You just need some time to rest and heal."

She didn't respond. The blank, white walls were closing in on her, trapping her in this tiny room, surrounded by machines and faces she didn't know.

"My name is Lily." The woman rested her hand on her arm. Hannah looked at her and in her eyes she saw something she hadn't seen in a long time. It called to her like a song long forgotten, a picture that shimmered at the edge of her memory, beyond the darkness and shame of the past few years, before she had come to Hollywood, a whisper of a time before she knew what real pain was. "My brother Noah found you and called the ambulance. It was a miracle he was there."

A miracle. Her throat tightened and she looked away. That was what she saw in those eyes. Faith. Hope. All the things she lost when she left home and headed for Hollywood.

"Found me where?" The cracked words scratched her throat, itching and burning past the raw skin as she whispered. Scattered images of the emergency room flashed through her mind. Doctors and nurses leaning over her, questions coming at her from every side, the stomach pump being forced down her throat. They were all so desperate to keep her alive, even when she told them to let her die.

"He found you at the Hollywood Mission. My dad is the pastor there. It was late, but Noah happened to be there when you . . . when . . . " Her words trailed off, but Hannah knew what it meant. When Lincoln found her in the backstage dressing room at Norma Jean's he wouldn't have bothered to call an ambulance, and he definitely wouldn't have called the cops. He just made sure he got rid of her body.

The calculated coldness of it should have hurt her. She didn't know what she had expected, but after all the years they had been together knowing that he had tossed her away should have been a betrayal. It should have devastated her. But it didn't. Not now. Not after she found out what he really was, what he was doing. She would have done anything to escape him.

Lily left the rest of the details unsaid. "Our family has been praying for you all night."

Hannah would have laughed if she hadn't been fighting tears. What would her father say if he knew she had been abandoned at a church and a family of strangers was praying for her? That after everything she had run from, everything she said she didn't believe in, she ended up in the middle of a family of Christians?

"Is there someone we can call for you? Someone who can take care of you?" Lily's smile was so kind, so sincere that she wanted to scream.

It wasn't comforting, it was condemning. She was everything Hannah could never be. Lily used words like *prayer* and *miracle* like they were true, like they were available to her, and it battered against her soul, a howling, bellowing reminder of the life she had thrown away. She couldn't bear it.

Hannah swallowed her tears and shook her head. She had nowhere to go. She couldn't go back to Lincoln and the life he forced on her. She wouldn't go back. She would rather die.

She had tried to die.

Memories of that night sprang to her thoughts. Was it last night? A week ago? She had no idea. But it was so clear. There hadn't been any other way out, not that she could see. Scouring the dressing room at Norma Jean's, she'd raided the other girls' purses, collecting pills until she thought she had enough. Clutching the fistful of colorful drugs, she had no idea what she was taking, she only hoped it would do the job.

A tear slipped down her cheek and she wiped it away, not caring about the pain it caused. She had failed at that, too.

Lily rested her hand on hers. "It's going to be okay."

Hannah recoiled before she could stop herself, pulling her hand away, burying it beneath the blanket that covered her broken body.

If Lily was offended, she didn't show it. She didn't yell or leave. She simply sat by her bed. "You're not alone in this, Hannah."

But she was. Hannah swiped at the tears that coursed down her face, furious with her own weakness. She was alone. She had nowhere to go and no one who cared. And it was all her fault.

Chapter Four

NOAH SAT ON THE FLOOR, his back resting against the soft cream sofa. He knew he should go to bed. He'd probably already be asleep on the couch if Lily and Ben hadn't taken up all the cushions and demoted him to the floor. He looked at the small loveseat across the room, but it was too far away and he was too tired to move.

Ben sat on one end of the sofa with Lily's feet in his lap. Noah watched as the man who was about to become his brother tenderly massaged her feet and calves, keeping the blood flow strong and healthy. Lily looked up at Ben and smiled, her face filled with love and Noah's heart constricted. When he thought of what could have happened, how close she had come to dying in that fire, he was too grateful to stay angry about the paralysis. The physical therapy seemed to be helping. She wasn't walking yet, but she was regaining more and more movement in her feet and legs. He held on to the hope that one day she would walk again. But even if she didn't, he knew Ben would make her happy. The same man who had pulled her from the fire would protect her and cherish her and love her every day of her life.

He couldn't ask for more than that. So, he would put up with their romantic displays and mushy sentiment and keep his petty jealousy to himself.

"What about pink?" Lily asked, turning the bridal magazine around so her fiancé could see it.

Ben leaned forward and looked at the bridesmaid dress she was showing him. Then he scrunched his nose in masculine distaste. "That's very pink."

Lily huffed in exasperation. "You know, we've got only three months to get this wedding planned. We don't have time to be picky."

"I'm not worried," Ben said and wiggled her toes, grinning when she managed to use her big toe to nudge his hand.

"Well, I'm worried," she said. She pointed to the spiral notebook that was by her side and jabbed at the long list of things left to do before the wedding, a list that seemed to grow every day. "Noah, what do you think?" She shoved the magazine and the pink dress in his face.

He didn't know anything about bridesmaid dresses, but he knew his sister's maid of honor. "Yuck." He shook his head at the bright pink picture floating in his vision. "Kate would kill you."

Lily frowned, then tilted her head as if trying to picture her best friend in the slim, pink dress. "You're right. She'd hate it. And then she'd hate me."

Ben took the end of the fuzzy blanket and covered her feet. "It will be nice to see her again, especially now that she doesn't have a plan to sue me or beat me to a bloody pulp."

"Or beat you to a bloody pulp and then sue you," Lily teased, her eyes already back on the magazine. "You never know."

Ben laughed, but the concern in his eyes was real. Noah didn't blame him. Kate was a spitfire even on her best day. "When does she arrive?"

Lily sighed and stared at the ceiling and he knew what that meant. Kate was being Kate. Stubborn, obstinate, set in her ways Kate. "She won't be here until the week before the wedding. She says she's too busy to get any more time off than that."

Noah stayed silent, his gaze focused on the fireplace and his thoughts far away in Boston. He had plenty to say about his sister's best friend, but he kept those thoughts to himself. Unfortunately, his silence was enough to get Lily's attention. She gave him a sympathetic smile that he tried to ignore. It was bad enough that Lily knew about his feelings for Kate. It was worse that they both knew Kate didn't feel the same way.

He was saved from having to talk about his hopeless love life when his dad walked in, fresh from after-dinner kitchen clean up duty.

"More wedding talk?" He asked as he sat in his favorite recliner and popped up the footrest.

Lily nodded. She dropped the magazine and picked up the notebook, staring grimly at her to-do list. "Who knew planning a wedding would be so complicated?"

Ben tugged the notebook out of her hands and scanned the lengthy, but neatly organized and color-coded list. "Everything is going to be fine. And you know, we could have this all done in less than a week if you let me hire the studio's event planner."

"Absolutely not." Lily crossed her arms, her lips set in a mutinous line, defiance sparking in her eyes. "I'll plan my own wedding, thank you very much. It's the only one I'm going to get."

Ben smiled and kissed her hand. "That's right because I'm never letting you go."

Rolling his eyes so hard they could have leapt from his face and danced across the floor, Noah groaned, then winced when his sister hit him on the head with the bridal magazine.

"You're just tired and grumpy," she declared.

Rubbing his head, he scowled at her. "Sitting up all night in a hospital will do that to a person."

The mood in the room sobered, like a rain cloud obscuring the sun. Ben kept Lily's hand in his, running his thumb along her knuckles. Noah could feel the memories winging though Ben's mind. The movie star had spent weeks in that same hospital waiting for news about Lily. Praying for the best and fearing the worst.

"How's the girl doing?" Ben asked.

Lily squeezed his hand as she filled him in. "She'll recover from the overdose and the doctor said she'll probably have a scar from the cut on her face. She's got a lot of bumps and bruises and a nasty concussion, but all the physical injuries will heal. It's the emotional side that I'm worried about. She acts tough, but she's very scared and very alone."

Standing abruptly, Noah paced to the fireplace. Resting his hands on the mantel he tried to forget the image of Hannah lying on the ground, her life ebbing away. If he hadn't been there that night she would have died. If he had arrived ten minutes later, or if he had left ten minutes earlier, she would be dead. A million little things could have gone differently, and she would have wound up dead on the doorstep of their church, a nameless statistic for the evening news. God's timing was perfect; he believed that, but he couldn't pretend he understood the reasons behind that timing.

"And you said she doesn't have any family out here?" His dad leaned forward, his arms resting on his knees. "No one who can take care of her?"

Lily shook her head. "No one that she was willing to mention. When I went into her room this afternoon she was ready to run."

Sitting back, his dad closed his eyes. Noah watched him, knowing he was praying. His dad had a special relationship with God. He heard God's leading in a way Noah never did, and he envied the peace and the certainty his dad had. In the face of his mother's cancer, his dad had never doubted. He had prayed for healing, prayed without ceasing, but even when his mom died, he never lost his faith. Evan Shaw was a man of God. Noah was just a man.

His dad nodded and opened his eyes. "We should invite her to stay here."

Three stunned faces turned to him.

Noah spoke first. "Are you sure that's a good idea?"

Ben followed. "What do you know about her?"

"That's a great idea." Noah and Ben stared at Lily's quick agreement, but she smiled as if they were discussing whether to have tacos or spaghetti for dinner the next night and not inviting a stranger they knew nothing about to move in with them.

"Well there you go," his dad said cheerfully. "You can't argue with the bride."

Noah rubbed his hands over his tired eyes, wishing he'd gone straight to bed. "I'm not sure this is a smart thing to do, Dad. We don't know what kind of trouble she might be in. We don't even know her last name."

"God knows who she is. And He brought her to our church for a reason." His dad was thoughtful and calm as he spoke, everything Noah wasn't.

Unease settled in his gut, a nervousness he couldn't articulate. They hadn't seen Hannah that night, death clinging to her, stalking her like a devouring shadow. Seeing her lying there had broken something open in him. He didn't know what having her here, in his home, everyday would do to him. It was selfish, he knew, but he didn't want to find out.

He pushed off the mantel, ready to give in to the exhaustion that had claimed him. "It's your call, Dad." Then he strode out of the room, desperate to escape the memory of Hannah's hand in his.

Chapter Five

A BRIGHT CIRCLE OF LIGHT danced across her vision as the doctor waved a pen light in front of her eyes. It was a fleeting spot of light that momentarily blocked out the hospital walls, the humming machines, and the doctor's disapproving stare.

"Physically, you're ready to be released, Miss . . . " He slipped his reading glasses onto his nose and glanced at the tablet in his hand before looking up at her from under arched brows. "Miss Smith."

Hannah ignored the suspicion in his voice. It didn't matter what he thought of her. She wouldn't be sticking around long enough to care. "Thank you."

"However." He tucked the glasses into the pocket of his plain white coat as he sat back and regarded her like a stray dog that had been brought into a shelter.

She recoiled from the pitying look on his face, steeling herself against it, building a wall of detachment around her heart. She didn't need his pity or his permission to leave. She was done letting men control her. Once she was out of this hospital, once she was free, she could disappear into the streets and start over. What was one more made up name?

"Given your condition when you arrived," the doctor continued. "I would like you to consider staying another forty-eight hours, under a psychiatric watch."

Hannah smiled weakly, plastering a repentant look on her face, the contrite expression she had perfected during the times her parents had lectured her, and nodded. "I understand, Doctor. I made a terrible mistake."

She had to get out of here. She had to convince the doctor to sign the discharge papers. She lowered her eyes, then lifted them again, a practiced expression of remorse that didn't reach her heart, the same show of repentance she used when she got caught sneaking out of class in high school, the same tactic she used when tourists turned and saw her reaching for their shopping bags.

"I'm grateful for everything you did for me. I just want to go home, to get back to my family."

Lie. Deny. Survive.

That was her mantra.

The doctor pursed his lips as he looked at her. She didn't fidget. She was used to the stares of men; it didn't affect her; it didn't touch her. Not anymore.

"Well, if you're determined to leave, I highly recommend that you seek professional counseling as soon as possible."

She nodded, but she had no intention of visiting a therapist or seeing her family. She had to get out of town before Lincoln found her and dragged her back to that club. The memory of Norma Jean's flooded her mind and she shivered in the warm room. The stink of sweat and desperation that filled the club, the dingy lights that surrounded the cracked mirrors in the tiny dressing room behind the stage, the crude comments from men sitting at stained and dirty tables, their leering gazes looking up at her as she danced. She wasn't going back there. And if acting like she agreed with the doctor was what it took to get him to sign the papers that would set her free, that was what she'd do.

With a heavy sigh, the doctor left the room, his lack of faith in her obvious. A nurse returned a few minutes later with her discharge papers and told her they'd send someone up with a wheelchair to escort her out of the hospital. Out of the hospital and onto the streets. She had a stack of papers full of prescriptions she couldn't afford, referrals she wouldn't use, and nothing else. No clothes, no phone, and nowhere to go.

The door closed behind the nurse with a soft thud. Hannah stood and found a plastic bag filled with her belongings stuffed in a corner of the small closet. The crumpled and stained dress she had been wearing the night she was admitted had been cut open, destroyed in the process of saving her life. Studying it, and the ragged slash that tore down the middle, she wondered how she was supposed to walk out of the hospital in a dress she would have to hold together. The thought of putting it on made her skin crawl, but what choice did she have. She couldn't wander the streets of Hollywood in a hospital gown.

Tears blurred her vision as she clutched the fabric in her hands. Lincoln had given it to her the first time he took her to Norma Jean's. It was the first time he forced her on stage. He'd made it seem like the dress was a gift, like it was something special and not a leash that would tie her to him and his life until death seemed like the only way out. She never wanted to see it again. Fisting her hands in the thin, black material she wanted to burn the dress and all the memories it held.

"Oh, God, what am I going to do?" The words slipped out before she could stop them. A prayer she had no right to pray. Looking at the ruined dress in her hands, she knew she had fallen too far to ask God for anything. God didn't listen to people like her, and she didn't blame Him. She didn't deserve His love nor His help. She never had. She was going to have to figure this out on her own.

"Hi, Hannah."

She shoved the ruined dress back in the plastic bag and wiped her eyes. The woman in the wheelchair was back. She remembered her kind smile and searched for her name, digging through the jumble of memories of the past two days. Lily. Her name was Lily.

She rolled her wheelchair across the waxy, tiled floor and stopped a few feet from her. Her light brown hair was swept back into a loose ponytail that hung over her shoulder. Up close, Hannah could see the resemblance between Lily and her brother especially in their eyes. They were the same color blue, like a tranquil, mountain lake. "So," she said, those blue eyes looking up at her from the chair. "It looks like today is the big day."

Hannah shook her head. Confusion wrinkled her forehead and she immediately regretted the action, the stitches in her forehead pinching and protesting the movement. "Sorry?"

"You're being released today, right?"

Hannah scooped up the plastic hospital bag, and crossed back to the bed, acting as though she had a plan, like she had an appointment to keep and didn't have time to chat with strangers, not even strangers who had been kind to her.

"Yes." She set the bag on the bed and straightened the edges, as if it held something valuable and not just the ruined remains of her shattered life. "The doctor just signed the papers. I can leave as soon as I'm ready."

Lily swung the wheelchair around and faced her. "Well, as fashionable as that hospital gown is, I thought you might need a change of clothes for your big escape."

Her head jerked up. Was it that obvious she was planning to run?

But Lily didn't seem to notice her reaction. She swiveled in the chair and grabbed a backpack from the basket beneath her seat. "I guessed at the sizes so everything might be too big, but it will be better than that hospital gown." She held a canvas bag out across the bed, offering it to her.

"You're giving me clothes?" Lacing her hands together, Hannah stared at the backpack. She couldn't accept it. She didn't deserve it. And she didn't want whatever strings came with it. The shredded dress in the plastic bag was reminder enough that every gift had a price. "Why?"

Wheeling closer to the bed, Lily set the backpack on the rumpled sheets between them. "Because you need them."

Hannah stepped back. If there was one thing she knew, it was that nothing was free. Everything came with a price. Especially in Hollywood. "You don't even know me." She didn't bother to conceal the suspicion in her voice.

"No, I don't. But God brought you to our church for a reason. You could have ended up anywhere."

You could have ended up dead. The words were unsaid, but they echoed in the confines of the small hospital room, a truth that hovered between them as obviously as the backpack that sat on the bed.

"But He brought you to us, to our church, to our family. We'd like to help you."

Understanding began to break through Hannah's resistance. They were a church family, a family who had reached out to the hurting and the lost. A family who believed they could make a difference. Like—

She cut the memory off. She refused to remember, refused to look back at a life that was gone. It was better to face reality in all its ugliness than wish for what was lost. And the reality was she had no money, no clothes. She had her pride, but her pride was what had gotten her in this mess in the first place.

She reached for the bag of clothes Lily brought, and her fingers brushed against the material, hesitant, as if the gift would disappear once it realized she was the intended recipient, as if even the clothes knew she was undeserving. "Thank you."

Lily smiled and she envied the peace she saw in it. Some people had it so easy. Then her gaze dropped to the wheelchair and she felt terrible for the bitter thought.

"So." Lily fussed with the sheets, her slim hands smoothing out the wrinkles. "Do you have somewhere to go?"

A lie leapt to her lips. She was good at lying, she always had been. Lies had come as naturally to her as drawing or music came to other people. Growing up, deception had been easy for her. A sweet smile, the right tone, and no one suspected a thing. When she ended up on the streets of Hollywood at eighteen, deception meant survival. When she found herself wrapped up in Lincoln's world, deception was the only way she could look at herself in the mirror, the only way she could face what she had become.

But the words died before she could say them, the lie turning sour in her mouth. Lily sat beside her bed yesterday. She had prayed for her, held her hand, kept her company so the loneliness of the hospital room didn't smother her. She gave her clothes just because she needed them. And then there was her brother.

An image of Noah filled her mind. The rumpled hair, the blood stained shirt. She could have died, but instead he found her. He'd saved her and stayed with her, even when he didn't know who she was. Or maybe he saved her because he didn't know who she was. If he had known what she was, the things she had done, maybe he would have left her there, let her finish what she had started when she swallowed those pills.

But she doubted it. He would have helped her no matter what.

She dropped her head, unwilling to step back into that life of duplicity and trickery. She didn't want to lie, not to these people, not after all they had done for her. "I'll figure something out."

Lily came around the bed, stopping beside her, planting herself on Hannah's side. "Well," she said, her tone matter of fact and strong, with none of the pity the doctor had used. "While you're figuring it out, I have a proposition for you."

She smiled and Hannah felt a tiny flicker of something long dead gasp for breath in her heart. Hope.

Chapter Six

HANNAH SAT IN THE QUIET of the Shaws' guest room. The full bed was soft and the comforter, decorated with twisting blue flowers, was thick and warm. It was a wonderful change from the sterile white sheets of the hospital room. The walls were a light coffee color and delicate curtains fluttered in the breeze coming from the open window. The sounds of the street were close but even they seemed softer and quieter in the peace of this house.

She didn't know what to do with herself. Lily's dad, Pastor Evan, drove them home from the hospital a few hours ago. He was a nice man, seemingly unruffled by the bandage on her face or the too-big, hand-me-down clothes she wore. He shook her hand and smiled like she was an honored guest and not a charity case. When they pulled up at the small yellow house, a swell of homesickness drenched her. She ached for her mother's touch, her gentle hand stroking her hair like she did when she was sick. Days listening to her mother sing in the kitchen while she ate soup and watched cartoons, her mother stopping to check on her, laying the back of her hand against her forehead and immediately knowing if she had a fever. The prayers she whispered over her as she fell asleep, knowing her mother would always take care of her.

But those days were gone. The memories were too painful, too hard to dwell on so she pushed them away, stuffing them into a corner of her mind and focused instead on the concrete steps and the wooden wheelchair ramp that led to the front porch of the yellow house and the cheerful sunflower wreath that hung on the door.

Once inside, Lily gave her a tour of the small house. It was warm and clean and filled with family memories. It was in the photos that decorated the walls and the mix of older, well-loved pieces of furniture and newer, practical things. Hannah hadn't missed the framed prints of Scripture that hung in every room, inescapable proof of their faith. Glancing to her left, she saw a rustic, wood sign mounted over the bed inscribed with the words, *For I know the plans I have for you, declares the Lord. Plans to prosper you and not harm you, plans to give you hope and a future - Jeremiah 29:11.*

Closing her eyes, she sighed. There was a time when she believed that. Now she knew better. Maybe when she was younger God had a plan for her life, but it was ruined now, left in broken pieces strewn along the road that had led her here. If there'd ever been a plan, she had messed it up beyond repair. Surely God had given up on her a long time ago. Everyone else had.

Regret and recrimination drifted through the room like the breeze coming from outside. It was her fault. She had squandered the life God gave her. She was rebellious and stubborn and thought she knew it all. Running away from home had been an easy decision for her. Fresh out of high school and eighteen she was suddenly free to do whatever she wanted. And she wanted to have an adventure. All the years she had spent trying to be the good pastor's daughter, living in her perfect older sister's shadow, it was all too much. She loved her family but they didn't understand her. No one in that tiny town did. So, when her boyfriend suggested they run away to Los Angeles, she jumped at the chance. With the windows of his car rolled down and the wind whipping through her hair as music blared through the speakers, she hadn't looked back as they drove out of town, leaving her childhood and her innocence behind.

There had been parties and life free from rules and restraint. But it couldn't last forever. Now five years later, she didn't know where he was or what he was doing. He was probably married and living two doors down from his parents in the same small town they had grown up in. It had been easier for him to go back, easier for him to forget what they had done.

He'd left her on a Sunday morning. It was the rumble of the car engine that had woken her up. One glance at the empty bed beside her and she knew he was gone, headed back to the life he said he hated. But she couldn't go home. Not after the bridges she'd burned and the hearts she'd broken. It was the first time in her life she had ever been truly alone. Trapped in a rundown motel on a dark alley in Hollywood with only a bag of stale bread and three dollars, the girl she had been disappeared and someone new was born. Someone who could survive, no matter what it cost.

But being here, in the Shaws' house, a house that was achingly familiar, was bringing up memories she wanted to forget, a life she lost and could never recover. Being so close to everything she had run from brought waves of shame that threatened to drown her. Guilt and loss stole her breath and squeezed her heart until she thought it would fracture, shatter into pieces, and leave her soul as broken as her body.

It was a cruel taunt of fate to dangle this life in front of her when she had no right to be here. She made her choices and she would live with the consequences. But how could she do that if she had to spend every day looking at what she had lost, if every minute was going to be a reminder of what she could never have again? It was too much. It would destroy the last remnant of strength she had. She couldn't face it.

She rose from the bed and straightened the comforter, smoothing out the wrinkles she had caused, making it look like she had never been there. She grabbed the plastic hospital bag she hadn't bothered to unpack and cracked the door open. Laughter coming from the kitchen echoed down the narrow hallway and the ache in her heart nearly made her turn back. Maybe she could stay here. Maybe she could be different. Maybe she could bury her mistakes and start over.

But as quickly as the thoughts sprang to life, she crushed them again. Some mistakes were unforgivable.

Keeping her feet on the thick carpet runner, she tiptoed down the hallway. She wouldn't go back to Lincoln, but she couldn't stay here. If she went back to Norma Jean's, Lincoln would find her. As far as he knew she was dead and she'd rather keep it that way. Once she made it out of the house, she'd figure something out. She always did.

Guilt gnawed at her as she crept towards the front door. Lily and her father had been nothing but kind to her. And her brother—Noah was the reason she was alive. Opening her eyes in the hospital room and seeing his face had been like waking up in the middle of a dream. If her life was a nightmare, he was the sunrise that banished the darkness. And this was how she repaid them, sneaking off like the thief that she was—the thief and con artist Lincoln had made her.

It wasn't fair of her to leave without saying goodbye, without even saying thank you, but what choice did she have? She had no place here and the longer she stayed, the greater the risk that Noah would figure out who she really was. That they would all find out. She doubted Lily would look at her the same way when she found out about her past. It was better to make the decision herself, to run rather than sit around and wait to be kicked out.

She crossed the small foyer and had nearly reached the front door when she spotted Lily's purse sitting on the table. Surrounded by a collection of framed family photos, the purse was unzipped and temptation seized her. A few dollars would help her make it through the night. A credit card would get her a hotel room. If she was quiet, she could grab the purse and be gone before anyone noticed.

It was what Lincoln would do.

It was what he had taught her to do.

It was something she had done hundreds of times before. Slipping her hand into a purse while the tourists were distracted, scooping up a shopping bag while the owner looked the other way. Liar, thief. Those were skills she had honed on the streets, skills Lincoln taught her and she hadn't refused. She never refused him.

Yet she hesitated. Even after everything else she had done, all the lies she'd told, the laws she'd broken, she couldn't do this. Not to this family. She'd find another way.

Leaving the purse untouched, she flipped the lock on the door. Turning the handle slowly, she held her breath, expecting to be caught, a part of her hoping she would be. But no one appeared. The voices from the kitchen kept up a constant stream of chatter, undisturbed by her furtive actions.

No one would even notice that she was gone. Bitterness flooded her heart as the vicious words ricocheted in her brain. They'd probably be relieved when they found the empty guest room.

She was no one. A burden. Expendable. She might as well slip into the night and disappear like the shadow that she had become.

The door opened on silent hinges, and a cool evening breeze rushed in as Hannah stepped into the night without looking back.

She carefully pulled the door closed behind her, turned away, and walked right into a strong, male chest. Terror flooded her veins and a strangled scream choked her throat. He'd found her.

She pulled away, her body tensing to run. She wouldn't go back. She'd take her chances on the streets before going back to that place.

"Leaving so soon?" A deep but gentle voice broke through her fear.

Lincoln had never spoken to her so kindly. Dragging her eyes up to his face, she blinked. Noah stared back at her, his jaw set in a hard line as his gaze swept from the bandage on her forehead down to Lily's shoes on her feet.

She took a quick step to the side, intending to walk past him, and dizziness engulfed over her, turning the world into a kaleidoscope of colors and spinning shapes.

The porch tipped and she felt weightless. She knew she was falling, the wooden slats of the porch rushing up to meet her, but she was helpless to stop it.

"Whoa there." Noah's quick reflexes paid off and he caught her before she collapsed, his arms wrapping around her and sweeping her off her feet. "I've got you."

The warmth of his chest pressed against her side and his shoulder cradled her head as he held her in his arms. The spice of his aftershave settled around her like a veil and the beat of his heart drummed steadily against her skin. Meeting his eyes, she tried to decipher what she saw there. It wasn't the hungry, selfish stare she was used to from men, and it wasn't the pitying look the doctor and nurses had given her. It was something else, something that chiseled away at the wall she built around herself, and that made it dangerous.

Warning bells echoed in her head and butterflies danced in her stomach. She shouldn't be here. She should go. She should leave before he found out what she had done, before he threw her out and slammed the door in her face. It would be easier to leave now, to never have to see disgust and condemnation written on his face when he looked at her.

But the words wouldn't come. She sank into the security of being in his arms, the peace that enveloped her and instead of running, she allowed herself to hope for one more day.

Chapter Seven

NOAH JUGGLED HANNAH'S WEIGHT IN his arms and frowned. She weighed less than some of the kids in children's church. She looked up at him as if he was some sort of savior, a hero out of a fairy tale, and that made him nervous. He was nobody's hero. He was just a confused limo driver who still didn't know what he wanted to be when he grew up, and considering the fact that he was almost thirty, that was a problem.

Better to get her back in the house, turn her over to Lily's care, and stay as far away from her as possible.

He pushed the front door open, and carried her into the living room. He laid her down on the couch and stuffed a pillow behind her head, trying to be careful as he moved her, worried about the concussion and the stitches, feeling like he was about to drop a china doll. "Just lay here and try not to run away again."

A racing blush colored her cheeks. He grinned at the innocence of it.

"I wasn't running away," she protested, even as the blush deepened. "I was . . ."

Noah tilted his head as he watched her search for right words. "Going for a quick nighttime stroll through downtown Hollywood with a concussion? That seems like a questionable life choice at the moment."

Mutiny flashed in her eyes as she stared up at him. "I was trying to not be a burden to your family."

"Maybe we should get a vote in that next time, before you decide to just disappear." Irritation made his words harsh, but he couldn't stop himself. "Did you even bother to say goodbye?"

Her gaze fell to her hands, clenched tightly together like she was trying to hold on to something that was slipping away. Silence stretched between them and he was struck again by how fragile she seemed. He knew there was fire underneath, he'd seen it for himself, but laying on that sofa, she looked frightened and alone.

The irritation left him, and the impulse to sit beside her, to tease her until she laughed, to whisper a smile back onto her face, rose swift and strong. Caught off-guard, he stepped back, widening the distance between them. That was the last thing he needed right now. It was the last thing she needed.

Hurt rippled across her face as she stared at his retreating feet.

"I'm sorry," she whispered, the words barely carrying across the room to him. They fell like withered rose petals blown by a careless breeze, dry and empty. "I was trying to do the right thing. I guess I don't know what that looks like anymore."

Noah rubbed the back of his neck, the tension of the past few days knotting his muscles into an unforgiving mess. He was at a loss, adrift in the midst of upheaval and uncertainty. Lily was getting married. Kate was coming out for the wedding. His father wanted him to assume more leadership in the church. And Hannah . . . Hannah was right in front of him, wounded, scared and just as lost as he was. Maybe more so.

Dropping his hands, he pulled a chair over beside the sofa. Wariness flickered behind her eyes as he sat down. He hated that she was so nervous, that she expected the worst. His eyes settled on the bandage that covered the left side of her forehead, knowing there were wounds that couldn't be healed with stitches and gauze.

"You're not a burden." Anxious for something to do, he stood up and grabbed a blanket off the back of the couch and laid it over her, bringing the edge up to her chin and tucking it in around her shoulders. Her dark lashes lifted, tears sparkling unshed in the brown depth of her eyes and a spark flickered to life in the pit of his stomach. He stepped back, and sat down again, fixing a smile on his face. "And you don't have to run away. We're happy to have you."

The words sounded trite. He knew it, and based on the coolness that shuttered her expression, she knew it, too. But better polite distance, than whatever it was that danced across his nerves when he was around her. He didn't know her. He didn't know what she had been through or what had driven her to try to take her own life or how she had ended up on the steps of the church. She needed a place to stay and a new start. She needed to know that God loved her. And that would have to be enough.

Hannah smiled, but it was a hollow gesture. The wall that had momentarily cracked was solid and strong again, and he was back on the other side of those hardened stones. But it was better that way.

The telltale squeak of Lily's wheelchair broke the silence and he looked up as Ben pushed her into the room.

Hannah turned and her mouth dropped into a stunned "O." Her hand flew to her head and she squeezed her eyes shut.

Noah was out of the chair and on his knees beside her immediately. "Are you okay? Is it your head?" Concern morphed into fear as she sucked in a breath, pressing her hand against her forehead, and shaking her head as if trying to clear away a fog.

Ben and Lily stopped at the other end of the sofa and his sister laid her hand on Hannah's foot. "Hannah, what's wrong?"

Shaking her head, she blinked rapidly. "I must have hit my head harder than I thought." She looked up at Ben, still standing behind the wheelchair, then rubbed her eyes. "I thought you were that movie star. The one who did that terrible space movie a few years ago. You look just like him."

Lily giggled and Ben shrugged. "Yeah, I get that a lot."

Covering his smile with his hand, surprised by the relief that washed through him, Noah sat back in the chair. This was going to be interesting.

"Hannah," Lily said and gestured to Ben. "This is my fiancé, Ben Prescott."

One second passed, then two. And then everything fell into place. Hannah blushed deep crimson and her eyes widened in horror. "You are him. You're the movie star. And I—I said—" She looked at him frantically, stumbling over her words, silently begging him for help, before turning back to Ben. "I can't believe I said that. I'm so sorry. Don't listen to me I'm sure it was a great movie."

Noah shook his head. "No, you're right. It was terrible." Lily rolled across the floor like her wheelchair was a racecar and smacked his leg, but he just laughed. "What? You didn't like it either."

Her eyes widened in betrayal, promising retribution, as Ben pulled the wheelchair back and spun it until she faced him. "Wait, you didn't like *SuperNova?*"

Noah nudged Hannah's arm, grinning at the embarrassed horror still written on her face, and whispered. "Watch this."

Lily reached for Ben's hand. "Honey, you know I like watching all of your movies. SuperNova was . . . umm . . . "

"Stupid?" Noah volunteered, folding his hands behind his head and thoroughly enjoying the show. Hannah's wide eyes bounced back and forth between them like she didn't know if this was going to end with laughter or violence.

His sister glared at him before turning back to her fiancé. "No. It's not stupid. But out of all your movies, that one isn't my favorite."

Ben stared at her for a moment, then sank to his knees in front of her. Taking her hand and bringing it to his lips, he planted a loud kiss on her knuckles. "You're right. It wasn't my best work. That's why you get script approval from now on."

Lily reached out her arms and Ben wrapped her in a hug, lifting her out of the wheelchair and settling her on his lap as he sat on the loveseat.

Rolling his eyes at the display, Noah moaned. "Oh just get married already and move out. I can't stand all this mushy stuff."

Hannah watched it all in mute disbelief, staying silent, making herself an invisible spectator to their family teasing. If she thought this was bad, she was in for a rude awakening when he and Lily really started in on each other.

Peeking over her shoulder, his little sister stuck her tongue out at him. "You're just jealous."

He scoffed and pulled his phone out of the pocket of his jeans. Absently scrolling through his notifications, not seeing any of them, he fought to keep his eyes on the screen. He was happy for his sister. She and Ben deserved each other. But the emptiness in his own heart yawned like a black hole in his chest. Kate would be coming out in less than three months. She'd be here for the wedding and if past history was any indication she'd be on the first flight out of LAX after Lily and Ben said "I do."

Uncertainty tugged at him. There wouldn't be much time for him to say what he wanted, what he needed, to say to her. The trouble was he still didn't know what that was.

Hannah rustled on the sofa beside him and his eyes drifted to hers. An unspoken bond stretched between them. It was tenuous, a shared memory of trauma that neither of them mentioned but that they would both carry for the rest of their lives. No matter how many years passed, he would never forget the sight of her lying in the parking lot, or the way he felt when her eyes finally opened in the hospital room. Like it or not, he felt responsible for her, as if she had been given into his care.

He sighed as he watched her snuggle deeper under the blanket, her eyes drifting closed. It was one more thing he didn't know how to fix.

Chapter Eight

OVER THE NEXT FEW WEEKS, Hannah fell into a comfortable routine at the Shaw house. Lily spent most of the day with her while Evan and Noah worked at the church. They baked together, watched wedding shows while Lily jotted down ideas in her ever-expanding wedding notebook, and they talked about everything and nothing. Lily shared stories of her mother and her battle with cancer, how she met Ben and her struggle after the fire at the church left her paralyzed.

Hannah was happy to listen, but she wasn't ready to share her story. Not yet. She still jumped at unexpected sounds or when the mailman knocked on the door. With each new day, her past seemed further and further way, but with one word, one memory that sprang up without warning from the depths of her mind, it all came crashing back. Lily didn't push and she was grateful for her new friend.

In the afternoon, Noah would come back and take Lily to the church for the aftercare classes she taught. In the quiet that followed Lily leaving, Hannah had no choice but to think about the future. She couldn't stay here forever, in this bubble of security and anonymity. The scar she saw in the mirror every morning wouldn't let her forget who she was or the life she had led. Staying with the Shaws was a temporary fix, and she had no idea what to do next.

The temptation to call her parents was there, an ever-present longing, but one she couldn't indulge. Maybe when she had her life figured out, when she had something to be proud of, when she could face them without shame, then she could call them. But right then, battered and scarred, broke and broken, she couldn't do it. She couldn't handle the sorrow she'd see on their faces, knowing she was the cause. She was their daughter, and she was their greatest disappointment.

So, she smiled when Lily talked about her mom, but she didn't offer any information about her own past. Someday, when she had fixed her mistakes, when she had put her life back together, then she would be able to talk about it. When it was all over, when it couldn't touch her anymore, then she could share it, but not before, not when it was still so close, so real, not when it still had the power to hurt her and those around her.

In the evenings, they all came home for dinner and most nights, Ben would join them. After they ate, Hannah enjoyed doing the dishes while the family sat at the table and talked. Evan shared stories from his day at the church, his conversations with young pastors in the area, or what he was learning in his sermon preparation. Noah was unusually quiet during these discussions. From her spot at the sink, she watched and listened, studying the Shaws and all their quirks.

She had learned to observe people from her time on the streets, how to pick a mark, how to know who to press and who wasn't going to be fooled. Noah was quick with a joke, he was funny and witty, and he picked on his sister mercilessly. Of course, Lily picked on him right back and it was obvious that they loved each other. But when the conversation shifted to the church, Noah fell silent. It was as if he didn't want to draw attention to himself, as if he was waiting for the topic to shift, afraid he would get sucked into something he couldn't get out of. He was a Christian so she couldn't figure out why talking about the church made him nervous.

Their conversations often went long into the night and the whole family welcomed her to join in. Other nights, they'd play a board game or watch a movie. Noah loved to play Ben's movies and provide color commentary until Lily threw popcorn at him or his dad shushed him. Ben took it all in stride and none of Noah's taunts seemed to bother him. It was as if they were already brothers, a family brought together by more than blood.

As a hot and muggy July gave way to an even hotter and muggier August, they sat at the kitchen table one night after dinner while Hannah dried the dishes. The small kitchen was the heart of their home. It was warm and inviting, the coffee was hot and the table was always ready for guests. Lily complained about the old appliances, but they all worked and no one ever went hungry in the Shaw house. It reminded Hannah of the kitchen in her parents' house. Late night conversations were always held there, gathered around a table just like this one, close to the coffee and the secret stash of cookies her mother kept hidden from her dad. Just like her parents' house, photos of families from the church littered the refrigerator until there wasn't an inch of the white finish left to be seen.

Evan, as always, had told Noah to help her with the dishes, but she shooed him away. It was getting harder for her to concentrate when he was around. He was always polite, always kind to her, but she sensed his distance, his reluctance to get too close to her. And of course that made her think of him even more. She spent every night lying in bed listing all the reasons why she shouldn't be attracted to him. Why she should stop thinking about him. She was leaving soon. He worked at a church. He didn't know about her past and once he found out he'd never look at her the same way again.

Even as her list grew, she couldn't stop the little flutter of excitement that leapt to life whenever he walked through the door. It was foolish and childish, but that didn't stop the butterflies in her stomach. It was self-preservation that made her refuse his help with the dishes every night. She dried the plates as they talked and tried to pretend that she was a part of the family, that she belonged here—even though she didn't.

Sitting in his usual spot at the table, Evan sipped his customary evening coffee. Lily had switched him to decaf two weeks ago when he complained about not getting enough sleep. Hannah had giggled as she helped her hide the evidence, carefully emptying one coffee can and replacing it with the decaf grounds from another. If Evan noticed the change, he hadn't said anything and he certainly looked more rested in the mornings.

"Remember, I'm leaving on Tuesday for the conference, and I'll be gone until Saturday night," he said. "So Noah I will need you at the church full-time while I'm gone."

Hannah didn't miss the way Noah hesitated before replying. "I've got bookings for the limo on Friday and Saturday night."

"That's fine," Evan replied. "I just need you there during the day and to lead the outreach Saturday morning, you'll be done in plenty of time for your limo jobs. Lily can help you."

"Of course I can help," Lily said. "I need to be there in the afternoons anyway to get the classrooms set up before the children arrive and Ben can drive me to physical therapy in the mornings, right?"

She turned to Ben who shook his head. "I'm leaving, too. We're doing re-shoots on location in New Zealand for three weeks."

Lily stared at him. "You're going to be gone for three weeks? Did I know that?"

Ben nodded and pointed to her battered notebook. "It's in there somewhere."

"Well," she said, her fingers drumming loudly on the cover of the notebook. Hannah recognized the nervous gesture and judging by the darted looks the guys gave each other over the table, they did, too. "That's a small complication."

Drum, drum, drum, her fingers thumped across the cover, picking up speed each time, no doubt trying to keep up with her racing thoughts.

"I can help." The words slipped from Hannah's lips before they registered in her brain. Everyone turned to stare at her, and she fidgeted with the plate in her hands, drying it over and over again. "I mean. I know how to drive. I can get Lily to the church and her doctor appointments and whatever." The stunned silence made her feel stupid for even suggesting it. Why would they trust her? She wasn't part of the family, she was a charity case, a broken girl they felt sorry for. She was not in a position to help anyone. Heat flooded her cheeks as they all looked at her. "Or not. It's no big deal. I just thought . . ."

"That's a great idea." Lily clapped her hands. "You can drive me to therapy and we can do a bunch of wedding stuff without listening to moaning and groaning from these guys."

"Hey!" Noah and Ben both protested, but Lily gave them a hard stare.

"Really? You want to go look at reception favors and photographers? Would you like to come to the florists and finalize the centerpieces for the reception, too?" When neither of them replied, she gave them a smug smile. "That's what I thought."

Wheeling away from the table and over to Hannah, she took her elbow and squeezed. "That would be a huge help. Thank you."

Embarrassment and relief rushed through her. She couldn't remember the last time she had a real friend and more than anything she didn't want to let her down.

Chapter Nine

HANNAH SAT BEHIND THE WHEEL of Noah's truck. It was old and had over two hundred thousand miles on it, but it was obviously well loved. In fact, she wasn't sure what he was more nervous about, letting her take his sister to physical therapy, or letting her drive his precious truck. He had handed Lily over a lot faster than he had handed over the keys with their superhero keychain.

"All right." He leaned in through the open window. "She's a little slow to accelerate, but once she gets going she'll take off. You have to keep an eye on your speed, you won't even know you've hit eighty until it's too late. Don't do anything crazy, keep it safe and easy."

He kept one hand on the wheel as he listed every idiosyncrasy of the vehicle, from the way the passenger window would occasionally stick, to the hum the carburetor made. Smothering a smile, she tried to look like she was taking his lecture seriously.

"The tires are good, but she skids a little in the rain so you have to be careful of the turns when the roads are wet or you'll end up drifting."

Hannah looked up at the cloudless sky in the middle of a Southern California summer, her eyebrows raised as she imagined the miracle it would take for rain to actually fall. But he was so serious, so concerned that she didn't point out the sunny day or the lack of clouds in the bright, blue sky.

"Oh, for goodness' sake, Noah, we'll be fine." Exasperated with the seemingly endless lecture, Lily tightened her ponytail and sighed. "Now go away or I'll be late."

"I'm just trying to help, Brat," he muttered, pulling his hand back from the wheel. "Drive safely, okay?" He looked at Hannah, intensity burning in his blue eyes and her heart skipped like a rock dancing across a lake. She nodded because she forgot how to form words. Then she mentally berated herself for being such a fool.

"I'll bring Lily to the church this afternoon for her class and drop off the keys," she said as she started the truck. It rumbled to life with a loud sputter, and she couldn't stop the grin that spread across her face. This was her kind of vehicle. It wasn't fancy, but it would get you where you needed to go and make sure the trip was fun. It reminded her of summer nights and dirt roads and the carefree days of her youth.

Noah glanced at the truck like he'd never see it again before stepping out of the way.

"Have fun being the pastor today," Lily called as they backed out the driveway and turned onto the street.

Noah made a decidedly unpastor-like face and waved, keeping his eye on them until they turned the corner and left the little yellow house behind.

Once they were out of earshot, Lily turned on the radio. Worship music filled the cab and spilled out the open windows to the streets outside. Hannah took a deep breath and let it out on a sigh of contentment. Driving a beat up truck with music playing was the best medicine, and she intended to enjoy every minute of it.

When they arrived at the hospital, it took Hannah a few tries to figure out how to get the wheelchair to open. Noah should have spent less time explaining how to adjust the seat on the truck and more time on how to operate the wheelchair, she thought, bouncing and yanking on it until it finally popped open. Even with the wheelchair complication, they managed to make it to Lily's appointment on time, though Hannah may have been pushing Lily a little faster than usual down the long hospital corridors.

The waiting room in the physical therapy office was small and clean. Tiny wooden tables covered with stacks of magazines and old newspapers sat beside the orderly rows of chairs. Lily rolled in and called a cheerful greeting to the nurse frowning behind the desk. The frown disappeared, replaced by a broad smile when she saw Lily. They chatted and the nurse asked about Lily's dad, her frown long forgotten. Lily's joy was infectious. People were drawn to her, drawn to the kindness she exuded.

After Lily signed in, she came back to wait with her. "I think that nurse has a crush on my dad," she whispered.

"Really?" Hannah stole a glance at the stern-faced nurse whose frown had returned with full force and tried to picture her with Pastor Evan. The image didn't fit at all.

"Your willingness to drive me here might be a blessing to him as well," Lily said with a wink.

The door opened and another nurse called Lily back.

Hannah hesitated. Was she supposed to wait in the small room with the frowning nurse or leave and come back later instead? "Should I wait out here?"

Hands frozen on the wheels of her chair, Lily considered her for a moment, her lips pursed in thought. "Can you keep a secret?"

Hannah laughed at the question. "Secrets are one thing I am very good at."

She tried to make the comment light-hearted even though she knew it wasn't something to be proud of. She'd been cultivating secrets as long as she could remember. Every lie she told her parents, every excuse she gave her teachers, each one became easier until sometimes she didn't know where the truth ended and her deceptions began.

"Then come on in." Lily disappeared into the therapy room while the surprised nurse held the door open and waited for her to catch up.

The physical therapy area was much brighter than Hannah had anticipated. She thought the room would be dark and sad, filled with wounded and injured people. Instead, light shone through the large windows that overlooked the city and lively, upbeat music played in the background. The therapists and assistants wore colorful scrubs and the conversations were sprinkled with laughter.

As she followed Lily to the far side of the room, she saw a man with prosthetic hands learning how to use a spoon. A child with arms that were bent and twisted at the elbows threw a large, red ball to a therapist. Another therapist was gently attempting to straighten the knee of a woman sitting on the edge of a purple padded table.

Surrounded by so many people who had endured trials she couldn't imagine, she didn't know where to look. Her first instinct was to help. To help the little girl with the ball, to help the man with the spoon, but she didn't know how and she'd probably end up doing the wrong thing, she always did.

She hurried to join Lily who had parked her wheelchair on the far side of the room and was talking with a tall, muscular man in bright yellow scrubs.

"Hannah, this is Andre. He's my therapist and my torturer."

Andre clasped a hand over his heart. "That hurts." He tapped his chest, but his eyes twinkled beneath his dark skin. "Right in the heart."

Then he extended his hand to Hannah. His grip was firm and warm as his hand swallowed hers. "It's nice to meet you. Lily doesn't usually let her family watch her therapy."

She caught the surprise in his voice and a feather of happiness took flight in her heart. If Lily trusted her enough to let her come with her maybe she was doing something right. She had no doubt Andre would toss her back into the waiting room and the frowning nurse at the counter would sit on her if Lily asked them to. Instead of tossing her out though Lily had invited her in, included her in a way not even Noah had been allowed to do.

Lily winked at the big man and tugged on her ponytail again, a soldier getting ready for battle. "Hannah volunteered to be my driver for the next few weeks and I hope she's going to help me with my big surprise."

"Sounds good to me," Andre said and flipped the locks on Lily's chair, making sure the wheels wouldn't move.

Hannah stepped out of the way, and found a chair in the corner. She sat down to wait, but she'd barely touched the chair before she leapt up again, panic thrumming in her chest, as Andre helped Lily out of the chair.

"Wait, should she be doing that?" Fear gripped her as she watched the gentle giant put his hands under her friend's arms and lift her up. What if she fell? What if she hurt herself? It would be her fault. How would she explain it to Evan and Noah? Heart pounding, Hannah took a step towards them. She didn't know what she expected therapy to look like, but it wasn't this.

"Just watch," Lily said with a grin. She didn't look scared, she looked . . . excited.

Andre helped her put her hands on the metal parallel bars in front of her. Using her arms, Lily pulled herself up, standing between the bars like a heavy weight fighter getting up after what should have been a knock out punch. Slowly, she took one hand off the bar. Hannah held her breath as Lily let the other hand fall to her side.

"Ta-da," she said, her smile lighting up the room as Andre stepped back and left her on her own.

Tears pricked Hannah's eyes. She wanted to celebrate, to jump up and down. She wanted to shout, to run up and hug her new friend, but she was immobile, transfixed by the sight in front of her.

Lily was standing.

*****

They sat in the little coffee shop across the street from the hospital, Hannah sipping her latte thoughtfully as Lily tore through a chocolate muffin. Clearly the exertion of half an hour of physical therapy followed by thirty more minutes of strength building made her hungry. Hannah was exhausted and all she had done was watch the grueling exercises Andre put Lily through. He'd been kind and encouraging, but he had pushed her. Telling her she could work harder, that she could stand a little longer, that even though her body was weak, her mind was strong. Over and over he told her to choose to take one more step, to choose to keep going when she wanted to quit. By the time the half-hour was up, Lily was sweating and her muscles trembled, but her smile was huge. She had definitely earned that muffin.

Their table was next to the window and from her seat Hannah could see the front of the hospital. The automatic doors opened and closed in an endless pattern. People coming and going, some rushing in, their phones clutched in tight fists, others walking out slowly, weighed down by worry or grief. The building itself seemed to vibrate with stories, with the lives of the people behind the concrete and glass, lives that would never be the same.

She should know. She went into that hospital one person and came out someone else entirely. Someone she barely recognized. It was as if two different lives had been forced together, like jigsaw pieces that looked similar but didn't quite match. She wanted the pieces to snap together neatly, to flow seamlessly, but the edges were off and the broken pieces of her two lives didn't fit.

It all went back to the day she left home. The day she ran away looking for adventure and found only regret. The girl she was before she got into that car and the woman she became on the streets of Hollywood came face-to-face in that hospital room, like distorted reflections in a fun house mirror, magnifying the worst parts of her soul.

Every part of her past was gone. Wiped out in a handful of pills. Everyone who had ever cared about her, or pretended to care, thought she was dead. The Hannah who grew up in church, the one who rebelled against her parents, the one who lied her way through school, was gone. And Sasha?

She shuddered as the name wound its way from the shadows of her past to the present, an echo that wouldn't end, always rebounding and finding its way back to her. She met Lincoln when she was waiting tables in a diner off Hollywood Boulevard, counting pennies to see if she had enough money to eat that night. He had promised her a life of glamour and excitement. If she went with him he would take care of her. With the right look, he promised, she could be a star. He dangled the promise of fame and money like bait on a hook and she was the guppy who swallowed the lie.

He'd made it all sound so easy, and she'd been desperate enough to believe him. There was nothing waiting for her in the small motel room her boyfriend had left her in. There was no reason to go back to scraping by, going hungry, and being alone. Lincoln promised her a way out and she took it.

She left the diner with him, drinking in the lies he told her like a woman dying of thirst. As he spun tales of television and movies, he told her she needed a new name, something exotic, something with flair, and she hadn't objected. When he stepped back and studied her, his eyes raking over her body, she silenced the warning bells that rang in her head. Under the yellow glow of a streetlight, he announced that her name would be Sasha, and her new life began. No one else cared about her; no one else cared if she lived or died. And Hannah? Naive, foolish Hannah? She left that name behind in the diner.

She became Sasha, the woman he groomed and trained, the one who followed his every order and sacrificed her soul to keep his love. There hadn't been fame or acting or agents. When the smooth talking, charming mask slipped and she saw who he really was, it was too late. She was in too deep. In the end, Sasha had died in the dressing room of a strip club and been tossed onto the street like trash.

But if she wasn't Hannah and she wasn't Sasha. Who was she? Where did she belong?

Tears stung her eyes and she turned back to the window so Lily wouldn't see. Lives were changing in that hospital at that very moment. Babies were being born, parents were dying, diagnoses were being given, entire lives were being altered, changed, and shattered all within those walls. How did anyone come back from that? How did someone pick up the pieces of a broken life and keep going?

"Sometimes it's hard to see, but God knows what He's doing."

The soft words drifted across the table and she turned to Lily. The muffin was gone and she was blowing across the steaming foam of her coffee. Calmness exuded from her, saturating the atmosphere like the scent of apples drifting through an orchard, something invisible but impossible to ignore.

She blinked, trying to separate the mess of her rambling thoughts and the words Lily had spoken. "What?"

Lily nodded towards the hospital. "When we see only the pain and the loss, it's hard to imagine there's a plan behind it all. When none of it makes sense, it's easy to believe that God isn't paying attention. That somehow things have gone too far, gotten too out of control, like there's no way back and He's given up."

Heat flooded Hannah's cheeks and she took a quick sip of her latte, trying to hide how much those words affected her. It was as if Lily could see into her soul and read every hurt that was written there, and she wasn't ready for that. This new friendship meant so much to her. She didn't want to lose it. She didn't want to see the change on Lily's face if she found out what Hannah had done, the life she'd led.

Clearing her throat, she tried to change the subject. "So why all the secrecy? Why not tell your family about your therapy? About how close you are to walking again?"

Lily sipped her coffee, not at all upset by the conversational diversion. "I don't want to get their hopes up. I want to walk down the aisle at my wedding. Walk. Not be wheeled down it or carried. I want to be standing when I say I do." An embarrassed smile crossed her lips. "I know it sounds silly. We'll still be married whether I'm sitting in this chair or standing next to him, but that's my hope. It's the picture I hold on to every time I go into that therapy room. I keep believing there's a reason for all the exercises and all the pain. I want to stand beside him, holding his hand and looking in his eyes that day. It's what has kept me going."

Hannah smiled. "I don't think it's silly."

Involuntarily, a prayer filled her heart, words she thought she had forgotten, words she hadn't said in a long time. She offered it to God, hoping He would hear it, not because she deserved it, but because Lily did.

Wrapping her hands around the paper cup, Lily hesitated. "I don't want to let them down. If I can't do it, if it doesn't work out, I don't want anyone to be disappointed. So I am keeping it secret . . . for now."

Looking at her friend, Hannah considered how much was at stake for her. How hard she was working, not knowing if it would turn out the way she wanted, but trying anyway. "I think you're very brave."

Lily looked at the busy hospital entrance across the street, her eyes following a man as he walked hurriedly to the door and disappeared inside. "God knows what He's doing," she said again, certainty filling her voice. "He's right here, beside us every moment, if we're just willing to hold out our hand, He'll take it and lead us home."

Hannah nodded because it was the right thing to do. It was what Lily expected. It was what everyone had always expected of her. Nod and act like she believed, even when she knew the truth. There were some things that were unforgivable. Sometimes there wasn't a way home.

Chapter Ten

THE ANCIENT TRUCK RUMBLED INTO the church parking lot, and Noah exhaled a sigh of relief. It wasn't that he didn't trust Hannah, not exactly. He just didn't know her. He didn't know who she was, where she was from, or what she was thinking half the time. The longer she stayed with them, the more she seemed to relax, but that didn't translate to sharing any of her past with them. And she wasn't only tight-lipped about her past with him. He'd asked Lily several times if Hannah had shared anything with her, anything that they could use to help her, but his sister's answer was always the same. "Not yet." As if she knew Hannah would open up one day, but the day simply hadn't come yet.

Noah wasn't so certain. It looked to him like Hannah was hiding, and he wasn't sure she wanted to be found.

Lily had always been the trusting one, willing to give everyone the benefit of the doubt. Well, everyone except Ben. Ben had been forced to work for it. But in every outreach ministry, in the children's classes, even when it came to buying food or clothes for a family in need, Lily was the trusting one, the giving one. She was like their dad, always willing to see the good in people, always able to see everyone as a child of God.

Not him. He was far too cynical.

Which was why he felt like such a fraud sitting in his dad's office at the church. He had no right to be there. It didn't matter that he'd been working at the church for over five years or that he helped build parts of it with his own hands. He'd helped his dad tear up the old laminate flooring and repaint the walls. He'd counseled drug addicts and men who just got out of prison, he'd led homeless men to the cross and praised God for the opportunity to serve Him, but now that he was in the office, sitting in the pastor's chair, he was at a loss.

Pastors were supposed to love everyone, to always know the right thing to say, to know God's will for every situation. He didn't even know what he was supposed to do with his own life, how was he supposed to know God's will for anyone else?

It was part of the reason he kept driving the limo. That business made sense. There were contracts and agreements. He knew where to go, what time to arrive, and when he would finish. It was all laid out, crystal clear, and signed on the dotted line. The limo's built-in GPS told him where to go, and he just had to follow the little neon arrow and the bright blue line. When he made a wrong turn or ended up going the wrong way, a robotic voice told him how to get back on track. If only it was that easy with God. He wanted to be obedient, he wanted to follow God's neon arrow, but he didn't know where it was or where it was leading him.

Laughter echoed down the corridor outside the office. Lily would be heading to her classroom to get it set up for the summer afternoon child care program. The parents who used their afterschool child care classes during the school year still needed a safe place for their children to go when the schools were out. They had a long wait list for the program, but until the church expanded, they would do the best they could with the space and teachers they had.

With his elbows propped on the table and his head cradled in his hands, he stared at the piles of paperwork in front of him. Budgets, offerings, tithes, bills. It was the administrative side of ministry, the behind the scenes workings of the church. Everything that kept the church going, everything that kept the doors open for the neighborhood. It was all numbers going in and numbers going out, and he hated numbers.

A soft knock brought his head up. Hannah peeked around the corner of the open door, her long hair swaying as she watched him. "Bad time?"

Sarcastic retorts leapt to his lips, but he bit them back. It wasn't her fault the church's budget made him crazy. Besides, his dad always made time for people. Evan Shaw made everyone feel welcome, as if their problems, their joys, and their sorrows were the only things that mattered in that moment. He never made anyone feel like they were intruding.

He looked at Hannah, unasked questions hovering in her deep brown eyes. The scar that cut across her forehead was slowly healing. For the first time, Noah discovered that the scar didn't take him back to the night he found her. Somewhere over the past few weeks, it had become a part of who she was, a testimony of God's protection instead of a reminder of trauma. She still messed with her hair, pulling it over to the side, allowing it to drape over the scar like a satiny curtain. Every time she did that, his hand itched to reach out and tuck the hair behind her ear, pulling it away from what she tried to hide. But he never did.

As her eyebrows raised, he realized he had never replied. He'd been sitting there staring at her like a fool. What was it about her that kept him so distracted?

"No. No, it's fine. I'm just . . . " He looked at the jumble of numbers spread out before him and sighed. "Drowning in math."

"Can I help?" She stepped into the office and Noah sat up straighter. She looked so much stronger now. Lily's pancakes and girl talk were obviously helping. The wary and timid Hannah they had brought home from the hospital was fading, slipping into the background, and he thought he might be getting a glimpse of the girl she was before she ended up on the doorstep of the church, before whatever demons dwelt in her past whispered suicide into her heart.

"I don't know," he said, tearing his mind away from the woman in front of him and back onto the piles of papers that littered the desk. "How are you with budgets?"

An excited twinkle danced in her eyes and Noah sucked in a breath. He'd never noticed the shine of gold in her eyes before. They were deep brown with hints of gold, like sunlight reflecting on the dark surface of a hidden forest. His train of thought shocked him and he shook his head, forcing himself to focus on her words instead.

"I'm actually awesome at budgets. Most of my friends in high school laughed at me, but I always loved math. History? Yuck. English? Boring. Biology? Gross." She shivered and Noah immediately thought of the frogs and eyeballs he'd had to dissect in his biology class. It hadn't been his favorite subject either.

"But math," she said with pride. "Math makes sense. The numbers add up. There are formulas to use and steps to follow. It's all very black and white. No subjective interpretations, no gray areas. Two plus two will always equal four." She stopped abruptly and a bright blush crept up her cheeks. "I'm rambling. Sorry."

The sight of her fidgeting hands, her face as pink as a sunset over the Pacific, wormed its way into his heart. The simple joy of seeing her smile, of hearing her speak without her voice being tinged by nervousness, it made him want to see it again, to see her smile without fear and laugh without reservation. He wanted to chase away the shadows that lingered and the fear that held on to her.

Standing, he pulled the rolling, padded chair away from the desk and waved his hand at it, inviting her to sit down. "Then it sounds like you are the perfect woman for the job."

Her eyes widened until he thought they might pop out of her head. "Really? Me?"

He stepped around the desk and took her hand. "I hate math. You love math. Clearly we need to switch places." Her hand trembled in his and he tightened his grip. Delicate fingers disappeared beneath his own as he pulled her over to the empty chair. "Have at it."

Standing behind the chair, she stared at him. "Are you serious?"

"Bills," he said and pointed to one stack of papers. "Offerings." He pointed to another pile. "Budget." His jabbed his finger at the spreadsheet open on the ancient laptop like it was his worst enemy.

Sinking into the worn leather chair, Hannah kept her hands clenched in her lap, as if she was afraid to touch anything on the desk. Noah saw her glance slide to the envelopes of cash in the donations pile and then dart quickly away. "Are you sure you want me to see all of this?"

Dragging a folding chair to the other side of the desk he sat across from her. "You're living in our house, you're taking my baby sister to therapy, and," his voice dropped to a low octave of seriousness, "I let you drive my truck. I trust you."

The words came out easily, so easily it surprised him. He remembered every cynical word he'd said about her, every skeptical thought he'd had, and now he was turning the church budget over to her. What would Kate say if she could see him now?

Kate. The name echoed in his mind and he pulled back. Loyalty tugged at his heart. He hadn't thought of her in days, maybe weeks. She was slipping from his thoughts right when she was so close to coming home.

Grabbing the church calendar, he looked away from Hannah and buried his nose in the messy pages, spending far too long studying the time schedule for their upcoming outreach.

For a long, silent moment, Hannah watched him. He could feel her gaze on him, but he refused to look up, refused to risk a glance into the mahogany depths of her eyes. He had a plan. Kate was coming back, and he had a plan. An important plan, a plan he had been holding onto for years. Thinking about Hannah's laugh and the strength that lay beneath her wary exterior would only complicate matters. She was a friend and nothing more.

One minute stretched into two and still she remained frozen in the chair. He could almost hear the confused war being waged in her head and he wondered which side was going to win. Then she reached for the first stack of papers and started sifting through the pile. From the corner of his eye, he saw her sorting and organizing the mess he'd made. They worked in silence, the desk separating them like neutral ground.

"Thank you." Her voice carried across the distance he put between them and drew him in. "For trusting me."

He looked up and fell into her gaze. Suddenly Kate was the last thing on his mind.

Chapter Eleven

AUGUST FLEW BY, THE HOT, summer days passing in a blur of activity. Hannah and Lily were caught up in a frantic flurry of wedding plans. Noah had complained for two days when they commandeered the kitchen table to painstakingly hand address the cream and gold invitations. She'd nearly spilled her lemonade over the pile of reception cards when she looked at the next name on her list and saw that it was director Chris Johnston.

"Oh, you'll love him" Lily said when she spotted her shocked expression. "He's the best man."

Noah had snorted at that and then ducked when Lily tossed a napkin at him.

Shaking her head, Hannah addressed the invitation, suddenly realizing that she now knew the home addresses of a number of Hollywood's most famous celebrities. Of every scam and con Lincoln had planned, he'd certainly never thought of anything like this. What would he do if he knew she had access to this kind of information? Wild plans and imaginings ran through her mind and turned her stomach, but she chased them away. She wasn't Sasha and Lincoln had no hold over her. Not anymore.

Noah's old truck was starting to feel like a second home to her as she served as Lily's driver and secret-keeper. Ben's shoot in New Zealand had been extended due to weather delays, but he swore that he would be back in plenty of time for the wedding. Pastor Evan was spending more and more time with young church plants in the area, encouraging and assisting their pastors as they tried to take root in neighborhoods that had been forgotten by so many other churches. His absence left Noah to assume more responsibility at The Hollywood Mission, and her heart ached for him as she saw the insecurity, doubt, and worry that clung to him as he tried to fill his father's shoes.

With Ben gone and Noah occupied at the church that left Hannah with the keys to the truck. She enjoyed the time she and Lily spent together, soaking up the new friendship like a person freed from years of solitary confinement. Lily pushed herself in physical therapy, sweating, crying, and praying her way through every exercise Andre gave her. The day she took her first step alone Hannah cheered so loudly everyone in the room turned to see Lily's triumph, then she burst into tears, overwhelmed with joy for her friend who was becoming more like a sister every day.

After therapy, she would leave Lily to the kids in her class and head to the small church office to help Noah. She didn't want to admit it, but the hours she spent sitting across from Noah, crunching numbers and organizing spreadsheets was her favorite part of the day. They had created two workspaces on one desk, their laptops sitting back to back formed the dividing line. Hannah's half of the desk was neat and tidy, papers stacked in specific piles, her collection of pens and pencils clustered in small mason jars she had scavenged from the church's craft closet. Noah's half of the desk was littered with random notes and scribbled messages trapped under books and half-empty coffee cups. He was still trying to keep his limo business running though he was having to turn down more clients as his hours spent at the church continued to grow.

Hannah watched him try to juggle both jobs and she did what she could to ease the burden. Noah didn't complain as she took over the majority of the church's administrative tasks. She was getting to know several of the church members as she returned their phone calls, helped schedule meetings, and answered questions. It felt good to be helping, and the Shaws treated her like family. It was only in the long, dark hours of the night that whispers of her past reminded her that she didn't belong, that she was lying to the very people who had given her their trust.

After the kids went home and the church was locked up, they would pile into Noah's truck for the short drive back to the Shaw house. Hannah sat in the middle to make room for Lily to get in and out of the truck, and every night she found herself inching closer to Noah. The warmth of his leg resting against hers and the distracted brush of his fingers against her hand sent tiny sparks dancing across her skin. He never seemed to notice, but every second she spent with him drew her in a little more until she knew every line of his face, the color of his five o'clock shadow, the way the blue of his eyes changed with his mood. She'd lay in bed at night and remember every word he said to her, every smile, every careless gesture. It was a fool's dream of course, but she clutched it tightly anyway, locking it away in her heart like a secret treasure no one else could find.

For the first time in years, she was happy . . . and that really terrified her. In her experience, happiness was always followed by crushing disappointment.

*****

"I know your secret."

Hannah jumped and nearly dropped the individual creamer cups she was adding to the wooden basket on the coffee table. The Sunday morning service had just ended and the coffee crowd was busier than usual. Autumn was creeping its way into the long days of the Southern California summer and people were excited for an excuse to dig out warm sweaters and drink hot coffee again.

Hannah was refilling supplies and chatting with church members when Noah snuck up behind her and whispered the ominous words.

"What?" She stammered, focusing on the coffee pots in front of her, as a finger of nerves wormed its way into her gut.

Noah took half the creamer cups from her and started refilling the French vanilla basket. "I said, I know your secret." A smug smile played on his face. He didn't look mad or disgusted, but she wasn't about to offer any information.

"And what secret is that?" Her mouth was dry and she remained perfectly still, afraid any movement would give her away. Whatever was coming next, she would find a way to explain. She would make him understand, even as her brain told her he never would.

Leaning in, his face hovered inches away from hers, so close the air between them warmed. The scent of his aftershave surrounded her and she took a step back, clenching her hand into a tight fist to keep from reaching up to touch him. He wasn't hers. He would never be hers.

Smirking, he leaned one hip against the table and crossed his arms. "You, my friend, are a PK."

Over the past few weeks, she'd planned a thousand different responses to questions about her background. As she got to know the Shaw family, she tiptoed along the line of honesty, deftly changing the subject or giving true, but vague answers when they asked about her family or her life before she came to Hollywood. No one ever asked about what she was doing before she ended up like trash abandoned on the steps of their church or why she'd tried to kill herself. It was like they knew the subject was off-limits, a part of her life she wasn't ready to share. What they didn't know was that her life before Hollywood was just as painful to remember, only for different reasons.

"PK?" she asked.

He nodded, secret knowledge glittering in his gaze. "You are a pastor's kid."

In every scenario she'd played out in her head, every response she'd planned, this hadn't been one of them. Heat bloomed in her face and she fought the urge to fan her cheeks. Instead she busied herself straightening the plastic stir sticks and shaking the insulated coffee carafes to make sure they were still full, even though she had refilled them only a few minutes earlier. "And what makes you say that?"

"My keen observational skills and years of experience having a pastor for a dad." He lifted his hand and ticked off a list of reasons on his fingers. "One, you know all the words to the classic worship songs. You only watch the screens for lyrics to the newest ones. Two, I've heard you on the phone with people and you understand Christian-speak, even from the people who go over the top with it. It doesn't throw you. Three, you are always serving. You see a need and you jump in, like you've been doing it your whole life, like you're used to being asked to fill in. It's second nature to you. All that," his voice was low, but triumphant, "adds up to pastor's kid."

She was saved from answering when an older woman came up to the table and smiled at them. She tucked her Bible under her arm and grabbed a disposable cup from the pile Hannah had just restocked. "And how are you today, sweetie?" she asked Hannah as the smell of fresh coffee mixed with the steam wafting up from the little white cup.

"Very well, thank you. How are you?" She felt Noah watching her, the weight of his gaze resting on her and she tried not to fidget. Lie. Deny. Survive. A thousand different excuses flew through her mind.

"Oh, I'm blessed. Blessed indeed." She added three sugar packets and four creamers to her coffee, swirling it with a stir stick and turning it into a barely beige concoction. "God is good."

"All the time." She was so distracted, the words slipped out in a reflex, an instinct Hannah was helpless to stop. She didn't hear Noah laugh, but she felt it vibrate in the space between them. With a quick step to her right, she kicked him under the table.

Hopping like he'd stepped on a tack, he shot her a dirty look as the women near the table stopped their conversations to stare at him. Maybe she was still fluent in Christian vocabulary, but that didn't mean her rebellious nature had completely vanished.

Noah stayed by her side, helping with the hospitality tables and making small talk. She had a distinct feeling he was keeping an eye on her, waiting to see if she'd bolt because he'd said too much about her past. She was grateful for the crowd and the busyness because it gave her time to think, to figure out what she wanted to say to him, how much she was prepared to reveal.

Lying had lost its appeal. Noah and his family had been kind to her. They'd taken her in and accepted her when they didn't have to, when any other person would have turned her away. They'd shared their home with her, welcomed her into their family, and while she knew it couldn't last forever, she wasn't ready to let go of it, not yet.

After all the church members had gone home and Pastor Evan was locking up, she found Noah sweeping the parking lot. Without a word, she picked up the dustpan and crouched down to scoop up the pile of trash and dirt he'd made. After tossing it in the dumpster, she held out her pinky finger towards him.

His eyebrows shot up in question, but he didn't hesitate to link his little finger with hers in an imitation of the schoolyard promise.

Nerves skittered through her body as she prepared to open the door, to let him in a little, to offer up a small part of her past, and hope that she wasn't making a mistake. "PK's," she said.

Noah grinned and tightened his pinky around hers, two children who took different paths meeting on common ground and forging a bond only they could understand, then he spun her out like they were dancing. The wind whipped her skirt and a laugh leapt from her soul.

It wasn't much of an admission, but it was real and it was true and it was her. It was a start.

Chapter Twelve

TWO WEEKS BEFORE THE WEDDING, even Noah was feeling the stress. In an attempt to keep the wedding date and location a secret from the press, most of the information for the guests had been left to the last minute. RSVPs were coming in every day, and Lily was obsessive about keeping track of everything in her notebook. Hannah was with her each step of the way and Noah was grateful for her steady presence. She always seemed to know the right thing to say when Lily started getting worried about a tiny detail that seemed inconsequential to him, but would apparently ruin the entire wedding if it wasn't exactly right.

Flower arrangements, candles, chair covers, the color of the napkins and tablecloths. It all seemed like a lot of nonsense to him. Lily and Ben would be getting married. They would go into the church as two single people and come out as husband and wife, joined together, a real-life happily ever after ending. To him, that was the only thing that really mattered. Everything else was fluff.

Of course, when he helpfully mentioned that small fact to Lily, his quiet and reserved sister tried to hit him with a unity candle. She would have succeeded if Hannah hadn't been sitting between them like a peace negotiator.

So, he left them to their endless online idea boards and the ever-growing pile of magazines spread across the living room table.

His little sister was getting married. To a movie star.

Staring into his coffee mug, he tried to dig up the excitement he had felt when she and Ben announced their engagement. But instead of excitement something else lurked there. A stab of loneliness had taken up residence in his heart.

Across the table, Hannah laughed and he followed the sound. In the past few months, everything about her had changed. The wariness was gone from her eyes, her too-pale skin had brightened, and twin circles of pink glowed on her cheeks. Smiling, he thought of how often that faint blush burned to a bright red when she was embarrassed. In the hospital and during the first few weeks she had been with them, she'd never smiled. Not a real smile, not the kind of smile that was free and unashamed. Now he saw it everyday. She'd stopped jumping at every sound as if she finally believed the monsters that had stalked her were gone. Even though she'd admitted to being raised by a pastor, he still didn't know why she ran away or what drove her to swallow the pills that nearly ended her life. He thought he was respecting her silence, giving her time to heal, but maybe he didn't ask because deep down he didn't want to know.

She was kind and efficient and she loved Lily. The two of them had become like sisters, giggling to themselves, changing the radio stations in his truck, disappearing for hours and coming back with nothing but stories of the people they had met. Meeting Hannah had been like finding a piece of their family he hadn't known was missing, but now that she was here, he couldn't imagine the house without her. It would be too quiet, too plain, too lonely.

Sitting on the sofa, he watched as Hannah and Lily hunched over the coffee table in the living room, studying photos of reception favors, weighing the pros and cons of candles versus picture frames, and ignoring his suggestion of those old-fashioned candy covered almonds. As they politely but firmly dismissed his idea to give every wedding guest a puppy, his dad came into the living room, sat in his recliner, and cleared his throat importantly.

All three of them looked up.

"It has come to my attention that someone here has been keeping a secret from me."

His dad levelled a hard stare at them and Noah hid his face in his coffee to keep from laughing at the panicked expressions on Hannah and Lily's faces. They both looked equally scared and equally guilty.

"I may be slow," his dad continued. "But eventually even I can see the writing on the wall."

"What's the matter, Dad?" Lily's voice shot up an octave and her face turned bright red.

He immediately wondered what his little sister was up to. She had always been a terrible liar and judging by the look on her face, she still was.

His dad didn't seem to notice Lily's tell-tale nervousness as he turned to Hannah. "It seems that Hannah here has been doing a lot more than just driving you around town."

Hannah froze like a startled deer, her body so still that Noah wasn't even sure she was breathing.

"It seems," he continued in his best pastor-voice. "That she has been very busy in the church office as well."

Color rushed to her face, but still she didn't move. She was tense and rigid, like a spring stretched to its limit. Her eyes darted to his like a co-conspirator, but Noah knew she'd never say it was his idea. If she thought there was trouble, she'd shoulder the blame herself.

Sure enough, she took a deep breath and faced his dad alone. "I am sorry, Pastor Evan. I should have asked first. I was just trying to help."

Noah tried to speak, but his dad held up a hand, stopping whatever he was about to say. "Hannah," his voice softened. "You misunderstand. I wasn't accusing you, I was trying to thank you. The office has never been more organized. Honestly, I can't remember the last time the church's monthly budget was done on time. You've been a huge blessing to us. In more ways than I can count."

Tears sparkled in her eyes as Lily reached over and held her hand.

"And that's why, I'd like to give you this." His dad held out an envelope, smiling as she took it from his hands.

When she peeked inside she gasped and tried to give it back. "I can't take this, Pastor Evan. Not after everything you all have done for me. It wouldn't be right."

"It's not a gift," his dad said. "That's your first paycheck. Well, pay cash . . . I wasn't sure if you had a checking account. If you're willing, I'd like to officially hire you as our church's administrative assistant."

Incredulous was the only word Noah could think of to describe her reaction. He wanted to memorize it. To be able to perfectly recall the parade of emotions that raced across her face like shooting stars flashing across the sky, disbelief followed by hope followed by worry followed by one more dash of hope. It must be what children look like on Christmas morning when they dare to believe their biggest wish might be sitting under the tree, but they're too afraid to open the gifts just in case it isn't there.

She stared at the envelope in her hands, holding it like she couldn't quite believe it was real. "Are you sure about this?"

And there it was. The unwillingness to believe, the dreadful fear of hope, the worry that if she allowed herself to dream it would all be taken away from her. He hated that she had become so jaded, so tormented by the world, so accustomed to disappointment and manipulation.

If his dad noticed her skepticism, he didn't acknowledge it. Instead he smiled broadly. "I am absolutely sure. You've done amazing work in the office, and we would be lucky to have you."

Lily squealed and threw her arms around Hannah. "Please say yes! This job is perfect for you. Plus, I need to see someone other than Noah every day."

"You know you love me, Brat," he replied, but his focus was on Hannah and the way she hesitated. She hadn't said yes. If she was going to leave, this would be the time. She had recovered, and she was strong enough to be on her own. With the money his dad had just given her, she could start over. There was no reason for her to stay any longer, unless she wanted to.

"This means so much to me. Really." She wiped at the tears that escaped down her cheeks. "But you might not want me there, not officially. You don't know . . . I mean, there are things I've done that I'm not proud of. The congregation, if they knew they might not . . . " Her voice disappeared in a whisper and she dropped her gaze, sinking onto the floor like she wanted to disappear.

The air conditioner switched on and hummed in the background as his dad considered his answer. "Believe it or not, Hannah, I wasn't always a pastor, and I have never been perfect. But I can tell you this, the mistakes of our past can become our greatest testimony if we surrender them to God and let Him redeem them." Leaning forward he rested his elbows on his knees. "Jacob was a liar. Rahab was a prostitute.

Peter was a coward. Paul threw Christians in prison. Nothing you have done is beyond His forgiveness."

The words settled over the room and Noah was humbled again by how his dad worked. He always knew the right thing to say. Hannah was silent and he could imagine the arguments running through her brain. For a moment he thought she was going to say no. That she was going to thank them in her self-deprecating way and mumble something about not wanting to be a burden and then pack her tiny bag and disappear into the night. That possibility scared him more than he thought it would. He was the one who hadn't wanted her to come here, and now he didn't want her to leave.

Tears shimmered in her eyes when she looked up again. "This means a lot to me," she said. "After everything you've already done for me, this is just . . . it's just . . . "

He sat in silence, surprised by how much he wanted her to say yes, by how much he wanted her to stay, but unable to say it out loud.

Taking a deep breath, she steadied herself, her gaze meeting his in a quick flash, a fleeting glance before she faced his dad and in that stolen glance he saw her answer. "It would be an honor to work at the Mission. Thank you so much."

His dad stood and gave her a hug as Lily whooped with joy.

"Let's go make brownies to celebrate." Lily clapped her hands then wheeled towards the door. "We can decide how to redecorate your new office while we bake." Disappearing into the kitchen, she was gone before Hannah had a chance to respond.

Still clutching the envelope in her hands, Hannah looked at Noah, uncertainty hovering in her eyes as if she was worried he would disapprove.

"Congratulations," he said. The word felt too small for what was happening at that moment, but nothing else seemed to fit. Nothing else could encompass it. There was a change in the air. He was witnessing a fresh start, a second chance, and there wasn't a greeting card word big enough for that. "You're going to do great."

He watched the empty doorway long after she had followed Lily into the kitchen, the sounds of laughter rising and falling like a song.

"That was a good suggestion." His dad sat down again in his ugly, but comfortable chair. His mom had tried for years to get rid of it, but according to his dad it was where he did his best thinking. Eventually she gave up arguing and started throwing colorful quilts over it instead. "I'm glad you told me how much she was doing at the church. I've been so busy with these young pastors, I didn't see what was right in front of me."

It was unintentional, but the words "young pastors" hit Noah with a wave of guilt. His dad hadn't meant anything by it, he knew that, but doubt latched on to him and wouldn't let go. His dad would love for him to be one of those young pastors, on fire for God and ready to change the world. But he couldn't. Not yet. Maybe not ever.

"They're lucky to have you," he said, lamely echoing the words his dad said to Hannah only minutes before.

"Are you doing okay?" His dad's perception was as sharp as ever. Even before he became a pastor, he had always known when something was going on with people. Noah had never been able to hide much from his dad, and apparently even as an adult, he still couldn't do it.

Sighing heavily, he sat on the sofa, ready to come clean. "Dad, I know how much you want me to join the ministry at the church and

I know I'm letting you down." Saying it out loud didn't make it better. In fact, it made it much worse. Guilt coated every word and he hated himself for being so selfish, so filled with doubt. "I just don't know if that's what I'm supposed to do. I'm sorry."

"Noah, you're my son, and I love you, no matter what. Pastor, limo driver, lawyer, construction worker, it doesn't matter. Do what God calls you to do, not what I want or what your sister wants, or what anyone else says you should you do. This is between you and the Lord."

It sounded so simple when his dad said it. But the more he tried to grasp it, the more he felt like it was slipping way. God's plan wasn't crystal clear, it wasn't written down as instructions for him to follow. He had no idea what he was supposed to do so he was paralyzed, stuck in limbo, afraid to take a step for fear he would be going in the wrong direction.

"I have no idea what He wants me to do."

"Son, God has a plan, you just need to be quiet long enough to hear Him share it with you."

"But the church—"

"The church will survive. Planting the Mission is what your mom and I were called to do. God might have something else in mind for you. If I have put too much pressure on you, that's my fault and I'm sorry. I appreciate everything you and Lily have done at the church. After your mom died, I desperately needed the help, and I have loved having you both by my side. But Lily is getting married and you're getting older. If this season is ending, then I will thank God for the time we've had and praise Him for whatever He's bringing next."

"I wish I knew what that was." From the kitchen, Hannah giggled, and he turned his head towards the sound. Maybe he was making it too complicated. Maybe he was overanalyzing and overthinking everything.

His dad sat back, looking completely undisturbed, completely at ease in his faith that God was in control. "You'll know it when you know it."

Chapter Thirteen

IT WAS STRANGE SEEING BEN Prescott, movie star and international celebrity, playing guitar during a Sunday morning service. Hannah wasn't sure she would ever get used to it, but apparently the rest of the church had. There was no screaming for autographs or flashes popping in his face. Ben was a part of The Hollywood Mission family, and his presence, however crazy it seemed to her, was no big deal to anyone else.

Lily was thrilled to have him home. The location shoot had been extended again and he finally made it back, only a week before the wedding and just before the bride completely freaked out. Lily had been in a state of perpetual nervousness, her words coming faster and faster with every passing day until Hannah could barely keep up with her. Even Andre had to tell her to stop and take a few deep breaths during their therapy sessions. As the days flew by, Lily's to-do list seemed to grow by leaps and bounds and her nervous energy made it impossible for her to keep still. Hannah was sure she had driven her across every inch of the greater Los Angeles area.

Having Ben back home seemed to help. His strong presence soothed her frazzled nerves and Hannah was happy to see her friend relax a little bit. As she sang with the congregation, she marveled at how Lily always looked right at home during worship. Sitting in the wheelchair at the front of the stage, her face was radiant as she sang, as if all the anxiety and stress disappeared and she was free.

Hannah sat in the front row with Noah during the service. She loved the warmth of his shoulder next to her as they listened to Pastor Evan's message. The church had welcomed her with open arms when she first started attending with the Shaws, and when Pastor Evan had announced her new position the church had cheered and applauded and the love was more than she had ever expected.

The Hollywood Mission felt more like home with each passing day. There were times that the cushioned chairs, the fresh coffee, and seeing the familiar faces every weekend made her long for the days she had taken for granted. Growing up she never realized what she had or how lucky she had been. She had been loved, protected, and trusted. Day by day, lie by lie, choice by choice she had destroyed it. She had run from the one place that had always welcomed her. Sure, some of the older church members had looked at her askance, knowing she was the pastor's rebellious daughter, the one who pushed the limits, but she had always known she could go to the church, even when she didn't want to, even when her parents had to drag her there, the doors were always open to her, she always had a place there. Until the day she turned away from God, too ashamed to call on Him, afraid of His rejection, embarrassed by what she had become.

Pastor Evan called the church to pray and as she stood, she felt the staggering weight of her loss, the consequences of her foolish choices. It was like a chain that held her down, links of condemnation that wrapped around her soul until she couldn't remember what it felt like to not be ashamed. Regret was her constant companion. Even as the pastor's soothing words filled the sanctuary, whispers of unworthiness echoed in her mind and tried to drown out his prayers.

The words of love were meant for someone else. They weren't for her, they would never be for her. She lost the right to speak to God, she had thrown it away with both hands and she had no right to call on the Father she had abandoned.

She stood with the congregation, her head bowed and eyes closed and accepted being an outsider. If this was as close as she could get to God, she would learn to be content with that. It was already more than she deserved.

Noah breathed, steady and even, beside her as Evan prayed for the church, his warm voice filling the sanctuary, reaching every row, every chair.

"It's no accident that you are here today. It's not a coincidence or random chance. God knew exactly where you'd be today. He's been with you every step of the way. Through every mistake you have made, every bad decision, God has been with you. You have never been alone."

Her heart beat rapidly in her chest, and tears gathered in her eyes as he spoke. Tingles of electricity shot through her legs as his words washed over her. Shame rose like quicksand, clawing at her, reminding her in an unending parade of mental images of every poor decision she had ever made. The disappointment on her dad's face when he caught her sneaking in after curfew. Smoking under the bleachers at school. The boys she flirted with and the one she ran away with.

Tears streamed down her face. God knew. He knew it all. There was no place to hide, no place she could run. It was too late, she was laid bare before God. She could hide who she was from Lily and Pastor Evan, she could even hide it from Noah, but she couldn't hide it from

God. There was nothing she could say, no defense she could offer to the One who had seen it happen, who had watched the drama of her life unfold.

"Whatever you've done, God was there. He wept with you. He walked with you even when you turned from Him. When you cursed Him, when you thought He'd left you all alone, He was with you."

There was the night Lincoln found her waiting tables in the rundown diner on a dark side street off Hollywood Boulevard wondering where her next meal would come from. He took her home, gave her a place to stay, and in exchange he took everything she had. He showed her how to steal, how to hustle, and how to make money on the streets.

"God never abandoned you."

The first night in Norma Jean's. When she had looked at the stage, the leering stares of the men waiting to watch her dance, and then run from the filthy dressing room to throw up in the bathroom. The numbness that engulfed her when she stepped on the stage and pretended she was invisible.

"God was there."

She choked back a sob, her hands shaking. God was there. In the midst of the darkness, He was there.

"And now He is waiting, with His arms open wide to bring you home."

She wanted to run. To cover her ears and block out the words. She had failed so badly. She had let everyone down. God gave her a chance and she blew it. She didn't deserve a second chance. Not after everything she had done. She wasn't worthy of His love.

"Your sins have been paid for. You don't have to live in bondage to your past. God has a plan for you. He has a purpose for you. No matter what you've done, it's not too late. You can start over today. Jesus has ransomed you and set you free. You can't earn His love, because you already have it. He has never stopped loving you and He has never stopped fighting for you. He's just waiting for you to say *yes*."

Hope burned in her heart. A hope she thought was dead breaking through the darkness that clouded her soul. It fought past the memories of her darkest days, past the whispered accusations that tried to distract her. It fell into her heart like a lifeline, like a rescue from the pit she had fallen into. Her hand twitched at her side. It was so close, it was within her grasp.

"Today is the day to let go of your past, to let go of the pain you've been carrying, to lay it at the cross and pick up the mantle of Christ instead. You are not your past, you are not your failures, you are not your regrets. You are who God says you are and He says you are His."

Tears rolled in a torrent down her cheeks, but she didn't care.

"If you are ready to give your life to Christ, to accept Him as your Savior, to receive the gift of His sacrifice and His grace, raise your hand right now."

As she lifted her hand the spark of hope that had whispered to life broke into a fire. It filled her heart, swallowing regret and doubt, banishing self-pity and silencing fear. As Evan led them in prayer, Noah's hand rested on her shoulder and she heard his whispered prayer for her. He stood with her, walking beside her. She didn't hesitate, she held nothing back, speaking the words boldly, surrendering her life to God and letting His grace wash her clean as she ran home to her Father.

*****

Hannah had never been hugged so much. Lily cried when she heard the news, and that made her start crying all over again. She was free.

The word reverberated in her mind. *Free.* Free from her past, free from her mistakes. God had never turned His back on her and even in her darkest moments, He had been there and He loved her. He had always loved her.

Noah was a protective presence, staying by her side as they cleaned up. Once the hospitality tables were put away and the coffee pots were washed and set out to dry, she stood on the covered dock outside the sanctuary and stared at the endless blue sky. She didn't see the chain link fence or the houses in the distance. She didn't hear the traffic or the distant thump of music blaring from a passing car. For the first time in years, she stared at the sky and didn't feel alone.

She wasn't a lost, rebellious girl filled with regret and too scared to go home. Not anymore. As a crisp autumn breeze drifted across her face, she closed her eyes and knew the truth. She was loved.

"Penny for your thoughts."

Noah had snuck up on her, but she didn't jump at the sound of his voice. It was as if she had been expecting him, waiting on that exact spot, knowing he would find her, knowing he would be there.

"It's been quite a day," she said, her gaze fixed on the sky and the puffy clouds that floated against the brilliant blue.

He stood close to her and for a crazy moment she thought about leaning into his side, resting against his chest and letting her head fall against his shoulder. Instead, she grasped the metal railing in front of her, tightening her grip when he took another step towards her.

"That was a big decision," he said. "I'm happy for you."

"During the altar call, how did you know? How did you know I raised my hand? Were you peeking?" Sunlight caught on the rough stubble on his face as she glanced sideways at him.

"No." He leaned against the railing beside her. "I didn't need to peek. You were sniffling up a storm."

"Shut up." She bounced her shoulder against his, giving him a hard bump that almost knocked him over.

He laughed as he straightened beside her. "At least this time they were happy tears, right?"

Embarrassment crawled through her. Noah had seen her at her very worst. He'd probably never be able to forget the night he found her. That might always be the way he thought of her, a broken girl left to die in the street.

She turned to go, but his hand on her arm stopped her. "I just meant that it's good to see you happy. You've been through so much, and you should know how special you are."

Words lodged in her throat and her stomach flipped. Attraction zipped through her until her toes curled.

She mumbled something that sounded like thank you, and then sucked in a breath when he pulled her against his side, wrapping his arm around her shoulder and resting his head on top of hers.

"It's only good things for you from now on," he said and squeezed her tight.

She leaned in to him, jealously guarding the feeling, committing it to her memory. It was a perfect day. The sun was shining, she had a fresh start on life, and she was in Noah's arms. Anything was possible.

"What's going on here?"

Thinly veiled suspicion broke the spell that had been woven around them. Noah dropped his arm as he turned and quickly stepped away from her.

A woman in a crisp black suit with hair the color of a sunset was standing on the other side of the dock, her hands planted on her hips as she watched them.

"Kate?" Noah raced across the distance and swept her up in his arms. "I thought you weren't getting in until tomorrow."

"Surprise." Her laughter rang out as Noah lifted her off her feet, crushing her against his chest in a way that made Hannah's heart ache. So this was Kate.

The red-haired beauty glanced over his shoulder, her sharp green eyes taking in every detail from Hannah's outfit to her smudged mascara before lingering on the scar above her eye.

Noah set her down, but kept his hands on her waist. "Does Lily know you're here?"

Kate's smile was radiant as she grinned up at him. "Not yet."

"She's going to be so excited. I think she's in the office." Noah grabbed her hand and started pulling her towards the church. Laughing, they disappeared through the side door.

Left alone on the empty dock, Hannah turned back to the cityscape spread before her. Disappointment curled in her stomach, and she tried to force it away. She had no right to be disappointed. Noah was a friend, that was all. He'd never pretended to be anything else, and she had no right to expect something more from him.

But no matter how many times she said it, she couldn't stop thinking about how quickly Noah had forgotten her.

Chapter Fourteen

WIND WHISTLED THROUGH THE CAB of Noah's truck as they flew down the 101. Kate's red hair whipped around her face, her left arm resting on the door as she darted through traffic with the practiced ease of someone used to the controlled chaos of Los Angeles freeways. Squeezed between Kate and Lily, Hannah couldn't believe how easily Noah had turned his keys over to the vibrant lawyer that morning. Lily was listing all the things left to do before the wedding on Saturday when Kate asked Noah if they could borrow his truck. He had tossed the keys across the kitchen table without question and without a lecture on tires, rain, or gas mileage.

Resentment settled in Hannah's gut as she thought back to the polite but skeptical interrogation she'd gone through before he relinquished those same keys to her. And she hadn't missed the cutting glance Kate sent her way when Lily invited her to join them for the day.

Maybe she deserved the suspicion. Maybe she could understand it. But it still hurt.

They were ahead of schedule when they finished with the photographer, the videographer, and the caterer so Lily suggested that they stop by the studio to see Ben before heading to her final wedding gown fitting. Kate jumped at the idea of going to a movie set and within minutes they were racing down the freeway like three college girls on spring break, determined to make the most of every minute of freedom.

Hannah was both terrified and thrilled by the prospect of visiting the set. She'd never been to a real movie studio, she'd never even been on any of the tourist tours of the studios, and the closer they got, the more the butterflies in her stomach multiplied. Playing board games with Ben Prescott was still a surreal and strange experience for her and she second guessed everything she said around him. He didn't act like a big shot celebrity and he wasn't what she expected from a major movie star, but his fame intimidated her, as if she were too inconsequential, too small for him to notice. She was sure she'd make a colossal fool of herself if they bumped into any other big stars, but even that fear couldn't stop the excited tapping of her toes against the floorboard.

When they pulled up to the security gate, Kate gave the security guard Lily's name and after a quick check, the wooden barrier that blocked the entrance to the studio lifted and they drove on to the lot.

From her phone, Lily read the directions Ben sent her. They all agreed it was a victory they got lost only once in the twisting maze of streets named after famous stars of the past before finding the right sound stage.

As Kate helped Lily into the wheelchair, Hannah stared at the building. The size of it overwhelmed her. From the outside it looked like a huge, concrete warehouse. The plain, industrial walls looked like every other building around it. Square, nondescript boxes dotted the landscape one after another in orderly rows, like a field planted with concrete seeds that one day sprouted into giant buildings. The only hint of what was going on behind their walls were the large blue numbers painted on each one. They found number twenty-three and walked up to the brown door carved into the side of the building. A sign warned them not to enter when the red light was on. They glanced at the red bulb beside the door, taking longer than necessary to make absolutely certain it was off before Kate grabbed the handle and pulled the door open with authority.

Stepping inside was like stepping into another world. When the heavy, metal door closed solidly behind them, the bright sunlight of Southern California, the smog tinted air, and the sounds of traffic melted away and they were swallowed by a world of make-believe. Cameras, cords, lights, and scaffolding surrounded them on every side. Burly men in stained jeans pushed huge set pieces from one side of the soundstage to the other while swarms of assistants wearing headsets and carrying clipboards walked quietly, but quickly, through the tangle of equipment. No one paid any attention to two wide-eyed women frozen in place and the slightly less-impressed woman in the wheelchair.

Hannah didn't know which way to look. It was huge, like a small city set up within the confines of the concrete box. Staring at the ceiling with its rows of multi-colored lights hanging from crisscrossing metal pipes, she nearly tripped over something that looked like a small railroad track that ran down the center of the floor.

"This way." Lily tried to pick her way through the cables and cords that littered the ground. They ended up taking the long way around the relatively clean perimeter of the soundstage so the wheelchair could get through without getting stuck or knocking over any of the equipment.

About halfway around the building, Lily spotted Ben. He was sitting in a folding chair looking over the script in his hand. When she called his name he looked up and the smile he gave her melted Hannah's heart. What would it be like to be with someone who looked at her that way? As if she was the answer to his every prayer and not just a means to an end. Ben loved Lily, it was obvious in everything he said, in the way he held her hand, in the way his eyes studied her as if he was memorizing every emotion, every expression that crossed her face.

He dropped the script on the chair, then dodged a stagehand coiling rope and waved away an anxious clipboard wielding young woman before joining them.

"I'm so glad you made it," he said, kissing Lily on the cheek.

Lily's smile was brighter than the lights that glowed overhead. "I'll take any chance I can get to see you."

"Oh ick." Kate rolled her eyes with enough drama to star in the movie. "Just get married already."

"It's nice to see you, too, Kate." Ben laughed and took her place behind Lily's wheelchair. He gave them a quick tour of the set, explaining technical terms that Hannah knew she'd never remember and introducing them to the people they passed. Ben knew everyone and it was obvious he was well-liked by the crew. He treated each of them with the same humor and kindness he gave her.

Everyone they met knew about Lily. She was welcomed to the set like a visiting dignitary and enveloped in the warmth of the close-knit movie family as they congratulated her on the upcoming wedding.

Ben found the director, Chris Johnston, huddled over a monitor watching scenes flicker before him on the tiny screen. He gave Hannah a broad smile and shook her hand, then stuttered and tripped over the leg of the table almost sending the small monitor crashing to the floor when he saw Kate. Glancing from Chris to Kate, she tried to keep her face composed. Chris was smitten, but if Kate noticed the effect she had on the director she didn't let on. It was the same with Noah. Kate was beautiful, intelligent, successful, and either oblivious, or indifferent, to the way men fell for her.

Jealousy sprouted, a prickly weed that burrowed into her heart, searching for fertile ground. She tried to ignore it, to reason her way out of it, but the more Chris stared at Kate, the more she remembered Noah hugging her on the dock and tossing her his keys that morning. Bitterness seeped in and she didn't know how to stop it. She was still on the outside looking in, peering through a window into a life she couldn't have.

As the four of them talked, she slipped away to the craft services area, astonished by the amount of food spread out before her. Her sweet tooth beckoned and she gave in. Nibbling on a chocolate chip cookie, she wandered around, absorbing the set, in awe of the amount of work that went into making a movie, and carefully avoiding bumping into anything as she waited for the group to finish chatting.

She was debating grabbing another cookie, or two, when a husky voice echoed behind her.

"Sasha?"

Habit made her turn before she could stop herself. Hearing the name transported her back in time, back into the shadows she thought she'd escaped. Dread coiled in her stomach and her legs turned to lead, too heavy to run, pinning her to the spot, paralyzed by the past.

A young man wearing a baseball cap emblazoned with a movie logo stood in front of her. A coiled cable hung over one shoulder, as if he'd been on his way to make a delivery and had suddenly taken a detour. An unkempt beard covered the lower half of his face, and a smile peeked through the scruff as he looked at her. "I thought I recognized you. From that club by the strip. NJ's right?"

Dryness caked her mouth, her words crumbling like dust on her tongue. Blood pulsed in her ears and spikes of fear shot through her limbs. He knew her. He knew who she was.

"Sorry?" She mumbled, her eyes searching for an escape.

"You're Sasha. I used to go to that club to watch you dance." He shifted his stance, stepping closer to her, closing the distance between them, his presence becoming a tangible thing, a press that vibrated against her skin even though he hadn't touched her. It repulsed her, it made her skin crawl, and her brain screamed for her to run.

Backing away, she shook her head. "I think you have me confused with someone else."

He laughed. "No, I remember cause I went to that place every night for like two weeks with a bunch of the guys from my last shoot." He leaned in like he was sharing a secret. "You were always my favorite." He said the words like a compliment, but all she could think about was how much he had seen. As his gaze drifted down her body, she felt sick.

"You used to wear those gold boots, and that black dress." Caught up in the memory, he rattled on, his voice too loud, too true. She had to get away. "You got like half my paycheck one time. All in singles of course."

She fought to control her breathing, searching for the detachment she had used on the stage. She wasn't here, not really, she was gone. Far away, hidden somewhere else, it was someone else's body on display, someone else being bought and sold. But he kept talking, kept stepping closer, pulling her into the present, the chains of her past wrapping tightly around her until there was no escape.

"You should come party with us tonight. Are you still at NJ's? Maybe we could hook up after—" Stopping suddenly, he looked at her, taking in her appearance, his memory of her at odds with what he was seeing now.

Sasha would never wear jeans and a baggy t-shirt. Her hair was brushed, but not styled and the only make-up she was wearing was lip gloss, no doubt a far cry from the heavy make-up she had been wearing the last time he saw her. She felt the change in his demeanor, saw it in the narrowing of his eyes, heard it in the suspicion in his voice. "How did you get in here?"

"I—um. I'm visiting a friend." Nausea rolled through her. She was drowning, swimming in waves of memories.

Stepping closer, he looked at her again. The humor in his gaze was gone, replaced by something else. Something hard and dark as he raked his eyes over her body. "Listen, Sasha—" He reached for her and she stepped back, hitting the table behind her and sending a stack of plastic cups crashing to the floor.

"I'm not Sasha. I'm not who you think I am."

Turning, she raced away and ran straight into Kate.

*****

Hannah stood in the dressing room, fastening the row of tiny, fabric covered buttons that ran down the back of Lily's wedding dress. It was a beautiful satin and lace gown. The A-line silhouette was classic, and the long, lace sleeves looked like something from old Hollywood, a nostalgic era of happy endings and true love. Intricate pearl designs decorated the hem and the short train. It was perfect for Lily, and she looked like a princess ready to marry her prince.

"So what did you think of Chris?" Lily's blue eyes twinkled in the mirror as she watched Hannah work.

She furrowed her brow, intent on the long line of buttons. "Who?"

"You just met him. The director. Ben's best friend. He's pretty cute, right?"

"Oh, I guess. I don't really remember." Truthfully, she didn't remember much about the visit to the movie set. The sudden reminder of her past had taken all of the joy out of the day. Anxiety filled her. How many people did the stagehand tell about her? Would word get back to Ben that his future wife had brought a stripper to the movie set? Would he put the pieces of her past together? Maybe it was already too late.

Kate's eyes had been sharp, watching her as they walked around the set, and Hannah wondered how much she had overheard. She had tried to relax, to keep a smile on her face, but it was impossible. Every shadow held a secret waiting to be told. She was certain Ben was going to kick her out at any moment, one of those clipboard wielding assistants was going to whisper in his ear and everyone would know the truth. She had nearly fainted from relief when Lily finally announced they had to leave for the bridal salon.

No matter how far she ran, she wouldn't ever be able to escape her past. God had forgiven her, she was sure of that, but she was equally sure that no one else would. She could only hope that Lily and Noah never found out.

"He's a really nice guy." Lily pulled on the sleeve of the dress, keeping up a steady stream of nervous chatter. "And he's a Christian. He normally attends our church but he's been gone so much with the new movie you haven't had a chance to meet him yet. I knew you'd like him. So, you know . . . "

Her voice trailed off teasingly, and Hannah looked up to meet her friend's reflection in the mirror. "What?"

Lily winked knowingly and Hannah scoffed. "Oh, come on. Me and Chris? I don't think so."

"Why not?" The genuine disappointment in Lily's voice was enough to make her laugh. Lily wanted to set her up with Chris. Apparently, romance was contagious.

"You're just obsessed with love because you're getting married." Shaking her head, she went back to the buttons, making a mental note of how long it was going to take to do this on the morning of the wedding and completely dismissing Lily's comments about the movie director.

"And what's wrong with that?" Lily asked. "So I want you to be happily married and blissfully in love. Ben and I are getting married. Noah has Kate. You could—"

Her hands stilled on the button as her heart fell. "Noah and Kate?" She should have known. The way he hugged her, the stories they shared, and the way she made him laugh. They were perfect for each other. Kate was everything Noah deserved. She was beautiful, successful, and smart and she was already a part of the family. Of course, they should be together.

"Well, not officially. But he's been in love with her for years," Lily whispered, both of them aware that Kate was outside the dressing room waiting to see Lily in her wedding gown. "It took me getting married to get her to leave Boston, but now that she's here, he finally has a chance to tell her how he feels."

Well, that was that. Hannah knew she'd been foolish for thinking that she could ever be with Noah, for letting herself dream about him.

At least now she knew. Noah would never see her that way because he was already in love with Kate. She wanted to be happy for him, but that didn't make it any less painful.

Keeping her head down so Lily wouldn't see the hurt, she finished the last few buttons and stepped back. "You look beautiful."

"I couldn't have done this without you," Lily said, and pulled her into a tight hug.

Fanning her face to stop the tears, Hannah handed her the veil and turned towards the door. "I'll be waiting outside with Kate for the big reveal."

She stepped into the waiting area and saw Kate standing on a small pedestal in front of a curved bank of mirrors. The seamstress was pinning and fitting the pale, blush bridesmaid dress. The dress flattered her every curve and softened the hard edge of her business-like persona. "She is almost ready," she said, meeting Kate's gaze in the mirrors.

The lawyer gave her a curt nod in acknowledgment, the chill in her eyes more than enough to tell Hannah that she'd made up her mind about her. This was the woman Noah loved. Hot embarrassment filled her, she'd never had a chance with him.

When the door to the dressing room opened, they both turned. Lily stood before them, glowing like only a bride can.

"You're standing." Kate whispered the words, as if she was afraid to say them too loudly, as if the force of her breath might knock her over.

Taking small, tentative steps, Lily made her way to the mirrors. Tears sparkled in her eyes when she saw herself standing in her wedding gown, fours days away from marrying Ben.

She took another step and wobbled. Hannah dashed to her side, and held her elbow. "I'm okay. Just a little misstep. My legs still feel new, like they don't quite belong to me."

After helping Lily on to the pedestal, Hannah stepped back and let the seamstress adjust the veil. It floated down like a cloud, enveloping Lily in a gauzy cocoon, wrapping her in a mist of lace and tulle.

Tears glistened in Kate's eyes as she stared at her friend. "How? When?"

Lily wiped her own tears away. "Hannah and I have been practicing and plotting."

Kate's sharp green eyes turned to her and Hannah couldn't decipher what she saw in their depths. She suddenly felt out of place, like she had intruded on a friendship, an interloper crashing a party she hadn't been invited to.

Lily turned carefully on the small step. "Hannah, you have been with me every step of the way . . . literally." She laughed and used a tissue to dry her cheeks. "And I would love for you to walk the rest of the way with me. I know it's last minute, but will you be one of my bridesmaids on Saturday?"

On cue, the saleslady returned with a copy of Kate's dress. Hannah stared at it, her fingers brushing against the soft fabric. Lily wanted her to be a bridesmaid, to stand beside her in the wedding.

The reality of the request hit her hard, and disjointed prayers began running through her mind. Just a few months ago she wanted to die. She hadn't seen any other way out of the life she was trapped in, but God had not only saved her life, He gave her friends who treated her like family. She didn't deserve any of it, but God had done it anyway.

She took the dress, struggling to form words against the tightness in her throat. "It would be my honor."

Lily cheered and hugged her, while Kate stood by silently. As she went to the dressing room to try on the dress, she felt Kate's hard stare following her.

Chapter Fifteen

"I'M JUST SAYING, HOW MUCH do you actually know about her?"

Noah withdrew as far as the hard metal back of the chair would allow and stared at his French fries. He'd lost his appetite. He should have known this was going to be an ambush. When Kate waltzed into the church office that morning and suggested they grab lunch to catch up, he hadn't hesitated. They wound up at an outside table at a restaurant on CityWalk, watching the vibrant life of Hollywood walk past. Now he was trapped, and she knew it.

"I thought we were having a nice lunch," he said, hoping she would drop it.

"We are." She picked up her milkshake and swirled the straw in the thick vanilla concoction. Her dark sunglasses hid her eyes but he knew there was suspicion lurking behind those lenses. "We're having lunch and talking about what in the world you were thinking bringing her into your house. A girl who overdosed in the church parking lot. A girl you know nothing about."

"It wasn't my idea." The words escaped before he thought about them, a reflex, and he instantly regretted them. It felt like a betrayal of Hannah, like he was implying that he hadn't wanted her there. Which, if he was honest, was true. But after everything they had been through, after everything she had done for their family, he didn't like the feeling.

Kate shook her head, sunlight catching on the red of her hair. "Noah, you and I are supposed to be the realists. Lily has always been soft-hearted. She's the one who rescues wounded birds and stray kittens. If Jack the Ripper said he was selling cookies was for a good cause, she'd buy them and then invite the guy in for coffee. Your dad is the same way. He thinks everyone is worth saving, and I love that about him, but some people don't deserve forgiveness."

The bite in her words and the harshness of her voice stunned him. Boston was supposed to have been a fresh start for her, a chance for her to heal, but she came back more embittered than ever. "You don't mean that."

"Yes, I do." Steel echoed back at him, unbending, unforgiving steel. He remembered the fun-loving, impulsive girl he had first met, the loud-talking, loud-laughing, optimistic college freshman Lily had brought to their house. Only a ghost of that girl remained, and he mourned her loss.

"Noah, Lily needs us to see the reality of the situation. We're supposed to protect her, even from herself." Sitting back, she waited for an explanation, but he didn't know how to start.

"My dad was the one who suggested it. He said God brought her to the church for a reason, and I agree with him." It wasn't much of a defense, but he was at a loss. On paper, it probably did sound like a foolish thing to do, letting Hannah stay with them, but she had been such a blessing to their family he couldn't believe it had been the wrong decision. He couldn't imagine the church or their house without her.

Kate stared across the decorative fence, the thin, iron line that separated them from the crowds on the other side. "I'm worried about you guys. I don't want anything to happen to you—any of you."

He reached across the table and patted her hand. "Nothing is going to happen to us. She's been with us for four months and she hasn't killed any of us. Yet." He laughed, but Kate didn't.

"This isn't a joke, Noah. This city, this place, bad stuff happens here all the time." She withdrew her hand and focused on her salad, stabbing pieces of lettuce with her fork.

The pain of her loss was still there, he saw it in the tense set of her jaw, heard it in the edge of her voice, bubbling under the surface, a roiling lake of anger waiting for a reason to erupt. He didn't know what to say, so he didn't say anything. Lily had been hurt, but she was still alive, he still had his little sister to pick on and rely on. Kate's little sister was gone. They had been in the wrong place at the wrong time, and only Kate survived.

Picking up her water glass, she swirled the ice cubes around and around. "I'm not saying she's planning anything terrible, but I don't like the chance you're taking with her. You don't even know her."

A million little details leapt to his mind. Didn't know her? He knew she liked mocha lattes in the morning, but she couldn't drink caffeine after noon or she wouldn't be able to sleep. He knew she liked to wear fuzzy socks around the house, and she hated broccoli. She tried to eat it when Lily cooked it, but he saw the grimace she made with every bite. He knew she loved math for some bizarre reason and she had all the state capitals memorized. She drummed her fingers on the desk when she was thinking, and she sorted her pens by color. She sang in the shower and sometimes she cried at night when she thought no one could hear. She was a pastor's daughter who had lost her way and was trying to find the road back. She made him laugh, and she loved his sister. She was the first to volunteer to help and the last one to leave. She was brave and selfless and she deserved a second chance.

No, he didn't know what high school she went to or if she had any pets growing up. And he didn't know how she ended up on the streets of Hollywood or why she wanted to end her own life. But know her? He knew what was important. The rest of it didn't matter.

"You don't have to worry," he said, making his voice light and care-free. "You can trust her."

Kate pushed her sunglasses on top of her head and crossed her arms, a defiant look etched on her face. "Trust her? Really?"

Swallowing hard, Noah suddenly realized what it must feel like to face off against her in a courtroom, and he didn't like it.

"So tell me, where is she from? How did she end up in the church parking lot? If she's really a pastor's kid, where's her family? Why hasn't she tried to contact them? If she's trying to repair her life, why doesn't she call her parents? Why doesn't she go home? Or maybe everything she's told you has been a lie."

The questions peppered him like rifle-fire, one after the other, planting seeds of doubt with every word, every enunciated syllable, until they throbbed in his brain.

"Do you even know her last name?" Kate demanded.

Noah rolled his neck, tension twisting the muscles into a tight knot. "Smith. Her last name is Smith."

Her eyebrows shot up in a look that stated exactly how stupid that sounded. "Smith? Really? I guess Jane Doe was already taken?"

"Stop it, Kate." He'd had enough. Hannah deserved her privacy. True, she hadn't shared anything about her past with them, but that was her choice. She'd tell them when she wanted to, when she was ready. Kate was wrong. Hannah wasn't a threat, she wasn't planning anything. If she wanted to hurt them or rob them she could have done it a hundred times by now. Unbidden, the memory of Lily's open purse by the door the first night Hannah had been in their house filled his mind. Maybe he should have asked Lily if anything was missing. Images of all the times Hannah had counted the donations and made the bank deposits ricocheted through his brain. Should he have been double checking her entries?

Nausea rolled in his stomach, and he pushed his plate away. He didn't want to believe it. And yet, Kate's questions remained, taking root in his heart, seeds of doubt finding fertile ground.

"I'm sorry, Noah. You guys are like family to me, and this whole thing . . . " She waved her hand and he knew she meant Hannah. "This whole thing is setting off red flags. The stuff she was doing, before you found her, couldn't have been good. A sweet little church girl doesn't end up overdosing in a church parking lot by accident. She was into something bad."

"You don't know that." Noah had imagined hundreds of different scenarios of what her life might have been like before that night. He'd seen enough of Hollywood to know what lurked on the streets when the tourists went home, but none of it mattered. Or maybe none of mattered because he didn't know the truth, it was all speculation, none of it was real. If he knew what happened to her, would it change how he felt about her?

Kate pursed her lips like she wanted to say more, but decided against it. Pushing her salad around on the plate, she stared at the people walking past. "Why is she still here? What's her angle?"

"She does not have an angle," he said wearily. "She was hurt and we helped. That's all there is. If anyone could understand what it is like to need to start over, to escape the past, I thought it would be you."

The words were unnecessarily harsh, but Kate accepted them. She didn't yell or fight or defend herself and that made him feel worse. "I'm sorry," he said softly. "That was uncalled for."

But she waved him off. "You're right. Boston was me starting over, trying to bury everything that happened out here. But the past never really goes away. It sits there, waiting for a chance to grab you again. That's why you need to be careful, Noah. Her past could ruin your family."

Her eyes drifted out over the crowd, searching, always searching.

"Kate, I know what you've been through. God can heal that hurt. You don't have to go through this alone."

"Don't," she said, sharp and quick, severing the conversation like scissors cutting string.

He let her. He sat in silence while her gaze picked out faces in the passing throng. Was she looking for her little sister? Hoping to catch one more glimpse of her? Or was it someone else she was searching for?

She sniffed and looked at him, the sea of faces beyond the fence passing in an unending river of humanity. "Besides, I'm not alone. I have you, right?"

He smiled, knowing the moment was here. There wouldn't be a better time to tell her how he felt. But he hesitated, stunned to realize that he didn't know how he felt anymore. He grasped for words, searching for something to say, but instead it was Hannah's face that flitted through his mind.

Chapter Sixteen

SATURDAY MORNING DAWNED CLEAR AND bright, the perfect day for a wedding. After everything Lily and Ben had been through to get to this day, even the weather decided to cooperate to give them the day they deserved. The October morning was crisp as Hannah and Kate checked and double checked to make sure they had everything they'd need for Lily to get ready at the church. Her wedding dress was tucked away in a garment bag from the bridal salon, and Kate kept a close eye on the duffle bag Lily had filled with her shoes, jewelry, make-up, an emergency sewing kit, breath mints, her barely holding together wedding notebook, and an embroidered handkerchief that had been her mom's.

Hannah was in charge of the bridesmaids' attire. She had both dresses in one of Noah's old garment bags and a shoulder bag filled with their accessories. Lily had packed and repacked every bag at least three times the night before, carefully putting each item into a bag, checking them off one by one on her list, and then in a panic unpacking it all, convinced she had forgotten something.

Hannah and Kate both reminded her over and over that the house was only a few minutes from the church. If they forgot anything that could literally run home, grab it, and be back at the church in under fifteen minutes, but Lily was in complete nervous bride mode, and instead of taking comfort in that knowledge, she unpacked and repacked their bags again until Kate finally took the bags away and stored them in the guest room.

They were all up early Saturday morning, watching the minutes slowly tick away. Noah had abandoned the house at Lily's first excited squeal, heading over to Ben's house to get ready with the guys. Evan gave his daughter a hug and promised to see her at the church before he left, too, the unmistakable sheen of tears glistening in his eyes. And she wasn't even in her dress yet. Hannah imagined what his reaction would be when he saw Lily standing her wedding gown and veil.

Standing.

Once they men were gone, Lily stood and practiced walking in her wedding shoes. She had chosen simple ballet flats for the day, not ready to risk high heels yet, and she had the sneakers she wore to physical therapy in her bag as well, just in case she needed more support.

At nine a.m., the limo arrived to drive them the two minutes to the church. Lily had protested when Ben made the arrangements, telling him it was wasteful and silly, but he had insisted. As they climbed into the limo, Hannah glimpsed the excited smile on her friend's face, and she was glad Ben hadn't budged. He had done everything in his power to make sure the day was special for his bride.

When they arrived at the church, Hannah juggled the bags while Kate wheeled Lily up the ramp so no one would suspect her surprise. Once they were settled in the music room where they would get ready, Hannah shoved the wheelchair into the corner, praying Lily would never need it again.

The next two hours passed in a blur of make-up, hairspray, and nervous giggles. Lily was too excited to eat and it took thirty minutes of badgering by both bridesmaids and the threat that she might pass out during the ceremony to get her to eat a banana. The photographer arrived and clicked away, posing and reposing the three of them until Hannah's face hurt from smiling. She couldn't remember ever being happier than she was that morning. She belonged. It might have only been for that morning, but as she fussed with Lily's veil, draping it down her back until it fell in floating, lacy waves, she felt like she was part of a family.

Catching a glimpse of her own reflection, she gasped, barely recognizing herself anymore. The bridesmaid dress fit her perfectly, thanks to some last-minute alterations, and her hair was twisted into a lovely up-do, the delicate, wispy brown curls framing her face in such a way that she didn't even notice the scar that cut across her forehead. Kate had done Lily's make-up and then offered to do her make-up as well. She was sure the lawyer didn't like her, but it was clear she would do anything to make Lily's wedding day perfect. So, Hannah sat still as Kate applied mascara and blush and a pale pink lipstick that complemented her skin.

A steady rumble of cars pulling into the parking lot echoed in the music room and Lily's flushed and excited cheeks faded to a slightly green shade of nervous terror.

"I'm getting married," she exclaimed, her voice suddenly filled with more disbelief than wonder. "I'm marrying a movie star. With the photographers and the media and the red carpets and . . . " She swayed on her feet and Hannah and Kate each grabbed an arm to keep her steady. "We should have eloped," she whispered.

"Lils," Kate said, authority ringing in her words. "You're going to be fine. This is your wedding day, and it is going to be wonderful."

Lily gripped their hands and took a deep breath. "You're right. I'm fine. We're fine. Everyone's fine. It's going to be great."

A heavy knock thumped against the door. "Are you ready, sweetheart?" Pastor Evan called through the thin wood.

Kate moved to the door, her hand resting on the handle as she waited for Lily's signal. Hannah fluffed the veil one last time and then stepped aside as Lily nodded and Kate opened the door.

Wearing a crisp black suit and tie, Evan took one step into the room and froze as he saw his daughter standing on her wedding day.

*****

There were tears, followed by a frantic reapplying of mascara as Evan wrapped his arms around Lily, stood back to look at her again, then hugged her once more. When Noah came to see what was taking so long, he took one look at Lily standing in front of him before grabbing her and swinging her in his arms with a loud whoop of joy. Then there were more tears as Lily explained why she had kept her walking a secret.

Hannah watched them with an ache in her heart, a dull throbbing that reminded of her what she had thrown away, the love she had taken for granted. Evan would walk Lily down the aisle, give her hand to Ben, and then officiate the ceremony himself, no doubt beaming with pride as he pronounced them man and wife.

She had imagined that scene herself countless times when she was a little girl. Her dad walking her down the aisle in the church she had grown up in, the only church she had ever known, the entire congregation gathered to watch as the pastor's daughter said her vows.

She remembered raiding the linen closet with her sister, the two of them wearing pillow cases on their heads like veils, practicing the bridal march they were sure they'd get to do one day.

As she got older, the dream seemed to fade and drift away. She didn't want to stay in that same small town, and she certainly didn't want the predictable life of a pastor's daughter. She wanted to be different, to find her own path. Maybe her sister could be happy being the perfect daughter and growing up to be the perfect wife, but Hannah had wanted something more. Contentment eluded her, it always had. Fear of missing out clawed at her, as if there was something better waiting around the next bend in the road, as if staying in one place was robbing her of all the possibility in life. And so, she dabbled, she experimented, she pushed the limits, and then she broke them entirely.

It was only now, years later, watching Lily rest her head on her dad's shoulder, soaking up the last few minutes of being his little girl, that Hannah finally started to see the treasure in that simplicity. In her quest to find what she was missing, she ended up missing the only thing that mattered.

She smiled as she picked up her bouquet and followed Lily out of the room, but the longing in her heart remained.

The double doors to the sanctuary were closed, but she could hear the rumble of the guests inside as the wedding party lined up in the foyer. Hannah and Noah stood together at the front of the line, Kate, as maid of honor, behind them and finally Evan with Lily on his arm.

Nerves raced through her stomach as she stared at the pattern of the wood grain on the door.

"Ready?" Noah asked and offered her his arm.

He grinned at her, and her heart thumped. She'd never seen him so dressed up. His hair was carefully combed and the black suit hung perfectly on him. The lines of his clean-shaven jaw called to her and she wanted to touch the smooth skin, to feel it under her hand. Out of the corner of her eye, she saw Kate shift her bouquet. Noah loved Kate, she reminded herself. They belonged together and she belonged . . . nowhere.

Refusing to let sadness into Lily's day, she focused on the wedding instead. "Ready," she replied, slipping her arm through his, her other hand clutching the bouquet tightly to keep it from slipping out of her sweaty palm.

As a beaming friend from church pulled the doors open, every head in the sanctuary turned towards them. A string quartet played softly in the background and stands of flowers dotted the aisle leading to the altar. Sprays of blush pink and white roses, hydrangeas, and cascades of lily of the valley blossoms decorated the church. Even though Hannah had helped pick out the flowers, seeing the beauty of it laid out before her took her breath away. It was like entering a secret garden.

She was so stunned by the sea of faces staring at her, she forgot to walk until Noah gently led her forward. Pasting a smile on her face, she matched his stride as they walked down the aisle. Even after all the Sundays she had spent in this sanctuary, all the times she had vacuumed it or walked to the front to take her seat for the service, the aisle had never seemed so long.

His arm was warm beneath her hand and the fabric of his suit was soft under her fingers. He walked with quiet assurance, and his confidence settled her nerves. Noah was the calm in the midst of the storm, a shelter against the wind, strong and steady beside her, her protector from that very first night. She knew she had no right to him, but she tightened her hand on his arm anyway. For this one walk, he was hers.

Ben and Chris were waiting at the front of the church, their black suits sharp and starched under the warm lights. Ben smiled at her as she took her place on the opposite side, then he turned his head towards Kate coming down the aisle by herself. Hannah didn't miss the way Chris' mouth dropped open at the sight of her, and she couldn't deny that Kate looked lovely. Her glossy hair was swept up in a regal design and she exuded grace as she strode down the aisle, heedless of, or indifferent to, the adoring looks she was receiving.

She stopped beside Hannah and as the string quartet played a rousing fanfare, everyone in the church stood. Evan and Lily stepped through the doorway and the gasps from the crowd nearly drowned out the music. Hannah glanced at Ben and the stunned look of disbelief on his face was enough to make her teary-eyed all over again. As Evan and Lily began the long walk to the altar, Ben took a step towards her, as if he was going to race up the aisle, but Chris laid a hand on his shoulder and stopped him. The disbelief on Ben's face turned to wonder and then to joy and then to something even more as he watched Lily walk towards him. Tears rolled down his cheeks and he didn't bother to wipe them away. All of his attention was focused on his bride and the radiant smile on her face.

When they reached the front, Evan placed Lily's hand in Ben's, but unable to contain himself, he pulled Lily into his arms and lifted her off her feet. In his arms, she whispered, "Surprise."

Ben set her down, peering through the gauzy veil into her eyes. "You are my miracle."

Chapter Seventeen

HANNAH STOOD WITH THE BRIDAL party in front of the altar and smiled. She moved when the photographer told her to move, smiled when she said "Smile," but her mind was back in the ceremony. It had been the most beautiful wedding. She couldn't remember ever seeing two people more in love as they promised to love one another through sickness and health, laughter and sorrow, pledging to be faithful, and to cherish their marriage no matter what. Hannah had never heard truer words. They had already loved each other through the worst of circumstances, they had lived their vows before ever speaking them out loud. They had been through so much, she couldn't imagine them ever facing anything worse. But through it all, God had been with them.

"One more please!"

The official photographer was packing up her bag to head to the reception, when a woman in a long, red dress raced to the front, holding a camera in her hand.

Lily turned to Ben, a question written on her face, and he shrugged sheepishly. "I did promise her an exclusive."

"Well, we can't have you break a promise on your wedding day." She laughed.

"Go ahead, Kiki," Ben said.

The wedding party gathered together again, and Hannah smiled as Kiki, whoever she was, snapped a quick series of shots. Then she shooed everyone else away to get a few photos of the bride and groom.

By the time they finished, most of the guests had already left for the reception. Hannah joined Kate, Chris, Noah, and Evan in the limo for the ride to the reception. They had chosen a secluded estate in the foothills overlooking the Pacific with a beautiful garden and a high wall to keep out the prying eyes of the paparazzi. Hannah hadn't understood the necessity of the extra security until the ceremony ended and she saw the swarm of photographers clustered outside the church's fence. Though they had asked their guests not to share the details of the wedding, clearly word had gotten out. There were even more photographers waiting outside the iron gate to the reception venue.

Flashes popped, racing across the dark windows of the limo and muffled voices echoed on every side. Once they made it through the gate, the flashes and voices disappeared. The winding drive past the gate was protected by an arching canopy of trees and gave the illusion that the reporters were farther away, as if Hollywood were in another world, and for Hannah it was.

Lifting her hem as she stepped across the rolling green lawn, she was in awe of the ocean waves that danced and rolled in the distance. When she'd first come to Los Angeles she went to the beach almost every day, entranced by the sound and smell of the sea. She'd learned not to come during the day when the sand was covered by tourists and beach towels. Instead, she went at sunset. Watching as the sky turned to fire and the water glowed golden and red. The further she fell into Lincoln's world, the less she went to the water. It was one more thing he stole from her. But not anymore. She watched her beloved waves roll against the rocks below, letting them carry her regrets away with them.

A sprawling, white tent had been set up in the midst of the garden. Elegant drapes lined the inside and covered the ceiling making her feel like she'd walked into a silken cloud. Fairy lights twinkled in the fabric like hidden stars. Flowers filled the tent, overflowing in the centerpieces and lining the walls. Uniformed caterers walked through the crowd passing out hors d'oeuvres, and Hannah smiled as she saw a tray of bite-sized sliders go by. Those had been her favorite when she and Lily visited the caterer to choose the menu.

Relief filled her as she looked around. The day had been perfect, and she couldn't be happier for Lily. The bride drifted through the crowd, smiling and chatting with the guests, her face radiant with joy. Ben was always at her side, never more than a few inches from his new wife, his hand on her lower back or touching her shoulder as if he couldn't believe she was real, like she was a dream that might vanish in the blink on an eye. But Hannah knew Lily wasn't going anywhere. Their journey was just beginning.

Sinking into her seat, she exhaled a long breath, the excitement and anxiety of the morning finally catching up with her. She sipped ice water, and the thin slice of lemon floating on the surface bumped her lip. How could she be so happy and exhausted at the same time? She nearly dropped the glass when Noah sat in the chair beside her.

"Some day, right?" He had loosened his tie and undone the top button on his dress shirt. She smiled into her water glass. At least he had waited until the photos were finished before undoing the buttons.

"It was perfect." She watched Lily and Ben wander in and out of the crowd. Once lunch had been served, Lily had popped up from the chair; clearly, she had been sitting long enough. Hannah hoped Ben would be able to keep up with her on their honeymoon. She wouldn't be surprised if Lily took up marathon running after all the months she had spent in a wheelchair. Even though she had promised Andre at their last physical therapy session that she would go slow and rest when she needed it, Hannah highly doubted Lily would follow through with that promise, and from the look Andre was giving her from his table near the dance floor, the therapist doubted it, too. Lily was walking, she was married, and as far as Hannah was concerned, her friend was unstoppable.

Noah glanced at his sister and her new husband, affection filling his eyes. "I think they're going to be happy together."

"And what about you?" Hannah asked, surprised by her own boldness. "What's it going to take to make you that happy?"

"I am happy," he protested. "My annoying little sister is married and moving out, and an angel of mercy showed up and took over all the administrative stuff at the church that I'm terrible at." He winked at her, then scooped up her hand and kissed her knuckles.

Electricity zipped along her arm, the warmth of his teasing kiss on her hand lingering far longer than it should have. His dark blond hair was neatly styled for the first time she could remember and she longed to run her fingers through it, to mess it up until it looked more natural, more Noah. She could imagine what it would feel like beneath her hand, the way his eyes would lift to hers, swallowing her in the blue, like a bird disappearing into the horizon.

"What more do I need?"

Hannah opened her mouth to answer, with absolutely no idea what she would say, but stopped when his eyes darted to the entrance of the tent. Kate walked in, her laughter carrying across the distance. Beautiful, confident Kate. He sat back, his hand slipping from under hers, and she tried not to wince at the loss. Jealousy stabbed her, hard and swift, words springing to life in her heart before she could stop them. *I'll never be good enough.*

*****

Noah stood and clapped with everyone else as the DJ, with the style and roar of a sports announcer during the World Series, requested Mr. and Mrs. Prescott's presence on the dance floor. Ben whisked Lily onto the shining wood floor, her dress billowing around her as she twirled in his arms. Music filled the tent as they danced, gazing into each other's eyes, whispering words of love no one else could hear, oblivious to the people surrounding them.

The song ended and the DJ asked for the wedding party to take their places on the dance floor. Suddenly, Noah was keenly, painfully aware of Hannah beside him. Chris was leading Kate out onto the dance floor, but Hannah hadn't moved. Quickly fixing his tie, he stood and extended his hand towards her. "May I have this dance?"

Hesitation lingered in her eyes as she looked up at him, and he wondered what put it there. She was beautiful, a vision in the bridesmaid dress, and her smile had been true and sincere during the ceremony, her love for his sister evident for all to see. The wedding had been amazing, and he knew she was just as responsible for the smooth organization as Lily had been. She should be happy, ecstatic.

Cautiously, she placed her hand in his, as light and tentative as a bird ready to fly off at the slightest sound. As they found their place on the dance floor, he pulled her close, one hand closing over hers as the other settled on the curve of her waist. The music started, and she looked anywhere but at him, her eyes suddenly overly interested in the pattern of the wood floor and the swoop of the white drapes overhead.

"Hannah," he said softly, waiting for her to drag her gaze to his. When she did, the rawness in her eyes burrowed into his heart. Hope, fear, nervousness, wonder, it was all there in her eyes. Every doubt, every concern Kate had brought up about who she was, where she came from, every question that was still unanswered fled from his mind as he looked into the innocence of her soft, brown eyes. She reminded him of a deer, a doe that had been chased, hunted, and was finally free. It was as if she couldn't quite trust the freedom before her, some part of her still fearing that it would be snatched away again.

She felt fragile in his arms, but he knew that wasn't right. Aside from Lily, he didn't know anyone who fought as hard as she had. He didn't know what haunted her, the secrets that plagued her, but when she was in his arms, none of it mattered. As he pulled her close, her skin was cool beneath the heat of his hands, a perfect compliment.

They swayed in small circles as she studied him. His own heart thundered in his chest as he looked at her. This wasn't what he planned. This wasn't what he wanted.

Or was it?

Unable to bear the clamor of his own thoughts any longer he searched for something to say. "Thank you," he stumbled, and her eyebrows shot up in surprise. "For everything you did for Lily. For helping her in so many ways."

She smiled, and he missed a step in the dance.

"I was happy to do it. Lily is amazing. Your whole family has been so kind to me." The hint of a promise sparkled in her expression, as if there was more she wanted to say, but it was gone before he could grab on to it.

Gentle notes of a love song floated around them as he guided her across the floor. They moved as one, perfectly paired, and he pulled her closer, yearning for more of her, to lose himself in her eyes, her laugh, her smile. There was so much about her he hadn't noticed before. The freckle on her cheek, the way her nose crinkled when she laughed. She moved like water in his arms, flowing with him, pulsing in his arms.

His heart beat faster as the feeling grew. He shook his head. This was Hannah. He shouldn't be thinking of her that way. But the feeling refused to be silenced. He searched for words, trying to articulate what he didn't understand. "You've been a good friend to her. And to me."

The smile on her face faded and he knew he'd said something stupid. She turned her face away and the sudden absence of her eyes, the loss of the warmth he'd seen there was like a cold wind blowing through the tent. The hint of something more he'd glimpsed was shuttered away, vanished in an instant. He fumbled for a way to get it back, to will her into looking at him that way again, but the moment was gone, and he wondered if he had imagined the whole thing.

"It must have been a shock to see her walking today," she said, her voice light, and the tension between them eased. "The first time I saw her standing at therapy, I freaked out and yelled for her to stop. Andre probably thought I was nuts."

Picturing the scene in his mind, he couldn't help but laugh. Across the dance floor, Kate glanced their way, a puzzled look on her face.

"You should dance with Kate next," Hannah said, the laughter gone from her words. "Maybe you can convince her to stay out here a little longer."

"I—" he began, the words a jumble in his mind, each one fighting for a way out, but it was too late. The song ended, and she walked away.

Chapter Eighteen

BEN AND LILY SNUCK AWAY before the reception ended. She whispered a quick goodbye to Hannah, and then they were gone, off on a month long honeymoon to an undisclosed location. Since Hannah had helped her pack, she knew they were going on a romantic private cruise in the Mediterranean, but no one outside the family knew where they were going or how to track them down. The paparazzi may have crashed the wedding, but if everything went according to plan, they wouldn't be able to find them during the honeymoon.

As the guests slowly departed and the venue staff began to clean up, Hannah and the rest of the family collected the gifts and piled them into two cars. She gathered Lily's wedding dress from the small room where she had changed and carefully put it back in the garment bag so it could be cleaned and preserved.

Evan, Noah, and Chris stopped her every few minutes holding up various wedding objects, asking if they should pack them up or leave them in the tent for the rental company to take away. The cake topper, yes. The centerpieces, no. The guest book, yes. The decorations, no. The wedding was over, but there was still work to do, and Lily was counting on her. So, Hannah pointed people in the right direction, answered questions, and ignored her aching feet.

By the time she climbed into Chris' car, surrounded by a mountain of white and silver wrapped gifts, she was exhausted, completely worn out by the stress, excitement, and joy of the day. Chris was quiet as he drove them into the Hollywood Hills. Noah, Evan, and Kate followed close behind. With Lily leaving the Shaw house for her honeymoon, they held a family meeting and agreed that Hannah would stay in Ben's house. She could housesit and keep an eye on things for the newlyweds. Kate was going to be spending the night there before her flight back to Boston the next day.

The car climbed higher and higher into the hills and Hannah wondered exactly how far up they were going to go. The sun had already set and the moon was unusually bright when Chris punched a code into the security box outside Ben's house and the heavy gate swung open. Chris drove like he had been there a hundred times before, which he probably had, but Hannah was unprepared for the house spread out before her. It was a rambling Spanish style with a traditional tile roof dotted with solar panels and a circular driveway that wound around a bubbling fountain surrounded by late blooming flowers.

The two cars rolled to a stop by the front door. Hannah unlocked the large double doors with the spare key Ben had given her and entered the code into the keypad for the security system. Her heart pounded a little too fast as she envisioned the alarm going off and a flood of police officers descending on the house. She held her breath until the keypad gave a happy beep and turned from a threatening red to a welcoming green.

They made trip after trip, unloading the presents and stacking them on the large island in the kitchen. She looked around and laughed, imagining Lily whipping up her famous pancakes using the sub-zero refrigerator and the massive chef style stove.

Hannah left the gifts where they were. She was too tired to do anything with them that night. She'd organize them someplace else tomorrow so the house wouldn't be such a mess when Ben and Lily returned. She'd never been married, but she guessed that the last thing a newly married couple would want to do when they came home was clean the house.

The guys mumbled their goodbyes and stumbled out the door, looking as tired as she felt. They'd all be back at church bright and early the next morning for Sunday service. She closed and locked the door behind them, re-armed the security system, and hoped she wouldn't forget to turn it off before she left the following morning.

"Look at this place!" Kate exclaimed, poking her head into every room. "This is incredible." She moved to the wall of windows in the living room. In the distance, the lights of the city burned bright against the blackness of the sky. "You must be able to see all of downtown from here. I can't wait to see what the view looks like during the day."

Hannah nodded in agreement, a movement Kate couldn't see as she stared out into the Los Angeles night. Even though Ben had been the one to suggest she housesit for him, and even though she had his permission to be here, she felt like an intruder. She couldn't even bring herself to open the cabinets to find a glass to get some water. Everything felt untouchable, as if she had no right to be there, a fraud that was sure to be discovered. How would she last a month in this house?

Kate didn't seem to have any problem at all with her temporary living situation. She bounded back into the kitchen, as energized as Hannah was exhausted. After pulling the massive refrigerator door open, she dug out a can of soda and popped the top. "So which bedroom do you want?"

Considering the fact that she hadn't even stepped out of the kitchen yet, she had no idea. "It doesn't matter to me. Pick whichever one you want."

"Thanks." Kate grabbed her bag and disappeared down the hallway.

Sighing in the empty kitchen, she kicked off her shoes. She stared at her painted toes against the marble tile floor, amazed at the fact that she was there, standing in a movie star's kitchen, surrounded by more wealth than she had ever imagined, overlooking the city that had broken her.

Carrying the high heels, she picked up her bag and wandered down the hall. Behind a closed door on the right, dresser drawers were opening and closing in loud succession, so she turned into one of the other rooms across the hall. Flicking on the light, she sucked in a quick breath. The room was lovely. It was simply decorated in a tasteful collection of neutral colors, from the dark wood furniture to the matching shades of beige and ivory on the bedspread and curtains. It had a masculine feel to it, as if the room was kept ready and waiting for male guests. She wondered if the room Kate was in was a feminine version of this one. Maybe with pinks and flowers instead of browns and stripes. Glancing at the walls, she wondered how long it would take for Lily to add Scripture verses in every room.

There was a private bathroom, also decorated in subdued colors, and Hannah looked at the big jacuzzi tub wistfully. She couldn't remember the last time she'd soaked in a bathtub. On the wall opposite the bed, a television was framed by two large bookcases. Skipping the TV, she studied the books lined up in neat rows. Mysteries, thrillers, history. Ben had an eclectic taste in literature. Deciding that a bath and a book was exactly what she needed, she selected a novel from the top shelf and set it on the bed before going to find Kate to say goodnight.

She found her back in the kitchen, rummaging in the refrigerator.

"I'm going to take a bath and go to bed," she said to Kate's back.

Kate turned around, a carton of ice cream in her hands. "Good night."

As she set the ice cream on the island and started opening cabinets, no doubt searching for a bowl, Hannah asked, "What time is your flight tomorrow?"

"Oh, I'm not leaving yet," Kate replied, as she located a white bowl and went to work opening drawers.

Hannah froze, staring at the back of Kate's head. She had assumed Kate was leaving, heading back to her successful career on the other side of the country. She'd been looking forward to seeing her go, to escaping the hard looks and the suspicious questions. "You're not?"

Kate found a spoon and set the bowl beside the ice cream on a small square of free space between the gifts piled up on the island. "No. I'll be staying in town for a while. To help keep an eye on things."

Her hands clenched at her sides, gripping the soft fabric of the bridesmaid dress in tight fists. The warning in Kate's words had been unmistakable. She wasn't keeping an eye on things, she was keeping an eye on her.

"Well, I'm sure Noah will be happy to see more of you," Hannah replied, not caring about the edge she heard in her words.

The spoon stilled, buried in a frozen mound of chocolate ice cream. Kate looked at her with the same hardness she's seen in the bridal salon and on the movie set, unapologetically and unashamedly appraising her. "The Shaws are my family. They're good people, trusting people, but sometimes trust is misplaced."

Resentment flooded through her. Maybe she wasn't part of the family, maybe she wasn't a lifelong best friend, maybe she was the screw up who needed to be rescued, but not this time. This time she had done the right thing. "And I guess you're the perfect one to judge that," she said and turned to go, anger seething in her blood, yearning for the freedom to rage.

The spoon clattered to the island behind her. "Why are you still here?" Kate demanded, the words hitting her back like daggers. "What do you want from them?"

Hannah stopped, looking at the reflection in the panoramic windows. Kate standing behind her, the lights of the kitchen casting haloes on the dark glass, and herself standing in the half-light between them. Why was she still here? For the past five years she had been running, moving from place to place, blindly following Lincoln wherever he went. But now . . . now she was daring to feel settled, daring to hope she belonged. Deep down she knew Kate was right, she had no right to feel at home here. She was on borrowed time, and they both knew it. Eventually she would have to leave, find her own place, and start over yet again. When she left, Kate would still be there, still a part of the family Hannah had come to love. When she had to leave, Kate would get to stay.

Biting back every harsh word she longed to say, she turned around, forcing a calm she didn't feel as she faced off against the lawyer. "I understand that you don't trust me. That you don't even like me, and that's fine, but I would never hurt them." She took one step towards the kitchen, then stopped, not trusting herself to go any further, as if the closer she got, the more likely her words would fly out of control. "I want you to know, these past four months, I was here for them.

Driving Lily to therapy, watching her struggle and fight, helping her with the wedding plans, working with Noah at the church . . . that was me. I was here for them. Where were you?"

Kate recoiled like she had been struck, the ice cream forgotten on the cold quartz island.

Hannah didn't wait for a response. She escaped down the hallway and slipped into the guest room. Closing the door behind her, she fought the urge to slam it. Conviction wrestled in her heart. That hadn't been fair of her. She should apologize. But she didn't want to, not yet. Adrenaline coursed through her veins, her temper looking for an excuse to rear its ugly head. Kate had every right to be protective of the Shaws, but it hurt. It hurt that she would always be the outsider, the trouble maker no one trusted. How long would it take to make up for her past?

Ignoring the book and the bath she dropped to her knees beside the bed and prayed. Tears rolled down her cheeks as she cried for everything she had lost, and for everything she could never have.

Chapter Nineteen

KATE DIDN'T JOIN THEM FOR church the next morning. She was still asleep when Hannah left, nervously taking the keys to one of Ben's cars for the drive back to the Hollywood Mission. Even with his permission to drive anything in the garage, she couldn't escape the guilt and anxiety that dogged every mile as she drove the fancy sedan into Hollywood. It was the most practical car he owned, but it had more buttons and screens than she'd ever seen in a car. She was already pressing her luck driving without her driver's license which had disappeared along with her purse and everything else she owned the night Lincoln abandoned her. She didn't want to imagine what would happen if she got pulled over in a borrowed car without identification. So she drove cautiously and made sure she stayed under the speed limit, while she longed for the simplicity and comfort of Noah's beat-up truck, even with its persnickety windows and unreliable air conditioning.

The morning service was full of familiar faces, but it wasn't the same without Lily and Ben on the worship team. It wasn't that the music suffered, it didn't, but she missed seeing Lily's joy as she sang and the sly, adoring glances Ben cast her way. Hannah missed seeing her friends up there. Even Ben had become a friend to her over the past few months, albeit an intimidating and slightly overwhelming friend, and that fact never ceased to amaze her. Never in her wildest dreams as a teenager reading fan magazines with a flashlight after bedtime, hidden under the covers in her bedroom in her parents' house had she imagined playing board games with one the world's biggest movie stars, let alone living in his house and driving his car.

Ben and Lily were married, enjoying their honeymoon, and she was happy for them. Closing her eyes, she let the worship roll over her. Circumstances change, people move on, but God is still God.

When the service ended, Evan and Noah both looked as exhausted as she felt. No one objected when she drove straight back to Ben's house after they finished cleaning and locking up. It was the first Sunday in over four months that she hadn't had dinner with the Shaw family. As she drove up the winding road towards the house, the distance between her and the little yellow house by the church grew by more than miles.

Things were changing, and even though she had known it was coming, even though she'd been a part of planning it all, it still took her by surprise, as if the world was spinning too quickly and decisions were coming at her too fast. The life she'd made with the Shaws was disappearing and she'd have to figure out what to do next. As a single woman, she couldn't stay with Evan and Noah, and once Ben and Lily returned, she couldn't stay with them like some interloping third wheel. The inescapable truth was she needed to find someplace else to go and she had only a month to figure it out. She'd been frugal with her money so she'd have enough to get by for a little while. She knew when she had to leave, but she didn't know where or how.

The sensation of time speeding up and carrying her along whether she wanted to go or not tugged on her for the rest of Sunday and long into the night. Where was she going to go? What was she going to do?

She loved her job at the church and she hoped she could keep it, but what if it was time to move on? What if that job had been a temporary bandage, an act of charity to help her get back on her feet? Did they really need her there? Would they miss her if she left? Would Noah think of her at all, or would he be relieved that she was gone?

The biggest question was if she could stay at the church and watch his relationship with Kate progress. Of all the changes she was facing, that one was the worst. Could she sit across from him every day and listen to him talk about Kate and the life they were going to build together? And how long would it be before the lawyer who hated her convinced Noah that she didn't belong there? If Noah had to choose between her and the woman he loved, she was sure she would lose.

The questions and the uncertainty were with her like constant companions, waking up with her on Monday morning and keeping her company as she sat at the kitchen island sipping coffee. It had taken her almost twenty minutes to figure out how Ben's high-end coffee maker worked, but all the frustration had been worth it. Sipping her heavily flavored coffee and looking out over the mist covered hills, she opened her Bible to the book of Psalms.

"I lift my up my eyes to the mountains—where does my help come from? My help comes from the Lord, the Maker of Heaven and earth." The words of the psalmist filled her soul and she welcomed the peace they brought. "The Lord will watch over your coming and going both now and forevermore."

Coming and going. Watching the early morning mist rise and vanish through the windows, she realized that coming and going summed up her life nicely. She'd been in and out of living situations most of her life, never staying in one place, never allowing herself to take root, always looking for the next opportunity, the next chance to try something new. Home had never meant permanence to her, it had never meant forever. Until now. She had come home to God. At least she finally got that part right. She'd been given a new start, a second chance with the Shaws. Now she had to do something with it and not let it go to waste.

"Looks like we're all famous now." Kate dropped a newspaper in front of her as she made a beeline for coffee machine.

Neither of them had mentioned the fight after the wedding. Though they certainly weren't friends, they had reached a kind of unspoken ceasefire. It wasn't exactly a truce, but they weren't firing at each other anymore, and Hannah was glad for the reprieve. Kate cared about Lily and Noah and Pastor Evan, and she was trying to protect them. Hannah just wished the pushy lawyer recognized that she cared about them, too.

As the scent of fresh coffee filled the kitchen, Hannah glanced at the newspaper Kate had dropped. Half of the front page of the Sunday paper had been dedicated to Ben and Lily's wedding. And there, right under the photo of the two of them looking blissfully in love and ridiculously gorgeous, was a photo of the wedding party. She blinked, certain she was seeing things, but the photo was still there when she opened her eyes again. There she was, standing next to Kate, smiling for the camera in her blush bridesmaid dress. Somehow the rebellious runaway from Northern California had made the front page. Her name wasn't mentioned anywhere, but she didn't care. It was a surreal and stunning feeling, evidence that she hadn't imagined this crazy turn her life had taken, proof that she hadn't imagined it all.

She ran her finger over the paper, wishing she could save it, keep it tucked away as a reminder for the time when she was no longer a part of the family, when she was on her own again. Her longing must have been obvious because as Kate poured her coffee into a mug emblazoned with a studio logo, she said, "You can keep that one. My parents must have bought a dozen copies."

"Thank you." She was genuinely grateful for the gesture, an olive branch in their tentative ceasefire.

But Kate waved her thanks away. "I've got one for Lily, too." She raised the coffee mug to her lips then lowered it before taking a sip. "Though I guess Ben has people to handle stuff like that."

Hannah traced an imaginary line from her to Noah, gauging the distance between them, knowing that it was much further than a few inches of newsprint. "I'm sure she'll appreciate it. It's different when it comes from your best friend."

Kate gave her a hesitant smile before taking her coffee and disappearing down the hallway.

An hour later, Kate emerged from the guest room, her hair and make-up done to perfection, saying she was going to spend the day with her family. She roared out of the garage in the fastest sports car in Ben's garage, apparently unhindered by the worry that Hannah wrestled with when she looked at the keys hanging on hooks in the garage. As the engine noise faded Hannah wondered if "family" meant Noah.

The big house in the hills was quiet. Monday was her day off and she had nowhere to go and no one to spend it with. She wandered aimlessly through the house, turned the TV on and flipped through the channels before turning it off again. Eventually, she took a book out to the pool. Sitting in a lounge chair and listening to the gentle lap of the water against the pebble coated sides, she stared at the words, but her mind was elsewhere.

She thought about the photo in the paper and wondered if her parents had seen it. Not that they got the Los Angeles papers up near their home, but maybe it was in another paper, maybe someone had spotted it and showed it to them. Maybe they saw it online. Would they even recognize her if they saw it? She barely recognized herself anymore.

Casting a look over her shoulder, back into the house, she saw the phone on the desk. She could call them.

The thought hit her with the force of a tidal wave. She could call her parents. Pick up the phone, dial their number, and hear her mother's voice.

Memories of the past few years slid by as she tried to remember the last time she had spoken to them. Three years ago, maybe four. It hadn't been a special occasion. She'd been in a dismal hotel room, hungry, alone, and the yearning to talk to her mom had overwhelmed her. It wasn't long after she'd met Lincoln. His lies about fame and fortune had devolved into stealing and hustling. Lincoln had gone out to buy food and she was alone, the dark and the quiet of the hotel room more condemning than any of the cruel words he threw at her. When her dad answered the phone, she started crying.

"Come home, honey." He repeated it over and over. "Come home, please come home."

But how could she go back? Even if she'd had the money for a bus ticket, which she didn't, how could she face them again? After everything she'd done, the mistakes she'd made, there was no way back. Once they heard about the things she'd done, they wouldn't want her. Her dad was a pastor, he couldn't have a thief and a liar for a daughter. As much as it hurt to be so far away, to be so utterly alone, it was better than going home only to be rejected and tossed into the streets. At least in that dirty hotel room with fresh bruises on her face and arms she was already as low as she could go. Or so she'd thought. But that was before Lincoln changed everything, before he demanded more of her.

She'd whispered an incoherent "I love you" and hung up. When Lincoln returned with a bag of fast food and a bottle of vodka, she slipped into the tiny motel bathroom and spent the rest of the night crying, realizing for the first time that she could never go home again.

As the water lapped at her feet and birds called overhead, she stepped out of the memory and turned away from the phone.

Chapter Twenty

NOAH WALKED TO THE CHURCH Tuesday morning unaccustomed to the quiet. For the past few months he'd been surrounded by Lily and Hannah and their unending chatter in the mornings. As many times as he'd joked about needing silence and being unable to hear himself think, now that he finally had that quiet, he didn't know what to do with it. Echoes of their laughter followed him, carried by the breeze, so close he was sure that if he turned his head they'd be there.

But they weren't. Lily was a married woman and Hannah . . . he hadn't seen or heard from her since Sunday. She'd left the church so quickly he thought she had a hot date lined up. Would she have told him if she did? He shook the thought away, not liking where that train of thought would end. His feelings for Hannah were a puzzle he hadn't figured out.

His dad left the house early that morning, heading back to one of the church plants he was helping in the area, leaving Noah in charge of the Mission. As he unlocked the gates and slid the heavy metal fence open, out of habit, he glanced back, expecting to see Hannah behind him, sliding into the driver's seat, ready to drive the truck in, but he was alone, the street and the sidewalk empty and deserted.

Walking through the halls, flipping on the lights, and getting the coffee started was a lonely task. He'd done it thousands of times before, but he'd grown accustomed to Hannah's presence, the routine they shared, the familiarity of her presence.

The little coffee pot on the table in the corner was just starting to percolate when he heard a car pull into the parking lot. He smiled as he looked at the clock. Of course Hannah would still be on time. He wondered how early she had left the house in the Hills to make it to the church at exactly nine a.m.

When she came into the office, he was pouring her the first cup of coffee. After adding two of the flavored creamers she liked, he offered it to her. "Right on time," he said as she dropped her purse onto their shared desk.

"Barely." She took the mug he held out and sipped it, sighing with contentment as the caffeine hit her system. "I thought I was going to be late. Traffic was crazy."

"It's LA. Traffic is always crazy," he replied and poured himself a cup, skipping the fancy creamer and drinking it black.

"Ben's house is amazing, but the commute is a killer." Sinking into her chair, she started up the laptop and waited for it to come to life.

"Maybe we should switch," he said, thinking a few days in the lap of luxury might be fun.

She didn't laugh like he thought she would. She stared at the computer screen as it slowly changed from black to gray to a photo of the ocean. "I'm sure Kate would prefer having you for a roommate instead of me."

His cell phone ringing in his pocket stopped him from replying. Seeing his dad's number, he answered. "Hey Dad, what's up?"

"I'm over at the church in Inglewood," he began. "Pastor Steve is sick, his wife, too."

"I'm sorry to hear that." Noah watched Hannah and the orderly way she started her day. First, she sorted the papers that had accumulated on her desk, then she would go through the church's emails. Next she'd check the voicemails and take down messages. Finally, she'd make a to-do list with deadlines and priorities. He'd seen her do it day after day, always the same order, and it brought a familiar sense of calm to him. So he was only half listening when his dad dropped a bomb on him.

"That's why I need you to bring the message on Sunday."

Noah's feet, which had been propped on his side of the desk, dropped to the floor with a loud thud that interrupted Hannah's paper stacking. Eyebrows raised in concern, she stopped sorting and watched his side of the unexpected conversation.

"What? Are you serious?" Any calm he'd felt watching Hannah and her morning routine was gone, replaced by something very close to panic.

"I know it's a lot to ask, Noah, but Steve is going to be out for a few days, and I would like to be here to help. This church is brand new and any interruption in the services could hurt what he and Christy are building."

The room was suddenly too small. Noah stood and paced to the open door, then back to the chair. He felt Hannah's eyes tracking him, no doubt wondering what was going on. On his second trip back to the door, his dad continued.

"I know I said I wouldn't pressure you, and I'm sorry if that's what this feels like. If you don't want to do it, I will understand. I can call someone else."

Responsibility shoved the panic aside just long enough for him to say, "No, Dad, don't worry. I can do it."

"Thank you, Noah." Relief washed through his dad's words. "Pray about it and see what God does. Maybe this will give you the answer you've been looking for."

After saying goodbye, Noah dropped into the chair and tossed his phone on the desk where it landed with a sad *thunk*.

Hannah continued watching him with worry in her eyes. "Bad news?"

"Terrible news," he said and pressed his palms against his eyes, wondering if it was too late to take it back. As soon as he had hung up, he had started second guessing his decision. Maybe his dad would make it back in time. Maybe Pastor Steve would recover and be back to preaching in a day or two. Maybe Jesus would come back before Sunday.

"Are you dying?" she asked, and part of him wanted to say yes. If he was dying he could get out of this.

"Worse," he said miserably. "I'm preaching."

*****

After an hour of blindly flipping through his Bible, the pages crinkling every few seconds as he scanned one page and then turned to the next, desperately hoping inspiration would jump off the page and hit him in the face, Hannah slapped her hand on the middle of the book, the pale pink polish on her fingernails blocking out the Psalms.

Looking up at her, he saw irritation staring back at him.

"If you flip one more page, I'm going to lose my mind." She withdrew her hand slowly, but it was obvious she was ready to snatch the Bible away if he went back to his flip, flip, flipping search for ideas.

"Sorry," he said and closed the book under her watchful eye. "I have no idea what I'm doing."

That wasn't exactly true. When his parents started the church, he'd gone through a ministry training program with them and he'd majored in Bible Studies in college, thinking he might follow his parents into the church. He had followed them, just not the way he had imagined. Doubt had settled on him from the start, and he hadn't been able to shake it. When he found a job as a limo driver, he took it thinking it would give him clarity. It hadn't.

Was this how God worked? After all the years of not knowing which way to go, what path to follow, was this how God answered him? To drop it in his lap? To push him into the deep end without warning?

What if he messed it up? What if he got up there on Sunday morning and bombed? Well, he supposed, that would be a pretty clear answer, too. How did his dad do this every week?

"You know," Hannah said. None of the nervousness he felt was reflected in her voice. "You might be overthinking it." She took the announcement of his preaching with perfect calm, as if this kind of thing happened all the time. Of course, she'd been raised by a pastor so maybe she was used to it. "I watched my dad prepare lots of sermons. His face buried in the Bible and piles of commentaries on his desk. He wanted so much to give the church what they needed. He wanted every sermon to be his best, the best he could offer. But in the end, he knew it wasn't about him. It was about what God wanted to say to each person. It wasn't his job to change people, it was his job to invite God in and let Him do the work."

Sighing, he reached for the Bible again, then stopped when she narrowed her eyes at him. "You make it sound so simple."

Discouragement colored his words. "I wasn't expecting this. I have no ideas, no plan, and I don't think winging it in front of the entire congregation is an option."

"You're worried about preaching to the whole church. Maybe you can focus on preaching to just one person instead."

He stared at her, his brows wrinkled in confusion. "But I will be preaching to whole church."

She glared at him, but there was laughter lurking her eyes. "I know that. But if you find a message for one person, a message that can impact one life, speak to one problem, encourage one person, then I'm willing to bet the whole church will benefit from it."

He was silent for a few moments, letting her words tumble around in his brain.

"Focus on the one," he said, the words tinged with contemplation. "That helps. Thank you."

She spun around her chair to the side, then stood and picked up her keys, extending her other hand toward him. "Come on. Let's get some fresh air."

Slipping his hand into hers he noticed how small her hand was, the delicate smoothness of her fingers against his. Once he was standing, she dropped his hand, and he fought the urge to reach for her again, to recapture that connection, but she was already walking to the door.

He followed her down the narrow hallway and out onto the concrete dock. Hannah and Lily had replanted most of the flowers and the bright spots of color, the unobtrusive fragrance of them eased his nerves. The church, even after all it had been through, the destruction, the loss, the months of work, it was still the same. It was his home in a way nothing and nowhere else had ever been.

And now he might let the church down. No, it wasn't that he *might* let the church down—he probably would. Definitely would. He wasn't ready for this. His dad had a calling to be a pastor. What did he have?

"Fresh air always helps," she said, leading them to one of the benches set up near the railing that protected the dock from a long drop to the parking lot below. "Now I'm going to go check the mailbox while you sit here and ponder the mysteries of the universe."

She left him on the bench, alone with his thoughts, as she disappeared around the front of the church. He didn't ponder the mysteries of the universe as she suggested, he pondered the mysteries of Hannah instead. Her words had helped more than he could express. She was encouraging and wise, exactly what he needed. Lily would have danced with excitement when their dad called and tried to sweep him up in her enthusiasm. She would have glossed over his nerves and told him to get on with it. But not Hannah. She hadn't pushed or judged, even in the face of his worst fears.

As she reappeared, her hands flipping through the letters that had accumulated in the mailbox, his heart did a funny skip in his chest. When had Hannah gone from being a friend to being something more? And what he going to do about it?

"Did you figure it out?" She smiled and his breath caught in his throat.

"Not even close." His sermon was the farthest thing from his mind.

Her forehead wrinkled as she stared at one of the letters in her hand. "This one is for you," she said and held it out to him.

He took the thick cream envelope, recognizing the embossed logo in the return address. He'd forgotten about it. Forgotten about the application he'd submitted last year. That was before the fire, before Lily had even met Ben. Before Hannah.

Nerves shot through his gut and he wasn't sure what he wanted the letter inside to say. Hannah was quiet as he turned the envelope over in his hands. So much had changed.

"Do you want me to leave?" she asked.

"No." The answer was swift and sure. That was the one thing he did know.

There was no point in stalling. He opened the envelope and pulled out the letter.

"I've been accepted to an MBA program." He scanned the letter, words like *congratulations, acceptance,* and *honor* jumping out at him. He'd been accepted. He couldn't believe it. He'd submitted the application on a desperate whim, a long shot hope that he'd figure out what he was supposed to do with his life. He didn't really believe they'd accept him.

"That's great!" Hannah's smile was huge and as she bent to hug him he was surrounded by lavender, wrapped in the scent and feel of her as her head rested against his.

Far from clarifying his future, the letter in his hand made it even muddier. Why today? Why did it have to arrive on the same day he was asked to preach? Both opportunities appearing before him, both paths showing up at the same time. What was he supposed to do with that?

Noah stood and crossed to the railing, the cool metal warming under his folded arms as the acceptance letter hung limply from his fingers.

"When would you start?" Hannah came to the railing and stood beside him, the breeze making her hair dance around her face.

"In January. Which isn't much time to pack, move, and try to find a place to live." He was thinking out loud, working through the logistics of it. It was overwhelming. It would be a huge change. When he'd applied to the program, he thought that a huge change was exactly what he wanted.

Those deep brown eyes turned to him, he could feel them, feel the weight of her gaze. "Move? Where's the school?"

"Boston."

Hannah stiffened beside him and looked away. "Boston?" The word was as icy as a New England winter and carried the same sting. "Well, at least you wouldn't be alone out there. You'd have Kate."

Noah squeezed his eyes shut. Kate was one more complication, one more thing he didn't know how to handle. She'd been a part of his decision to apply to the graduate program, a big part of it. If he was going to move anywhere, he might as well move close to the woman he thought he loved. But that had been almost a year ago. "This isn't about Kate."

She searched his face, looking for an answer he didn't have. "Are you sure?"

She turned to go, and he reached for her hand, his fingers closing over her wrist. "I don't know what to do." The words he couldn't say to anyone else came easily, and he gave them to her, entrusting them to her. "It's why I have kept the limo business going, why I applied to this program. Maybe I'm not meant to be a pastor. The thought of it—of actually standing up on the platform, trying to fill my dad's shoes . . . " His words trailed off, hollow and empty. His dad was the best man he knew. He could never come close to that, and he knew it.

"You don't have to fill his shoes," she said. "God doesn't need another Pastor Evan. He needs you."

Dropping his head, he studied the fresh asphalt below. The burns and water damage of the fire had been washed away and paved over. No one could see the scars but they were there, buried beneath layer after layer of new paving. Not forgotten, but a foundation they were building upon.

"Do you want to be a pastor?" There wasn't any judgment in her tone, no expectation that he should answer one way or the other. That gentleness, that acceptance, encouraged him more than anything else, as if both paths were open to him, knowing that in her eyes, at least, whichever he chose would be the right one.

He turned and leaned his hip against the rail. "I don't know. I've thought about it. I haven't thought about much else for the past two years. Lily thinks I should do it. She thinks she's being subtle, but she drops enough hints that I know exactly what she wants me to do. My dad says it's up to me."

"And what do you want?" She stepped closer, her shoulder nearly touching his. Strands of her dark brown hair crossed the distance and brushed against him, and he wondered what it would feel like to run those dancing tresses through his fingers. To pull her close and inhale her lavender scent again, to be wrapped in the softness of her hair.

His eyes met hers and he saw the expectation there, the patient anticipation of an answer and his brain jolted, a sudden awareness of what he'd been thinking, of where his mind had gone, snapping him back to the conversation, to the coolness of the breeze, the solid concrete beneath his feet, the metal at his back.

What did he want? He swallowed his answer, unwilling to speak it, to give it life, but realizing for the first time the thing he wanted most was standing right in front of him.

Chapter Twenty-One

HANNAH WATCHED NOAH STRUGGLE AS he spent the week studying and preparing. He wrote endless notes, crossed things out, and crumpled sheets of paper in frustration. She didn't offer any more advice, and she didn't ask if he'd made a decision about the program in Boston. It wasn't any of her business and even though the thought of him moving—the idea of him following Kate back to Boston—kept her up at night, she bit her tongue and focused on her job.

Sunday arrived with a gray, overcast sky and a bite to the air. It was as close to fall as they were going to get so Hannah took advantage of the weather and bundled up in a cable knit sweater and boots. She'd probably be roasting by the time church ended and the sun finally made an appearance, but it would be worth it.

Driving past the still-green palm trees and the tourists dressed in shorts and flip-flops, a wave of homesickness for the changing leaves of her Northern California hometown washed over her. It wasn't a sweeping panorama of colors like the East Coast would get, but it was color nonetheless. There would be a fire in the fireplace and cider on the stove. Her mom was probably busy planning the big Thanksgiving dinner they hosted every year. Peeling potatoes had been such a chore when she was growing up. Now, as her fingers gripped the steering wheel, they itched to feel once again the rough skin of an endless pile of potatoes and the cool metal of the old-fashioned peeler she'd been using since she needed a stepstool to reach the kitchen counter.

Shaking off the thoughts she couldn't do anything about, she pulled into the church parking lot and found a spot next to Noah's truck. She wondered briefly how early he'd gotten there and smiled. He'd been so nervous these past few days. She'd prayed for him constantly, watching him dig through commentaries and never complaining as his books took up more and more of their shared desk in the church office. However things went this morning, no one would be able to say he hadn't poured his heart into this message.

By the time she'd helped with the set up and gone over a few things left on her desk, people had started to arrive. Making her way down to the front row, she waited for the service to start.

When Noah appeared by her side and slid into his usual spot she leaned over and whispered, making sure the people behind them couldn't hear. "Are you ready?"

He gave her a look that said no as he tugged on his tie. Pastor Evan wasn't usually so dressed up when he preached, but she imagined Noah wanted to make a good impression. He'd ditched his usual jeans and button-down shirt for slacks that he'd actually ironed and a dark blue tie.

"As ready as I'll ever be," he replied.

"You're going to do great." She patted his hand and almost yelped when he gripped her fingers and held on tightly. Her heart thundered in her chest when he didn't let go, when he kept her hand in his until worship started. As they stood with the rest of the congregation, his hand fell away, but even then, the memory of his touch lingered like a glove over her hand, a warm whisper of a memory that clung to her skin.

When he took the platform to preach, her stomach somersaulted, and she had to clench her hands together, certain everyone in the church could hear the wild beating of her heart and see what she had been so desperately trying to hide.

She was in love with him.

*****

Hannah stood by the coffee table, knowing she was smiling like a fool. Noah had been great. Better than great, he'd been amazing. And she was fairly certain that she wasn't being biased. Based on the hugs and handshakes he was receiving from the congregation his words had been well received.

She didn't want to be arrogant, but there was a part of her that thought his message had been for her. Focus on the one she'd told him, and listening to him preach on Philippians three, verses thirteen and fourteen, she thought, however selfishly, that the words might have been for her. "Forgetting what is behind and straining towards what is ahead, I press on to win the prize for which God has called me heavenward in Christ Jesus."

Forgetting the past. Isn't that what she had been trying to do? Isn't that what she wanted? To lay it all to rest and focus on a new start, a new life. She watched Noah walk through the crowd, slowly making his way towards her, accepting the compliments even though she knew he was probably embarrassed by all the attention.

How she wished Lily and Evan could have seen him. She'd have to tell Chris to save the video she'd secretly asked him to make so she could show it to them later. Noah would hate it, but Ben would love to see it. After all the commentary Noah provided during his movies she was sure Ben would have a thing or two to say while they watched Noah's first sermon.

Yet nothing Ben said would change how she felt at that moment. She, more than anyone, knew how nervous he'd been, how hard he'd worked, and it had been worth it. All of it. She couldn't wait to tell him, but she kept to her post by the coffee table, refilling the supplies and chatting with people as she waited for him to cross the sea of well-wishers.

He accepted a few more handshakes, a couple of hugs and a ferocious cheek pinching by a wrinkled older lady, then finally he was in front of her, standing only a foot away, his cheeks flushed in the cool air.

"Having fun?" She laughed and offered him a cup of coffee, black. "It looks like you were a hit," she said as he gulped the coffee, wincing as it scalded its way down his throat.

"Well, let's wait for the emails," he said with trepidation. "No one ever says anything bad to your face. They wait and email it to you on Monday morning."

"Seriously?" Looking out over the people still milling around the dock and clustered in the parking lot she wondered who could have anything negative to say about his sermon.

Noah nodded. "My dad dreaded checking his email on Monday. Someone always finds something to criticize."

"Well, I don't think you have to worry about it. It was a great message."

"You think so?" The yearning in his eyes melted her heart. He was so worried, so anxious to prove himself.

The butterflies in her stomach fluttered as she tried to formulate everything she wanted to say to him, to let him know how much it had meant to her, how his words had touched her heart. She wanted to tell him that even if no one else appreciated his words, she did and she would remember them forever. But she never got a chance.

"Noah!" Kate ran across the dock and threw her arms around his neck, planting a loud kiss on his cheek. "You were amazing!"

Noah shook his head as if he couldn't figure out how she'd gotten there. "I didn't even know you were here," he said, looking at her like she was a puzzle piece that was out of place.

"I snuck in and sat in the back. I didn't want to miss your first sermon." Kate slipped her arm through his and squeezed. She hadn't indulged in the fall weather, opting for black skinny jeans and a flowing white blouse. Hannah tugged on the baggy sweater she'd been so excited to wear, feeling frumpy and out of date.

Every word Lily had told her about them, about the crush Noah had nurtured for so long, about Lily dreaming of the possibility of Kate becoming her sister-in-law, it all roared through her head. In just a few months Noah could be living in Boston, meeting Kate for coffee, and walking through the snow with her to his way to a new life, far from the church and far from her. Jealousy curdled in her stomach, but she kept a smile on her face, refusing to spoil Noah's big day with her crushed dreams.

"So, do you have any plans for the afternoon?" Kate asked, her arm still linked with his, and Noah glanced her way.

Hannah didn't reply. They hadn't made any plans. She didn't have a claim on his time, he could do whatever he wanted with whomever he wanted. If being with Kate was what he wanted, she wouldn't stop him. Standing as still as a statue, a piece of the backdrop as they played out their scene, Hannah refused to let her disappointment show.

"Not yet," he said and bumped Kate's shoulder with his. "What did you have in mind?"

"Well," Kate said flirtatiously and Hannah wanted to smack her. She immediately regretted the uncharitable thought. After all, Kate had come all the way down here to support him. She should be nicer to her, even if every instinct in her body screamed against it. "I was hoping to kidnap you."

Noah laughed. "Is it really kidnapping if I go willingly?"

Hannah refrained from rolling her eyes and decided that was a mark of great personal growth. She would not be bitter, she repeated to herself. She would not dwell on what she couldn't have. Always wanting something more, chasing after something new was what had gotten her in this whole mess of a life in the first place. Content. She would be content with what she had and the second chance she had been given.

"I'm all yours," he said and Kate grinned. "Let me help Hannah clean up and then we can go."

"Don't worry about it," Hannah blurted, clumsily joining the conversation she hadn't really been a part of. "I can handle it. Why don't you two go ahead and take off." There was no way she wanted to watch them flirting and teasing as they cleaned and locked up the church. She wanted to pout and feel sorry for herself and go back to Ben's house and eat a pint of that gourmet ice cream Kate had found in the freezer.

Noah turned to her. "Are you sure?" Guilt radiated from him as he looked at her.

But she plastered an even bigger fake smile on her face and waved them away. "I wouldn't want you to be late for your own kidnapping."

Kate was watching her carefully, but she didn't care. Let her wonder why she was being so accommodating. Let her be suspicious and skeptical. It wasn't Kate's heart that was breaking over stir sticks and sugar packets.

"Thanks." Noah handed her the keys so she could lock up. "I guess I'll see you Tuesday," he said and she wondered if she was imagining the hesitation in his voice, if once again she was wishing for something that wasn't there.

"Have fun." She started collecting the coffee table supplies to put away until next week, looking anywhere but at the two of them. Cleaning up by herself would take a bit longer than usual, but it was worth it not to have to see Kate and Noah together, to watch them laugh and tease and pretend like her heart wasn't shattering like broken glass.

Still Noah waited. She looked up ready to shoo him away again, needing him to go, needing him to take Kate far away, then stopped when she saw the gentleness on his face.

"I couldn't have done this without you." His eyes bore deep into her own, the sincerity reflected there burrowing into her, finding the cracks in her defenses and pushing right through. "Thank you."

He walked away before she could reply. Which was just as well since she had no idea what she would have said anyway.

Watching them disappear around the corner, she called herself every kind of fool for falling for him.

"Want some help?" Chris Johnston smiled down at her, his eyebrows shooting up at the sight of her hands full of cream and sugar.

"That would be great." She dropped the condiments into his hands and pulled out a box from under the table, hidden by the linen table-cloth. As she set it on the table she caught Chris staring in the direction Noah and Kate had gone, his eyes tracking them with a longing she hadn't expected, but one that she recognized.

Chapter Twenty-Two

KATE PRESSED A BUTTON ON the key fob and a black sports car beeped to life in welcome.

"Nice choice," he said. His brother-in-law had excellent taste in cars. "Where are we headed?"

"To visit Megan," she said solemnly as she slid behind the wheel.

Noah didn't reply as he got in beside her. The engine roared to life and Kate stepped on the gas.

She drove in silence, whipping the sleek sports car through the light Sunday morning traffic on the 101 as they sped north to the San Fernando Valley. Noah didn't ask questions, he was too busy gripping the door handle and trying not to yelp as she darted between cars, zigzagging across the wide lanes.

As the 101 met the 5, they left the smog of downtown behind and started a gentle climb up and then a fast descent down into the suburbs north of Los Angeles they had both grown up in. Their families had lived only a few cities apart, which made them almost neighbors in the congested clutter of the greater Los Angeles area. Though they'd been only a short drive away from each other, they hadn't met until Lily and Kate ended up at UCLA together. By that time Noah and his family were living in the small house near the church while Kate's family had stayed up north. Whenever Lily came home to visit, do laundry for free, or get a home cooked meal, Kate had been in tow.

She'd slipped right into their family, and Noah had been smitten with the feisty redhead from the start.

Kate was vivacious and free. A wild spirit soaking up everything life had to offer. She laughed loud and often. She was fearless and pursued joy like a hunter chases prey. She had taken his reserved sister, shy and quiet Lily, under her wing. Noah was certain they had gotten into their fair share of trouble, but Kate had always looked after Lily and protected her. It was one of the things he adored about her—her love for his family.

And then everything changed. One night was all it had taken for the bright and sparkling Kate to vanish, replaced by hard edges and bitterness. Her laughter was gone, taken along with her little sister.

He glanced at her as she drove, her focus on the road before them. There was something driving her, propelling her to visit Megan's grave, whether she was running toward that force or trying to escape it, was up for debate. She wasn't ready to talk about it, and he wasn't about to ask, so he sat in silence beside her and prayed they would make it to the cemetery in one piece as they ate up the asphalt miles that would take them to her childhood home.

They turned into the memorial park and drove past the perfectly maintained rolling lawns. White stones and statues spread in every direction, and scattered spots of colors from flower arrangements broke up the endless quilt of green and white. She parked the car and sat in the driver's seat, her hands gripping the wheel so tightly her knuckles turned as white as the gravestones spread out before them.

She turned the car off, but she didn't move. Sitting in the leather seat, staring out across the sea of endless names, she looked lonely and lost.

"Are you okay?"

Dropping her head onto the wheel, she closed her eyes and took two deep breaths. Putting his hand on her shoulder, he squeezed gently, a reminder that he was there. That he'd been there through it all and he wouldn't leave her now. He remembered being in their house the day after Megan died. His father sat with her parents, speaking words of comfort in hushed tones while he and Lily sat at the kitchen table with Kate. The light had gone out of her eyes and shadows haunted their depths. When his dad had asked to pray for them, her mom had stormed out, stomping up their stairs and slamming the bedroom door. Kate hadn't flinched. It was the first thread of many to snap.

She sat up quickly and wiped her cheeks, heedless of the black lines of mascara that streaked her face. Nodding to herself as if she'd made a decision, she opened the door and stepped into the cool afternoon. Noah followed as she walked across the impossibly green grass. He didn't know how long it had been since she'd visited Megan's grave, but she didn't hesitate as she walked, picking her way through the resting places, past the bright, fresh flowers and the faded, long forgotten ones.

Megan was buried in a flat section of grass, surrounded by names Noah didn't recognize, the rolling foothills rising in the distance. He remembered the day of the funeral, sitting in a plastic chair in almost the same spot where he stood now, dumbfounded that someone so young could be gone so quickly. It was the last time he saw Kate's parents together. They split up less than a year after burying their youngest daughter, the stress of her death and the ensuing investigation into the crash had damaged their marriage. Then Kate left, too. That one night, that one terrible night, destroyed not one, but four lives.

They stood in silence a few feet from the tombstone. Noah read the words carved into the gray and white marble. *Beloved daughter and sister.* Four words. Only four words to summarize a life that had been cut tragically short.

His mom didn't have a tombstone. When she died, they'd scattered her ashes in the Pacific. His dad, Lily, and he stood together by the sun-bleached railing of the small boat and watched as the ashes floated away, knowing that his mom was already in Heaven, had already heard the words "Well done," from her Savior, and he knew Megan was there, too. But he also knew that wouldn't be a comfort to Kate. She was like her mother, still angry, still blaming God for what happened, demanding to know why He hadn't stopped it.

She stared at the stone as if she could wring answers from it by the sheer force of her will. "Whenever I'm back here I spend every day searching all the faces I see. Walking, driving, at the grocery store. All of them. I keep thinking I'm going to see him, thinking he'll suddenly show up at the coffee shop or at the gas station. That I'll see him and know. I'll know it's him."

He didn't need to ask to know she was talking about the man who had been driving the car that hit them, the car that caused the crash that ended her sister's life and changed her own forever. The man had never been caught. He'd slipped away into the night, leaving tragedy behind him on a lonely road.

He stepped toward her and pulled her to his side, wrapping his arm around her shoulder and holding her close. He expected her to cry, he was prepared for sobs, for sorrow. He wasn't prepared for the hardness, the steel that left her rigid against him. No wonder she had stayed away for so long.

"Is that why you're still here? Why you haven't gone back to Boston?" He held her against his side, aching for her loss, understanding the anger that threatened to consume her. He'd felt the same way after the fire at the church. He'd wanted revenge, to make someone pay for what happened. As angry as he'd been, he'd had his dad to talk to, to pray with him. And he still had his sister.

She was quiet for a long moment and when she spoke her voice was less certain. "No. I was supposed to already be back at work. My boss has been blowing up my cell phone wanting to know when I'm coming back. I just . . . " She hesitated, then looked up, her green eyes meeting his. Gone was the tough talking Kate he had always known. The confident, brash woman who grabbed what she wanted without excuse. Instead he saw vulnerability and an insecurity he'd never seen before. "I thought there might be something here worth staying for . . . some*one* worth staying for."

Noah sucked in a breath. He stared over her head, over the soft, red waves that curled under his chin. He stepped back, but her hands rested on his arms, keeping him close even as he moved away.

"Is there, Noah? Is there something worth staying for?"

"Kate, I—" But the words wouldn't come. Everything he'd planned to say, everything he told himself he wanted, disintegrated on his tongue. Even as he saw for the first time a glimmer of hope in the way she looked at him, his mind took him back to the small office in the church, to the woman working at his desk, to her shy brown eyes and the way she ducked her head when he complimented her.

The dream of Kate he had held onto for so long had vanished. He didn't even know when it slipped away. It had faded day by day into a memory. And now that he was here with her, now that she was close enough to step into his arms, there was only one place he wanted to be.

Taking her hand, he stared at the red polish on her fingernails. "If you only knew how long I have wanted to hear you say that."

"Oh I knew," she said, and his gaze flew to her face. The laughter he saw there eased the tension, unraveling it like a string that had been pulled free.

"You knew? This whole time?"

"Well, I don't know about the *whole* time, but at least since junior year."

Something more than embarrassment grabbed him and he groaned. "So much for being sly and mysterious."

She shook her head. "You have a terrible poker face." With a sigh she stepped away and he let her go. "I guess I thought you would always be there. That I would always have a chance, but when I came back and saw that smitten look on your face—it wasn't for me. Not anymore. I guess I got jealous."

Sadness tinged her words as she knelt by Megan's tombstone.

"Kate, I'm sorry."

She shrugged at his apology. "There's nothing to be sorry for. Things change. I might want to punch you for a few days, but I get it." Using her hand, she brushed the dust and crushed leaves off the stone, letting her fingers linger over the word *sister*.

Brushing the dirt and dust off her hands, she stood and faced him. There was no condemnation, no betrayal, just an acceptance of what was and what would never be. "I want you to be happy, Noah. I really do, but be careful with Hannah. I know you don't believe me, but there's something off with her story. I don't want to see you get hurt. And I'd hate to have to kill her if she broke your heart."

He laughed and hugged her, knowing she'd made the same threat against Ben, repeatedly, and taking it as a sign that their friendship would survive. "I'll be fine. Besides, she might not even be interested in me. I'm kind of a handful."

Kate shook her head, the movement reverberating against his chest, and he could feel the smile on her face. "I think you'll be fine. But," she pulled away and looked up at him. "If you really care about her, maybe don't wait seven years to say something this time."

Chapter Twenty-Three

NOAH MARCHED INTO THE CHURCH Tuesday morning with Kate's words, if not her blessing, propelling him on. He understood her concerns, he appreciated the way she worried about him, but he wasn't going to let that stop him. He walked down the hallway certain of his next move, but his resolve faltered as soon as he entered the office.

Hannah was already there, sitting at their shared desk, her hair pulled up into some sort of bun with a pencil sticking out one side. She was focused on the computer, entering numbers then stopping to check the paper beside her before typing some more. She hadn't heard him enter so he stood there, soaking up the sight of her, knowing he was about to change everything. A frantic whisper echoed in the back of his mind telling him he could back out, slip out the door and disappear before she saw him and pretend like nothing had happened. Like he hadn't been standing on the edge of something dangerous.

But did he really want to go back to the way things were?

Before he gave in to fear, he took another step into the office. He was going to do this whether he was ready for it or not. Her head popped up, those deep brown eyes focusing on his, the hint of a smile ghosting on her lips as she saw him.

"Have dinner with me," he blurted, the words exploding like soda from a can someone had shaken, and he immediately wished he could take them back and start over. So much for the smooth and charming speech he'd practiced in the car.

Grooves etched into her forehead as she stared at him. She might have been assessing his mental state, wondering if he'd lost his mind. And a part of him wondered the same thing. "Excuse me?"

This wasn't his first date, why was he acting like such an idiot? Taking a quick breath, he tried again. "Would you like to have dinner with me? Tonight?"

She blinked. Then blinked again, her hands hovering over the keyboard, whatever task she had been doing forgotten in the face of his clumsy invitation. If his stomach hadn't been in knots, he would have laughed at the shocked expression on her face. The longer she stayed silent, the tighter the knots got, each passing second twisting them in his gut.

She was going to say no. Of course, she was going to say no. He was going to have to figure out how to work with her every day, sitting across from her, staring at the back of her laptop, acting like he hadn't just made a colossal fool out of himself. Lily would feel sorry for him. Kate would laugh at him and Hannah . . .

"Um, sure." It sounded like more of a question than an enthusiastic agreement, but he'd take it.

Relief flooded through his veins and he felt a hundred pounds lighter, the weight of potential rejection had lifted and he could breathe again. "Great. How about we take off when the afterschool childcare teachers show up? Then we can come back and lock up after." He rocked on his heels, trying for casual and confident, and knowing he was failing. Nervous and uncertain was probably closer to the mark.

"All right." She was still in that same frozen position, still staring at him with a combination of confusion and surprise written on her face. "Excellent. See you then." Nodding once, as if they'd come to a business arrangement, he stepped back into the hallway and walked away, not stopping until he was sure she couldn't see or hear him. Leaning against the wall he ran his hands through his hair, and smiled. It hadn't been pretty, but at least she'd said yes. Now he needed to plan a first date she'd never forget.

*****

Her hands were sweating. Wiping them on her faded jeans, she wished for the hundredth time that she had worn something else to work. But how could she have known Noah was going to ask her out? When she woke up that morning and pulled out her favorite jeans and a soft beige sweater, she didn't think she had any plans at all for the night. Just work and then back to Ben's house for a night spent with a microwave pizza and a movie. She certainly hadn't expected dinner with Noah, especially after he had disappeared with Kate Sunday morning and she hadn't seen or heard from him or Kate since. If anything, she expected him to show up at the church and tell her all about the wonderful weekend they'd spent together. She imagined they'd run off on some romantic getaway. She'd lain in bed torturing herself with endless possibilities of where they'd gone and what they'd done. They might have eloped in Vegas for all she knew. She'd been planning for a day of misery and disappointment, nursing her broken heart and calling herself every sort of fool.

Instead he'd asked her out.

Her.

A tingle of excitement coiled in her stomach then spread like electricity through her body. Noah had asked her out.

At least she thought he asked her out. She was pretty sure it was a date. Not one hundred percent sure, but pretty sure.

She tried to do something with her hair, but it wasn't cooperating. Using the small brush in her purse she smoothed it down as best she could, attempting to tame the natural curls that got even more curly in the humidity of early fall. When that didn't work, she dug out a hair tie and pulled her hair into a loose bun, hoping it was a style that conveyed "cute and casual" instead of "long day at work."

The only make-up she had in her bag was a small tube of lip gloss Lily had given her. She ran it over her lips, the light pink shine giving her a bit of color. It would have to do.

Staring at her reflection in the small mirror in the ladies' room, she shook her head. This was Noah. He'd been with her at her worst. No amount of lip glass could cover up the memory of what he'd already seen.

Besides it probably wasn't even a real date.

It took a full minute to talk herself into leaving the small bathroom, but she did it.

Noah was waiting for her in the church office, wearing the same jeans and sweatshirt he'd had on that morning and she was relieved he hadn't changed. She felt less underdressed staring at the sports team logo on his chest.

"Ready to go?"

"Yes." She closed the laptop, and switched off the light. Noah shut the office door behind her and then led the way to the parking lot.

The silence between them was awkward, heavy with uncertainty and tinged with nervousness. It was the giddy feeling of standing on the edge of something that definitely felt like a date, and she wondered if he felt the same, like they were getting dangerously close to a precipice, a great unknown looming in front of them, and every step they took would make it harder to go back.

He opened the passenger side door to his truck and helped her in. The smell of Chinese food enveloped her and her stomach rumbled.

"I hope you don't mind," he said as he climbed into the driver's side and gestured to the plastic bag full of small white boxes sitting between them. "I've got something I want to show you and they don't offer food there."

"I'm up for anything," she said and meant it. She'd have been happy to sit in the truck with him eating Chinese food and staring at the side of the church. He grinned at her as he started the truck, and her heart flipped. She desperately hoped this was a date.

She lost track of where they were as the congested, traffic-snarled streets faded away and the truck climbed up a quiet canyon road. Houses and billboards gave way to scrub brush and rocks as Noah drove them up a steep road, winding in and out of rolling hills covered with summer scorched grass. Cresting a hill, they reached a secluded overlook. Noah backed the truck into a parking space and they got out.

As he walked to the back of the truck and dropped the tailgate, she marveled at the canyon spread out before them. In the distance, the sprawling urban jungle of Los Angeles unfolded like a concrete blanket, but right here, right at their feet, hills and valleys filled with green and brown rolled away in gentle waves.

It was one more sight she'd never seen, one more secret part of Hollywood she'd never explored. The fact that there could be such undisturbed beauty, such untouched wild in the heart of skyscrapers and neon signs and endless traffic jams astounded her.

She turned back to see that Noah had spread a blanket over the bed of the truck and was setting up the boxes of Chinese food like a picnic. Climbing in beside him, she helped open the boxes, nearly squealing with joy when she saw both kung pao chicken and vegetable lo mein.

"How did you know?" Her mouth watered as she broke apart the disposable wooden chopsticks that had been tucked in the bag.

He shrugged. "You always ordered the same thing when we had Chinese food at the house. I figured those were your favorites."

A jolt of pleasure spread through her, not at the food, though they were indeed her favorites, but because he'd noticed. All those nights of sitting with Lily and Evan, passing the boxes around their kitchen table, and he'd noticed. Somewhere in the midst of it, he saw her, knew her. That realization more than anything else caused her toes to curl inside her tennis shoes.

They sat with their legs dangling off the end of the tailgate, the Chinese food boxes scattered between them. A breeze drifted across the canyon, tugging on her hair and filling the air with the smell of orange chicken and egg rolls and something else, something uniquely Noah, a blend of soap and spice that would always remind her of him.

As they ate, the sun started its slow descent, igniting the sky in a riot of color. Someone once told her that it was the smog in the air that gave Los Angeles such beautiful sunsets, but she didn't believe that. Sitting in the bed of the truck facing the setting sun, bathed in red and orange skylight, they watched the day fade away and the night move in.

"This place is beautiful," she whispered as she tipped her head to the sky.

"My mom used to bring us up here," he replied. "There's a trail you can hike all the way into the canyon. When you go far enough you can't even see the city anymore. The hills block everything else out. It's almost enough to convince yourself that you're someplace else, someplace far away from all of that." He pointed towards the city skyline, and the long winding snake of traffic that led in and out of it, an endless stretch of red and white lights crawling along, everyone in a hurry to get somewhere, and everyone stuck in traffic. She knew firsthand there was never a quiet moment down there, never a second of peace, never a minute when bustling, frantic activity stopped.

But up here it was different. A breath of fresh air in a city choked by smog. A moment of stillness in a city that never slept. And the man beside her?

She looked at him, stunned to see he was watching her, the intensity of his eyes focused only on her. The heat of a blush crept up her cheeks and she brushed an errant piece of hair behind her ear.

"This reminds me of . . ." *home.* The word stuck on her tongue and she bit it back. "Where I grew up," she finally said. "We had the same kind of hidden trails and roads that led to the most amazing sights. But you had to know where to look."

Noah leaned back on his elbow, never taking his eyes off of her. "And where's that?" he asked.

Warning bells rang in her head. She'd been so careful to keep her past to herself, to keep that door closed and locked tight. As she looked at him, his face colored by the fiery sky, doubt roared through her head and she retreated. "A little town in Northern California no one has ever heard of."

Evade, distract, after all these months she was still closed off, unwilling to open herself up, even to Noah. Especially to Noah. Sitting in his truck at the edge of a cliff the fear of losing him was stronger than ever.

If he noticed the vague answer he didn't mention it. He never did. He never pushed, never pressed for more. She didn't deserve his trust and she knew it.

"So how did you end up here?"

She looked past him to the families that were packing up their cars, preparing to head back down the hill, back into the busyness of life, wherever that was for them. "That's a long story."

"I'd like to hear it."

Looking into his eyes, she believed him. That he wanted to hear her story, not out of suspicion or curiosity or because she was the broken girl he rescued all those months ago, but because he was interested, because that was what you did on a first date. You asked questions, you learned about the other person, you shared little bits of yourself. After all they'd been through, he knew everything and nothing about her. Maybe it was finally time to change that.

She drew her knees up to her chest and wrapped her arms around her legs, becoming a tight ball of nerves. She stared at the darkening sky, and as the sun sank lower in the west, so did her resolve. Maybe she didn't want to keep her past a secret anymore. Maybe she could find a way to be honest and not lose Noah in the process.

Taking a deep breath, she focused on the hills, watching the sun slip away as the shadows lengthened. She didn't want to see his face, she didn't want to see the way he was looking at her change.

"I wanted an adventure. You know my dad was a pastor, but I wasn't the best daughter. I pushed the limits, got in trouble. A lot.

By the time I was eighteen, I was tired of being known as the pastor's rebellious daughter, of everyone in town knowing my name and whispering about my mistakes. I wanted to live life the way *I* wanted with no one bossing me around or telling me what to do. I wanted freedom. So, after graduation, when my boyfriend suggested we run away to LA, I packed a bag and jumped in the car with him."

The stupidity of that moment weighed on her. If she'd only known, if she'd only listened, but she had been stubborn and selfish and unreachable, convinced she knew best and that everyone who tried to talk some sense into her was old-fashioned, boring, and out of touch. If only she could go back. She'd listen to every word and do it all differently. But it was too late for that now.

"My parents tried to help me. I wouldn't listen. And in the end, I didn't even say goodbye. I left them a note and hit the road." What had her parents thought when they found that note? When they looked into her room and saw she was gone? How much hurt had she caused them? How long had it taken for them to move on and forget their wayward daughter?

"Have you been back home since then?"

It sounded so easy when he said it. Leave and go back, run away and go home, but the tangle of regret and shame in her heart reminded her that it wasn't as simple as that. She couldn't cross a bridge she'd burned. And burned it she had. She wouldn't hurt her family any more, she wouldn't make them pay for her mistakes. She'd decided long ago that she would live with the consequences of her choices. Until that night in Norma Jean's when dying had seemed like a better choice, like her only choice. Until Noah found her and brought her back.

But she didn't say any of that. She shook her head and watched the sun burn low on the horizon, disappearing from its place in the sky and letting the night come in. As the darkness grew, swallowing up the remains of the day, the temperature dropped, settling on them with a chill that brought goose bumps to her arms.

He was waiting for her answer and she didn't have one. Not a good one. "No, I haven't been back. It's far away and I've been gone too long. I guess this is my home now."

She turned to look at him, surprised to see him already staring at her, the blue of his eyes bright with the promise of something she couldn't identify. Reaching out, he brushed his hand down her cheek, the lightest touch, a trail of warmth in the cool of the evening. "Then I hope you'll stay."

The words were a whisper against her heart, a knock against the walls she'd built. As she looked into his eyes, she hoped it, too.

Chapter Twenty-Four

THEY DROVE BACK TO THE church talking of less weighty things. Church business, what Lily and Ben might be doing, the church plants in the area Evan was working so hard to build. It had been a wonderful night and Hannah wasn't ready for it to end. She hadn't told him everything, but she'd made a start.

Sitting in his truck, the cool night air drifting through the open windows, the warm timbre of his voice washing over her like music, it was perfect. For the first time since she'd come to Hollywood, she was glad for the congested roads and densely packed cars, happy for the extra time it gave her with him.

"So, what did you think about preaching on Sunday?" she asked as they left the high traffic areas behind and drove into the church's neighborhood.

He hadn't said anything about it while they were at the overlook and she wondered if he was still worried about how it had gone She didn't have the heart to ask about any critical emails that may have appeared in Pastor Evan's account, though she also couldn't imagine anyone having something negative to say about Noah or his message.

She'd assumed Kate would have had done something to celebrate his big preaching moment when they disappeared that afternoon, but instead of coming back Tuesday morning with tales of a celebration, he'd come back and asked her out. Her! Just thinking about him standing in the office doorway, the rush of his questions, the worry that she might say no, made her smile and the date wasn't even over yet.

"It was better than I thought it would be. Being up there, it was . . ." He searched for the right word and she waited. "It was good. I actually enjoyed it." He darted a glance her way, a quick flash of blue as his eyes met hers.

A question burned in her throat, words aching to be set free, but she was afraid to give them voice. Afraid she wouldn't like the answer. Afraid that the whole night might come crashing down around her. "And graduate school? What about Boston?"

The seconds ticked by, each one feeling like a lifetime. The longer the silence lasted, the worse her fears became. Her heart was already lost, it had been from the moment she woke up in the hospital and saw his face and felt his hand in hers, but if it was hopeless, if he was leaving, following Kate to Boston, she needed to know. If this one night was all she was going to get with him, so be it. She'd make the memory of it last.

Noah stared straight ahead, his hands tightening on the wheel and she regretted the question. She thought she wanted to know what was coming, but maybe she was wrong.

"I don't know." His words were honest, devoid of confidence, as if the question was too big for him to figure out. "It would be a great opportunity. I'd learn a lot about how to grow the limo business, maybe hire some additional drivers. I could make it into something successful."

Loss pulled at her, slipping away like the tide, receding inch by inch. "I'm sure Kate would be happy to have you there."

"I'm not so sure about that. Kate's pretty annoyed with me at the moment." They pulled into the church parking lot, the old truck bumping over the pavement. Noah parked his truck next to the car she borrowed from Ben. Bracing his arm on the steering wheel, he swiveled in the seat until he faced her. "I always thought preaching would be the hardest part of ministry. It terrified me. I was so sure I would mess it up and let everyone down. But when I was up there, I felt comfortable, like maybe that was where I was supposed to be." With a self-conscious laugh that made her want to wrap her arms around him, he looked away and turned off the ignition. "It turns out preaching isn't so bad, it's all the administrative stuff I struggle with. And now that I have you, I don't have to worry about that."

Now that I have you. Warmth tingled in her limbs at the words as he leapt out of the truck and dashed around the hood to open her door before she could touch the handle. Putting her hand in his extended one, she couldn't help the tingly excitement that danced in her heart. "Thank you," she whispered.

He kept her hand in his as they walked to the front of the church. "A gentleman always escorts a lady to the door on a first date."

She stopped, searching his eyes, every cell of her body aware of his nearness. Looking down, she realized they were standing only inches away from where he'd first found her, from the spot where her life had nearly ended. If she looked hard enough would she be able to see the stain of her blood on the dark asphalt? She paused, drawn to the spot, but afraid to go near it. Did Noah remember? Did he still see her as that broken, hopeless girl? Maybe she was imagining all of this, making it into something it wasn't.

"Is that what this was?" The words were tentative, filled with the anxiety she felt, a whispered breath that might blow away the fragile dream she held. "A first date?"

Noah ran his thumb over her knuckles, and she was spellbound by the movement, shocked by how such a small touch could radiate so far. "That's what I was going for," he said and she could have stayed lost in the way he looked at her, happily and blissfully lost. "With maybe a second date tomorrow night?"

She couldn't stop the smile that spread across her face, the joy that leapt in her heart, the riot of nerves that sizzled through her body. Noah hadn't just asked her out once, he'd asked her out twice. Before she could stop it a wild flare of hope ignited in a place she'd thought was dead.

"I'd like that," she said, amazed at the calmness in her voice, when all she wanted to do was shout and laugh and dance her way in to the church. She wished Lily were home so she could tell her. She hoped her friend would approve. After all the years she'd spent hoping that Kate would one day return Noah's feelings, would she be disappointed to come home and find Noah with her?

Was he with her?

The newness of it struck her. It was strange and foreign, but exciting too. She would do things differently this time, do things right.

With a gentle squeeze, he let go of her hand, oblivious to her leaping thoughts. "I'll start locking up," he said. "When you're done here maybe we can head home and see if Dad is up for a movie."

She nodded because words were too hard. As he disappeared into the church, she barely resisted the urge to do a jig in the parking lot. Her mind sped ahead to the little yellow house, to popcorn and a movie, she and Noah curled up on the comfortable couch while Evan sat in his recliner.

Walking to Ben's car, a rush of nervous energy seized her. What had been such a simple part of her routine just a few weeks ago, movie night with the Shaws, suddenly had new meaning. She already knew Pastor Evan so he wasn't really introducing her to his dad, but she wondered what Noah was going to say. Would they be keeping this, whatever this was, a secret? What would Evan think about seeing them together?

The thought of Pastor Evan looking at her not just as a church employee, but as the woman his son was dating, caused her to trip over her own feet as she unlocked the car to drop off her purse.

She was so focused on imagining Pastor Evan's reaction that she didn't notice the young girl who appeared by her side in the shadows of the empty parking lot. "Do you work here?"

She was thin and young with the haunted look of a girl who had seen the dark side of Hollywood. It was a look Hannah recognized, a look she had seen in the mirror every day for years. "Yes, I do. Can I help you?"

Glancing from side to side, the girl checked her surroundings and Hannah wondered if she should call Noah back, although he probably wouldn't be able to hear her. They often had people show up at the church who needed help, people who heard about The Mission and knew it was a place to go where they could get food and a list of local resources. Hannah had directed people to different community services and she knew they still had some food left in the free pantry they tried to keep stocked for the neighborhood.

But the girl shook her head and pulled an envelope from the back pocket of her very short shorts. "This is for you," she said.

As soon as Hannah took it, the girl fled, disappearing into the growing darkness.

She turned the envelope in her hand, wondering if she should have gone after the girl. If someone had reached out to her, offered her a way out, would she have taken it? The thought hovered in her mind as she tried to figure out what it would have taken for her to ask for help. How many girls were still out there? Trapped by hopelessness, prisoners of lies and deceit.

The lights in the church switched off. Noah would be back any minute. Maybe she should give the envelope to him. She turned it over. It didn't have a name or an address. It might be private, something for a pastor to see.

A pastor. She smiled at the thought. Noah had enjoyed preaching. If he had enjoyed it, maybe that would be enough to keep him here. But he didn't like the administrative stuff. She didn't want to hand it to him and give him a reason to run away to Boston, to choose business over ministry. *Now that I have you.* The words danced through her mind, and she held on to them.

Distracted by the memory of his words, she opened the envelope and pulled out a single sheet of paper. She unfolded it and panic clutched at her chest, strangling her breath, and draining the strength from her legs so quickly she fell against the car, unable to stand, unable to face the ugliness in front of her.

Her hands trembled as she held a copy of Ben and Lily's wedding party photo, the same photo she'd so carefully clipped out of the newspaper and pressed between the pages of a book for safekeeping. This one had been one printed from a website, the colors faded and dull, except for the blood red ink that wound in circles around her face, over and over, surrounding her like a target, like a noose waiting to be tightened. Scrawled below the photo, a message written just for her, dragging her back into the past, back to the darkness she thought she'd escaped and a voice she thought she'd never hear again.

I found you, Sasha.

Chapter Twenty-Five

SOMETHING WAS WRONG.

Noah knew it. Felt it. But he didn't know how to fix it.

He replayed they evening they spent at the overlook time and time again, trying to figure out where it all went wrong. It had seemed like the perfect night, the perfect start to something new. They'd gone back to the church to lock up and he suggested they go back to his house for a movie or a board game. When he finished locking up and was ready to go, Hannah complained of a headache, saying she wasn't up for a movie and that she'd rather go back to Ben's house and sleep.

It hadn't struck him as a lie at the time. He hadn't had any reason not to believe her. So he said goodnight and watched her drive off.

But when she showed up for work the next day, she was different. She was there, but not really. It was like a light had gone out, like she was only a shell of what she'd been the night before. He hadn't seen her so guarded and wary since the first day in the hospital.

Something had happened but he didn't know what. And if he didn't know what it was, he couldn't help. Whenever he approached her, she found an excuse to be someplace else. The teasing lilt in her voice was gone. She was all business and as soon as she was done for the day, she disappeared, driving off into the darkness, leaving him standing in the parking lot with no idea what to do next or what he'd done wrong.

Was it him? Had he come on too strong? Maybe he'd misread her feelings. Maybe he was an idiot to believe she could care for him. Maybe Kate had been right all along.

Ensconced in his limo, his chauffeur's hat discarded on the passenger seat, he stared at the letter in his hand. Business school. Boston. They were waiting for a decision, and he needed to make it soon.

Guilt nibbled away at him. He should talk to his dad, let him know about the acceptance. He told himself that he hadn't brought it up because his dad had been busy, investing all of his time with the new pastors, trying to help them take root and establish churches. He didn't want to bother him or distract him. But that was a lie. He was afraid of what that conversation would mean. He couldn't keep sitting on the fence, stalling, and vacillating between options.

A neglected notebook sat on the passenger seat and he glanced at it. He was supposed to be multi-tasking. Technically, he was still on duty, having dropped off his client at an after-party for a big movie premiere. Now sitting in the dark parking lot with all the other limos and luxury cars waiting for the call to pick him up again, he had time to think, too much of it. When he accepted the gig, the plan had been to spend the down time working on his next sermon. His dad had been thrilled to hear how well last Sunday had gone, and Noah hadn't hesitated when his dad asked if he would fill in for him again. But as he stared at the letter in his hand and the blank paper beside him, the only thing on his mind was Hannah and how badly things had gone.

He was intensely dissecting every word he'd said to her, so focused on figuring out where things went wrong, that he nearly jumped when the back door to the limo opened and shut with a resounding thud.

Spinning around to peer behind him, he saw Chris Johnston drop into an exhausted slump on the back seat.

Noah checked the bright blue clock on the dashboard. "You're supposed to be in there for another hour," he said.

The director gave him a pitiful look. "No way. I wouldn't have made it five more minutes with those people."

Tossing the acceptance letter onto the still blank notebook, Noah started the car, not bothering to put the chauffeur's hat back on. Chris wasn't a stickler for protocol or keeping up appearances. "You know, *those people* are your people." He grinned in the rearview mirror and laughed when Chris scowled back at him. "Everything okay?"

Yanking on his tie until the knot loosened, Chris pulled it apart and stuffed it in the side pocket of his jacket. "Everything is good," he said. "Too good. I couldn't walk two steps without someone pitching me a script or suggesting an up and coming actress for me to screen test. I spent more time dodging potential projects than actually talking to people."

"So, basically you're just too darn successful and everyone wants to work with you. Whatever will you do?" Noah guided the limo between the other cars and out onto the street.

Chris sighed heavily and rubbed his knuckles against his eyes. "I suppose when you put it that way I shouldn't be complaining."

"Don't mind me, complain away. I'd appreciate the company in my sad pit of misery." He turned onto the freeway, easing into traffic, as comfortable in the stretch limo as he was in his truck. "Home then?"

"Actually," the conspiratorial tone of the word got Noah's attention. "Can we stop for a burger? I'm starving."

*****

In any other city, the sight of a limo parked outside a fast food restaurant might have been shocking. In Hollywood, it was barely worth mentioning. Noah and Chris sat on a pair of hard concrete benches in the crisp fall air, cheeseburgers and French fries spread out on the matching concrete table in front of them. No one glanced twice at the movie director and his chauffeur hanging out under the yellow-tinged light of the fast food restaurant sign.

It wasn't the first time Noah had hung out with Chris. Usually Ben was around to join them, but Noah liked the director. His faith was evident in everything he did and he'd been a welcome addition to The Hollywood Mission family. Like Ben, he became a part of the church without fanfare or celebrity status. He spent most services in the tech booth, helping run the media team and managing all the buttons and switches that Noah found a bit intimidating. He was in the process of trying to convince Evan to put his sermons online so people could watch from anywhere in the world. His latest line of persuasion had been to tell him how nice it would be for Lily and Ben to be able to watch him preach while they were on their honeymoon. Evan hadn't agreed yet, but he also hadn't immediately said no, which Noah considered to be a sign of progress. He had to give the director credit, he knew his dad's soft spot.

"Isn't networking the point of these parties?" Noah asked, savoring the perfectly cooked cheeseburger from a uniquely California restaurant chain. He didn't know how people in other states lived knowing they were missing out on this kind of bliss.

"It's not the networking that bugs me." Chris took a sip of his soda then put the red and white paper cup back down. "It's the projects they keep throwing at me. Thanks to the success of Ben's last action movie, the only scripts I'm getting are explosions, car chases, and aliens."

"Car chases with exploding aliens? I'd watch that in a heartbeat." Noah laughed and dunked a fry in ketchup, trying but failing to understand the problem. If someone wanted to pay him a bucket load of money to make a movie about aliens, he'd jump at the chance.

"Well, then there are definitely some projects in the works that you're going to enjoy." Chris stared into the parking lot, his food forgotten on the table. "I just . . . I thought once I'd made it this far, once I'd paid my dues, that I'd be able to make the movies that mattered to me, tell the stories that are important to me. I have a film I've wanted to make for years and no one would touch it. Everyone said I had to wait my turn, make a name for myself before I could take a chance like this. And now, it feels like I'm stuck on a treadmill that keeps speeding up, like there's no way off, no chance to stop and reevaluate. You know?"

Chris lapsed into silence and Noah nodded. He did know. He knew exactly what the director was feeling. That sensation of life sweeping him up and carrying him along, the sense that the days were flying by, faster and faster, like a current propelling him forward and never giving him a chance to swim to shore, to see where he was or where the river was taking him.

He needed to choose a direction, but he couldn't get his bearing long enough to figure it out. The longer he waited, the more likely it was that he was going to be carried along until it was too late to turn back and he found himself twenty years down the road in a life he didn't choose, but wasn't strong enough to walk away from. Was he going to join his dad in ministry? Is that what he wanted? What God wanted for him? Or should he accept the business school offer and put his energy into building a business, being an entrepreneur? He couldn't keep juggling both jobs, not anymore. Business school meant moving to Boston and moving to Boston meant leaving Hannah behind. Given the past few days, he wondered if Hannah even wanted him around. She might the first one to help him pack and send him on his way.

"Yeah," he said, wiping the salt and grease from his fingers. "I get it. Maybe it's time for you to follow your own path. If there's a film you really want to make, maybe it's time to make it. I mean you did just walk out of a pretty high-profile premiere party to have cheeseburgers and fries with a limo driver. You're kind of already doing your own thing."

The thoughtful look on Chris' face turned towards him. "But what if I mess it up? This isn't exactly a blockbuster type of movie. It's small and controversial. What if I tank my career and there's no way back? Hollywood has a pretty short memory and once you're gone, you're gone."

Noah took a breath, knowing his next answer was important, feeling the weight of the moment. He watched the yellow light play across the table and then, without warning, the certainty of what he wanted to say was there, a nudge that became a push until the words were as clear as day. "And what if you don't?"

He could see the list of objections that leapt to the director's tongue, ready to give him reason after reason why he couldn't step out on his own, why he shouldn't do it, and he held up a hand, stopping the torrent of excuses before they started. "Chris, I know everything you're going to say, every reason you have for staying put, for plopping down right in the middle of your comfort zone and refusing to move. It's safe and predictable. You know what to expect." Laughing, he shook his head, recognizing that he'd been doing the exact same thing. Hesitating and stalling not out of indecision but out of fear.

"God always calls us out of our comfort zones. Leading us to new projects, new territory, new challenges because that's when we need Him the most. When we step out in faith, when we hear His voice and follow it, that's when we need His strength more than ever." Conviction filled his voice, the words coming up from somewhere deep inside him, or maybe not from him at all. "The things we can do only with His leading, His help, and His guidance, those are the things that bring us closer to Him. So maybe think of this secret project of yours as less of a movie and more of a chance to collaborate with God. I bet He's a pretty good director Himself."

Cars drove past and disappeared again, people walked into the restaurant and others left while the tables around them stayed empty and quiet. Chris crossed his arms, resting his elbows on the table and stared at him. "Not bad, Pastor Noah. Not bad at all."

If he'd been eating he would have choked. Pastor Noah. He tried out the words in his mind letting them roll around, hoping for . . . for what? A sign? A bolt of lightning or a letter to fall from Heaven telling him, *Yes, that's right?*

No lightning flashed, no letter fell into his lap, but a tiny thread of peace wove itself into his soul. And for now, that was enough.

Chapter Twenty-Six

EACH DAY HANNAH SPENT AT the church became an agony of waiting. Lincoln wasn't through with her. There was more coming, she was sure of it. Stress and anxiety enveloped her until she could barely concentrate. She made sure to beat Noah to work every morning, checking the doors for evidence of letters, going through the mail before he could, shuffling through the bills and junk mail, searching for anything that might be from Lincoln.

When the phone rang she answered it with trepidation, expecting to hear his voice in every call. But no more letters arrived, no phone calls came. Every day the waiting grew worse.

Noah was worried about her. He kept asking if she was all right, but she brushed him off. There was no way to explain. When he asked her to dinner again, she made up an excuse. Hurt rippled across his face, but she ignored it. She couldn't focus, she didn't trust herself with him, afraid of what she might say. So, she didn't say anything, and eventually he stopped asking.

She was losing him, and she couldn't stop it. The memory of the letter haunted her, it hung over everything she did, a sword ready to drop and destroy the life she had tried to build. It was like a trap closing in around her, the walls pressing in until eventually they'd crush her.

The numbers on the computer screen blurred and faded away. She wasn't sleeping, fear and accusation kept her company in the dark of the guest room, keeping her awake, reliving every stupid mistake, every bad choice she had ever made until the sun broke through the clouds and she dragged herself out of bed to face the day.

Rubbing her hands against her eyes, she tried to clear the fog away. She focused on the donation entries, getting ready to make the weekly deposit. Finishing one entry, she opened the next envelope, counted the cash inside and then pulled up the database record for the family so she could update their giving for the end of the year tax record.

"Well, well, well. Aren't you the professional now?"

Her heart thundered then dropped, sinking like a stone in her chest. Panic ran through her body like an icy river and her hands began to shake. Fear squeezed her chest and she couldn't breath. She couldn't move.

Lincoln.

He strode into the office like he owned it. His black hair was combed back and slick with gel. A gold chain shone beneath the open collar of his shirt, and a diamond earring glittered in one ear. He was tall and muscular, exuding an arrogance that was usually enough to convince anyone contemplating a fight to reconsider. The very things that had drawn her to him, the promise of protection and security, were the very things that now made her silently pray for help.

"Not even a *hello* for an old friend?" His crooked teeth flashed in a cruel smile below the hard steel of his eyes as he raked his gaze over her. She held perfectly still, dormant habits born out of years of fear flying once again to the surface. Her mouth was so dry she couldn't even swallow. If she'd wanted to yell for help she wouldn't have had the breath to do it.

"What are you doing here?" There wasn't any force behind her words, and she hated how small she sounded. Her eyes darted to the door, but there was no one there, no one to step in, no one to rescue her. Noah had gone back to the house to get his phone, and she was alone in the church. Lincoln glanced over his shoulder and smirked, knowing what she was doing, but also knowing there was no one to help her. How long had he been watching? Waiting for a chance to catch her by herself.

"It's a shame your boyfriend left you here all alone. I would never have done that. There's dangerous people around, you know." He closed the distance between them until he sat on the edge of the desk, his knee only inches from hers, the overpowering scent of his cologne, the same brand he'd always worn, the same chemically created facsimile of the wealth and superiority filling the space between them.

"You know," he began thoughtfully, as if they were simply two old friends who'd bumped into each other, catching up on the days gone by. "When I dropped you off here, I didn't think you'd stay."

"Dropped me off?" Anger broke through the fear, just enough to fill her with a burst of fire, a tiny spark of defiance. "Is that what you call it? You left me here to die."

Something cold and hard descended over his eyes, like a brick wall shutting out the light. His big hands clenched and unclenched and she couldn't help but watch. She knew the pain those hands could deliver. "And whose fault was that?" The words were quiet, deadly and she sat back as far as the chair would allow. "You caused me an awful lot of trouble that night."

She refused to apologize, to take the blame, even when the words leapt to her tongue, an impulse, a trained reaction, an instinct honed over the years to protect herself from whatever was going to come. Apologize, appease, survive. But she wouldn't do it again.

"What do you want?" The boldness of her words surprised her, and she clung to that sliver of confidence with every shred of her being. She was not the same scared girl Lincoln had found all those years ago, and she was not the hopeless, broken woman he'd created. She was not alone. God would not abandon her.

Crossing his arms, he stared down at her, evaluating her, measuring her, and she endured it. He could not touch her, not here, not anymore. "So you finally grew some backbone? Well, that should make this easy."

Worry speared through her but she kept her face blank. Noah would be back soon. She just had to hold on for a little while longer. Lincoln couldn't stay here forever.

"I think we can come to an arrangement." His tone was all business, like he was an executive negotiating a contract. "Seeing as how you've landed in the middle of some seriously rich people and also seeing as how I took care of you for all those years, you owe me a cut of your new-found fame and fortune."

"Where do you see fame and fortune? This is a church." Glancing again at the door, she struggled to find a way out of this mess.

Lincoln pulled another copy of the wedding photo from his jacket and laid it on the desk. "You've got connections. And unless you want them all to find out who you really are you'll cooperate."

Dread settled like cement in her stomach. Noah, Lily, Evan, Ben. Everyone who had been kind to her. Lincoln would destroy them, and it would be her fault. She couldn't let it happen. She wouldn't. "I'm not going to help you hurt them. They're good people."

He laughed, a harsh, biting sound. "Good people? And what do you think your pastor boyfriend will say when he finds out he's dating a stripper? What do you think will happen to this church when everyone finds out they hired a thief and a runaway to handle the money?" He flicked the wedding photo in her face. "And I don't think your movie star best friend with his do-gooder conversion story will appreciate it when I tell every gossip and reporter in town that he had a stripper in his wedding party. I wonder what that headline will look like."

The trap snapped shut, clamping her in its jaws. He could destroy the church, ruin Ben's career, crush the entire Shaw family, and there was no way she could stop it. "Lincoln, please . . . " She would beg. For the Shaw family, she would beg.

"Look, Sasha." He smiled again, a sly, evil grin. "You've got a sweet set-up here. If you want to pretend like you're some innocent church girl, that's fine. I won't tell anyone who you are and what you've done. You can sit here with your Bible thumpers and sing hymns for the rest of your life. As long as you pay me what you owe me."

"I don't owe you anything." But the fire was dying, the boldness was wilting.

Before she could react, before she could run, his hand flashed like a viper striking its prey. Gripping her chin roughly, his fingers squeezing, the metal of his rings digging into her skin, he was every inch the man she remembered. The man who terrorized her into stealing, who forced her onto the stage at Norma Jean's, the man who took every dirty dollar she made and then tossed her away. She was here because of him. She was damaged and scarred and haunted because of him. And he wanted to do it again.

"Don't push me, Sasha. Unless you want your new boyfriend to end up in the hospital." He tightened his grip until she thought her jaw would break, then shoved her head away, her neck whipping to the side.

Standing, he glanced at the open bank deposit envelope sitting beside the computer. She couldn't speak, couldn't breathe as he dug out the cash. "Let's call this a down payment."

He walked towards the door, stuffing the wad of cash into his pocket. "I'll be seeing you, Sasha." Then he disappeared, the echo of a whistle lingering as his footsteps faded away.

Shaking.

She couldn't stop shaking. Her stomach roiled and she thought she might throw up. This couldn't be happening.

She had to think. She had to plan.

But all she could remember was the low rumble of his voice, the feel of his dry hand on her face, the familiar fear that leapt to life when she saw him. Tears stung her eyes and she forced herself to take a breath. That was the only thing she could do. Breathe.

As her stomach settled, she looked at the empty deposit bag. It was her fault. All of this was her fault. She had led him to the church, made it a target, but at least that was something she could fix. Reaching into her purse, she grabbed a handful of bills. This was one thing she could make right.

Double checking the deposit on the computer screen, she counted out the right amount and slipped it into the bank deposit bag. She wouldn't let the church suffer for her mistakes.

"How's it going?"

She jumped, the tension and tightness of her muscles reacting before she could process it.

Noah was leaning on the doorjamb, the familiar pensive look on his face that had been there since she had first received Lincoln's letter.

"Good," she stammered, zipping the deposit bag closed and stuffing the leftover money back into her purse. "I'm just going to the bank to make the deposit. I'll be back soon."

He watched her, the silence pregnant with things that remained unsaid. She crossed the room and stood before him, longing to explain, to tell him the truth, to reach across the distance that separated them, but Lincoln's words echoed in her mind. If she explained, she would lose him. She would lose everything.

Without a word, he stepped aside and let her go.

Chapter Twenty-Seven

HANNAH SAT IN THE GUEST room, staring at the closed desk drawer. She should burn the letter. Turn it to ash and let it scatter in the Santa Ana winds.

But she didn't.

There was no point in burning it. She couldn't outrun her past. All this time she'd been kidding herself. Thinking that waking up in the hospital had been some sort of clean slate, pretending she could start over and be someone new.

She opened the drawer and pulled the letter out again, staring at the words he'd written.

Lincoln.

He'd been more than happy to dump her body when he'd thought she was dead. More than happy to toss her aside. But now that he'd found her . . .

She stuffed the paper back into the darkness and slammed the drawer shut. He'd always said that he would never let her go. That she belonged to him. He'd promised to make her a star, instead he'd made her a thief and a stripper.

Fear settled itself around her. A fear that she had forgotten while she'd been with the Shaws. That ever-present anxiety, a constant waiting for something bad to happen, waiting for the world to collapse around her, she'd left that behind with the shredded black dress. With one look at the photo and Lincoln's message, it had all come crashing back. Her chin throbbed like he was still digging his fingers into her flesh, like she carried a brand, a mark on her skin. She'd never really escaped. She'd just been hiding, a temporary reprieve in the midst of the disaster she'd made of her life, and now the bill was due.

She'd brought it all right to the steps of the church, right into the lives of her friends. She put every one of them at risk and now they were going to pay for her mistakes. She could either betray her friends, use them, con them and buy Lincoln's silence, or risk what he would do to them if she refused.

She didn't doubt his threats. Lincoln would ruin Ben's career. Ben had given her a place to stay, trusted her with his cars, his house, and Lincoln would destroy it, trash his reputation, and end his career. He would drag The Hollywood Mission through the mud, and Pastor Evan would be heartbroken watching what he had built be torn down brick by brick. Lily would never forgive her. And Noah. Lincoln's threat echoed in her head and made her sick to her stomach.

Stupid. She was stupid to think she was safe, that the worst part of her life was over, that by God's grace she'd survived and made it to the other side. There was no other side, not for her. She'd drown on this side of the river, glimpsing a land of freedom and second chances, but never actually getting there.

The sun had set long ago, but she didn't get up to turn on the light. It had taken her nearly three hours to drive home as she switched directions and doubled back, making sure Lincoln hadn't followed her to Ben's house. Waiting for the gate to close behind her, shutting out the world had been a temporary relief. Lincoln may not have followed her but his promises of violence had.

Sitting in the dark, she heard Kate in the kitchen. Successful Kate who had it all together. She wouldn't be one bit surprised to find out about this. Somehow Kate had always known what she was, that she didn't deserve the love and kindness the Shaw family had given her. Kate was right. She'd always been right.

She laughed dryly, the sound heavy with tears. Kate would certainly have one giant *I-told-you-so* for Noah.

Pain sliced through her. Longing, regret, and loss wound in ribbons around her heart until she thought it would burst. What would he say when he found out? She'd seen the look in his eyes, the concern and confusion there. They'd had a great night, one perfect night, embracing the wonder of possibility, and then she'd shut it all down. There had been no explanation, no reason, because what could she say? He was lost to her no matter what. She might as well let him go now, while he still thought well of her, before she saw the disgust on his face when he found out who she was and what she had done. Before Lincoln could hurt him.

Run.

The word repeated in her mind, an endless loop that urged her on. She needed to run. She couldn't stay here, not when Lincoln knew where she worked, not when he knew where to find her. She had to get away. If she was gone, Noah would be safe.

She dragged a bag out from under the bed. Just a few weeks ago she had packed that same bag with everything she owned so she could move over here. A few weeks that seemed like a year ago. She tossed whatever clothes she could find into the bag, then moved to the bathroom and unceremoniously dumped all of her toiletries and make-up on top of the clothes. She didn't stop to check the drawers or the closet, whatever she missed she'd replace later. She had to go.

Emptying her purse onto the bed, she counted the money she had left. She still hadn't opened a checking account, that was a little hard to do without any identification, and Pastor Evan had continued to pay her in cash, never once questioning her about it. Habit made her keep all of the money with her, tucked away in a hand-me-down purse Lily had given her. After replacing what Lincoln had stolen from the church, her funds were depleted, but she had enough to run, enough to make it until she could get to a new town and find a job. Maybe Nevada, maybe Arizona. Maybe further. It didn't matter, as long as she was far away from the Shaws.

Stacking the bills into piles on the soft comforter she tried to focus, to come up with a plan.

There was a sharp knock on the door and her hands froze, sudden and relentless panic stealing her breath. It swung open before she had a chance to say anything.

Kate stood in the doorway, her silhouette framed by the hallway lights shining behind her. Warm light spilled into the room and onto the bed, onto the neat piles of cash she'd made. Kate's gaze drifted from the bed and up to her face, questions she didn't ask leaping in the space between them.

Scooping up the bills, she stuffed them back into her purse. "Did you need something?" Shame burned her cheeks and she hated that she couldn't stop it.

The familiar hardness of Kate's stare bore into her. "Noah's on the phone. Again."

She swallowed and stood, looping her purse over her shoulder and picking up the hastily-packed duffel bag. "Um, could you take a message? I was just going . . . out." She took a step towards the door, then stopped and went back to the desk. Slipping the letter from the drawer, she folded it and tucked it away in her purse.

She didn't stop on her way past Kate, and headed straight for the garage. She didn't hear what Kate said into the phone, what explanation she'd given to Noah. It didn't matter. Nothing mattered except getting away. Revving the engine of Ben's car, she left the high gates and walls of the borrowed house behind and sped into the night.

*****

Noah ended the call and stared at the phone in his hand. Kate told him that Hannah had taken off, dashed out of the house carrying a bag and not saying a word about where she was going.

And the cash.

There was a disappointed smugness in Kate's words when she explained about seeing Hannah stuff a bunch of cash in her purse and then take one of Ben's cars, a tone that conveyed both her conviction that everything she had warned him about was coming to pass and the poorly disguised pity she felt for him. He'd been used, lied to, and now ditched.

He couldn't believe it, couldn't believe it had all been an act, a long con game featuring him as the sucker.

Tucking his cell phone in his back pocket, he wandered into the living room. His dad was already settled in his comfortable recliner, the news playing on the television across the room, the volume turned down low. Noah sank onto the sofa and stared without seeing at the swift moving pictures and the nodding, grave-faced news anchors. He wished Lily were there. She would tease him, but she'd listen. She would know how to get to the bottom of this mess.

But it was two more weeks until Lily and Ben returned. By that time Thanksgiving would be approaching and then the whirlwind of Christmas. He sat back and rubbed the knots of tension bunching together in his neck. He thought Hannah would be there for Christmas, that she would be a part of their family celebration, all the silliness and joy of it. She'd become a part of their family, a part of him, but it had all been an act.

He'd fallen for it. Every bit of it.

And now she was gone.

Was it about the money? Had it always been about the money? Recrimination assaulted him from every side and he closed his eyes, as if the darkness could keep the voice of regret away. He'd been blind, he'd been a fool.

"Are you okay, Son?"

He didn't want to open his eyes. Didn't want to see his dad's concerned look, but bad news didn't get better with age. Opening his eyes, he stared at the ceiling. There was no point in waiting. Hannah had played them and she wasn't coming back. She took off and left him to pick up the pieces.

"Hannah's gone." The words were flat and empty, as if by sticking to the facts, treating it like he was talking about someone else, he could keep the truth of how much those words hurt hidden.

"What do you mean, 'she's gone'?" Muting the TV, his dad leaned forward, intent on hearing an explanation Noah had no desire to give.

He studied the living room, the farmhouse style artwork his mom had picked out and his dad refused to change, their framed wedding photo still sitting on the mantel where a matching one of Lily and Ben would soon join it. He thought of the first night Hannah had been in the house, when he caught her trying to sneak out. She'd fallen into his arms and he'd brought her back here, laid her in the very spot where he was sitting. She'd seemed so fragile and he'd wanted to comfort her, to protect her, to shield her from whatever ghosts were haunting her.

Out of everything in his life that had been so murky, all the paths he was trying to find, the choices he had to make, Hannah had been the one thing he was certain of, the one pinprick of clarity in a fog of uncertainty.

But none of it had been real, not for her anyway. Was she laughing at him? Rolling her eyes at the gullible man she'd duped, the church she'd swindled. She deserved an Academy Award for that performance.

He couldn't face his dad as he spoke. "I called the house and Kate said Hannah left. She packed a bag and took off without saying a word."

"That doesn't sound like our Hannah."

The way his dad referred to her as "our Hannah" cut him up anew. Somewhere along the way she'd become "his Hannah," a presence he counted on, the warmth of her smile and the easy way they spoke and laughed, it had all been his. For a fleeting precious moment, it had been his, and now she was gone.

In spite of everything, his dad didn't look worried. "Maybe after all this time she decided to visit her family. I'm sure she'll be back."

There was that faith again That unwavering faith. How Noah envied him. He didn't have the heart to tell him about the money. Tomorrow morning he'd go to the church and check the bank deposit records. All this time she'd hinted about her past, that she had done some less-than-honest things, things she was ashamed of. He never once thought she'd go back to that life. She'd seemed so sincere, so committed to changing, to starting over.

He didn't reply to his dad. Instead he stared at the TV, letting the images distract him, looking for a way to keep his mind off Hannah, to stop wondering where she was and why she'd left. But no matter how hard he tried he couldn't escape the vision of the empty desk that would be waiting for him the next morning.

*****

She drove aimlessly while the moon tracked its way across the sky, the few stars bright enough to pierce the neon glow of Hollywood twinkling in the sky yet leading her nowhere.

She couldn't just drive away, not in a car that didn't belong to her. She could take it to the bus station or the airport and call Noah to let him know where it was. She would be long gone before he ever arrived, before he had a chance to ask where she was going or why. Before he had a chance to talk her out of it.

She didn't go to the airport or the bus station. She kept driving, winding in and out of empty streets, coasting along the freeways that were free of traffic in the dark hours of the night, until she found herself following the snaking canyon road that led to the overlook Noah had shown her. Higher and higher she went with no idea why.

A sign posted at the entrance said the overlook was closed for the night, but she didn't care. Turning into the empty parking lot, she pulled to the rim of the canyon, the edge of the yawning black space, empty of light, stretching on until the bright lights of the city in the distance staked their claim on the night.

She'd been so close. A new life, a new start, it had all been so close. This was her home, the home she'd made, the home the Shaws had given her, and now it was gone. Stolen by her past, ripped away by mistakes she couldn't change. It wasn't fair.

She shook her head at the thought. If her dad heard her complaining of the injustice of the situation, he would remind her that life isn't fair, but God is good. How many times had she heard him say those very words? When she came home whining that a teacher had been unfair or that another girl had been cruel to her, she'd vent and rage and make sure he knew that it wasn't fair. When she was done, he'd gather her in his arms and remind her over and over, life isn't fair but God is good. Even in the ugliness, even in the suffering, God is still good. Then he'd pray for her.

Looking out into the empty sky, she did what her father would have done. She prayed. She emptied her heart, laying it all at the feet of God. She cried for the foolish decisions she'd made, the regrets and disappointments she carried. She asked forgiveness for the people she had hurt, the pain she had caused. At the edge of the abyss, she praised Him through her tears because that was all she had left.

In the midst of the darkness, she felt a whisper in her soul, a gentle touch that spoke truth and peace.

Stay.

The word settled in her heart with a certainty she'd never known before.

Stay.

Staying didn't make any sense. If she were smart she'd leave town that night, be gone before the sun came up, before Lincoln could make his next move, before Kate put the pieces together, before Noah turned his back on her. Surely, Ben would understand about the car, and she'd make sure it was returned to him. Leaving was the logical choice, the safe choice.

But the more she planned her escape, the more she imagined herself starting the car and driving away, leaving Hollywood far behind, the more her heart ached. She didn't want to lose what she'd built here. She had a job she loved, friends who cared about her, and Noah.

The thought of never seeing him again, of never hearing his voice or feeling the warmth of his presence beside her, hollowed her out, like leaving would carve away a piece of her soul that she would never get back. But how could she stay and put her friends at risk? It was a selfish desire, asking them to bear the burden of her mistakes. She needed to go.

Stay.

Getting out of the car, she slammed the door behind her, the sound echoing in the desolation of the canyon. The night was cold and she wrapped her arms around her chest to keep warm. Far below her, hidden from view, a coyote howled, the mournful sound rising from the canyon floor. The plaintive wail resonated within her, a howl for home, a cry to be found.

Tears streamed down her cheeks. She didn't want to be lost anymore. Staring into the horizon, she wiped her tears and asked God for the strength to face what lay ahead.

Chapter Twenty-Eight

IT WAS THE SMELL OF coffee that convinced him to open his eyes. He hadn't slept well, waking up every few hours to stare into the darkness and be reminded of everything that had happened, searching the ceiling for answers that wouldn't come before falling back into a fitful and restless sleep. He wasn't exactly enthusiastic about going to the church and seeing an empty chair instead of Hannah. He needed to double check all the work she'd done over the past few months, go over every bank deposit and donation record. If she had conned him, this was the perfect final insult, making him sift through all the numbers she knew he hated. In the quiet, black shadows of the night he was sure he could hear her laughter ringing in his ears.

The possibility of having his worst fears confirmed, finding evidence of her duplicity, staring at the black and white confirmation of his own stupidity, wasn't appealing. So, he banged on his alarm clock until it stopped beeping and tried to go back to sleep, but the tantalizing scent of fresh coffee from the high-end coffee maker he and Lily had given their dad last Christmas had him tossing the rumpled sheets back and his feet hitting the floor. Getting out of bed to get hot coffee was better than being stuck with cold coffee an hour later. It didn't matter how long he tried to put it off, eventually he was going to have to face the truth. And that truth would be easier to face with coffee.

He was halfway down the hallway when he heard voices. A man and a woman were talking in hushed tones in the kitchen. He didn't want to eavesdrop but he also didn't want to barge in unannounced if his dad was counseling someone. He walked a little louder, the noise of his heavy steps giving them time to prepare.

But *he* was the one who needed to prepare.

Hannah sat at the kitchen table, in the chair that had been hers while she stayed with them, the chair she sat in for dinner and when she helped Lily address the wedding invitations. It was like he had slipped back in time, back before he talked to Kate, before his world had shattered. Her eyes were red-rimmed and puffy, her hands wrapped around a cup of coffee. His dad sat across from her, still in his pajamas and the faded blue bathrobe he'd worn for over a decade. When she saw him in the doorway, shock and shame crossed her face and his dad turned. He reached across the table and rested his hand on Hannah's arm.

"You are always welcome here," he said, his voice gentle and unwavering in its strength.

Fresh tears glistened in her eyes as his dad picked up his coffee cup and walked towards Noah. There was both a warning and sympathy in the look he gave him as he slipped past him and disappeared down the hall. Noah had the distinct feeling the warning was for him to tread lightly, but he didn't know if he could. After a sleepless night filled with regret and doubt, he didn't know how to tread lightly. All he wanted to do was demand answers.

He hesitated in the doorway, unsure if he was willing to take the next step, not knowing what was waiting for him. Relief, anger, confusion, and a tangle of other emotions he couldn't decipher warred within him as he looked at Hannah. His Hannah.

She sat at the table looking once again like a lost, little girl. The bag she'd packed was on the floor by her feet and he couldn't stop his eyes from lingering on it, the evidence of her willingness to leave all of this behind, to leave him behind. It would be easier if he walked away. If he turned around and refused to listen to whatever explanation she had to give. He'd already offered her his heart once and she'd been willing to leave without even saying goodbye. Walking away would be the smart thing to do.

But when she looked up at him, the brown pools of her eyes as familiar to him as his own reflection, his resolve crumbled. He recognized the pain reflected there, the fear and the uncertainty. He could walk in, sit down, and listen. Let her tell her story, be the man he wanted to be. Or he could walk away. Shut her out and move on. She'd been willing to walk away from him, why should he be any different?

She didn't say anything. She sat at the table and waited. If he walked away he knew she wouldn't stop him. He took one step, then another, his mind screaming that he was making a mistake, yet he kept going, putting one foot in front of the other, refusing to consider the consequences, ignoring his better judgement, until he was sitting across from her.

*****

It wasn't anger that radiated off of Noah as he sat down, it was hurt. She had hurt him, and judging by the hard set of his jaw and the way he kept glancing at the bag by her feet, she had hurt him badly. Whatever Kate had told him last night clearly hit the mark. He sat at the table, his hands folded tightly in front of him, not saying a word. The silence was worse than any yelling or shouting he could have done. But he didn't have to say anything. She was the one who made this giant mess, and she was the one who had to fix it.

Pastor Evan had been sympathetic when she laid her past bare before him. She held nothing back, every mistake, every shameful detail, she told him all of it. He'd listened with the patience of a pastor and the love of a father. He hadn't fired her or kicked her out of his home, though she deserved both. His kindness was more than she expected, more than she had dared to hope for when she climbed the steps of the porch and knocked softly on the weathered front door. The Shaws had given her a home, and that was where she went.

But telling Noah . . . that would be much harder.

Looking at the pain etched on his face, pain she had caused, her courage faltered. Staring into the cup she clutched in her hands, she searched for the right words, the right way to start, but there was no right way, there would be no easy path this time.

"You weren't even going to say goodbye." His voice was low and quiet, but the words stung, hitting her like shards of ice in a winter storm.

His eyes fell once again to the bag on the floor, evidence enough that he was right, that every bit of anger and hurt that laced his words was justified.

"I'm so sorry." Her voice cracked, the weariness of a sleepless night catching up with her. "I should have told you all of this a long time ago. I just didn't want to think about it. I wanted to forget. I thought I could pretend like it never happened, like I could start over."

His face was impassive as he listened and she tried to convince herself that the fact that he hadn't already gotten up and walked out was a good sign. She cleared her throat, seeking a way to unlock the memories she had kept buried for too long.

"I told you that I came to LA with my high school boyfriend. We didn't have a plan. We just started driving south and thought we'd figure something out when we got here. It was impulsive and stupid, but I didn't see it at the time. I saw a chance to get away from my hometown and my parents, and I took it." She would never stop regretting that decision. She'd barely given it a thought before she left. Standing in her teenage bedroom, scribbling a note to her parents, she'd had no idea what that one decision would cost.

"At first everything was great. It was all fun and parties, like a vacation. Then the money ran out. We couldn't afford a place to stay, we didn't have jobs. He wanted to go home, but I . . . I couldn't. Not after everything I'd done, the things I'd said to my family." Echoes of the fights she'd had with her parents loomed in the dark corners of her mind. They'd tried to warn her, they'd begged her to turn from the path she was on, and she'd thrown that love in their faces. She'd been resentful and angry, blaming them for the mistakes she'd made, accusing them when the fault had been hers. She couldn't go back, she couldn't face them again. She couldn't bear to see the disappointment on their faces when they looked at her, or heard the excuses they would make for her.

"We were out of cash, we had no way to pay for another night in the cheapest hotel we could find, no food, so he took off. I guess he went back home, but I stayed. I was broke, barely scraping by with a part time waitressing job. I was about to get kicked out of the hotel I was staying in and I had no idea where I was going to go. Then I met Lincoln." His name was like acid on her tongue, like salt on a wound that wouldn't heal. Her hands started to tremble and she gripped the coffee mug tighter, her brain telling her to stop talking, to keep it inside, to stay hidden. Because when he knew it all, when he knew what she had done, how far she had sunk, he'd never look at her the same way again.

"You don't have to tell me," Noah said, as if he could hear the desperation in her thoughts, the fear that threatened to smother her. He didn't press and she knew he wouldn't. But if she didn't say it, if she didn't tell him the truth, it would be over. How far could they go, how close could they get with a wall of secrets between them?

"Lincoln," she paused. How could she explain what it had been like to meet him? He was charismatic and controlling. He'd found her at her lowest and given her a new name and a new life. He'd whispered promises of stardom and wealth. For a brief moment she had felt special and cherished, but the moment had ended, and she knew she wasn't special, she wasn't loved. She was being used. By then she was in too deep and she didn't know how to escape. Until that last night at Norma Jean's, when death had seemed better than one more night in the darkness that had enveloped her.

"I was alone, lost, and he offered me a way out. Except it wasn't a way out. It was like being trapped in a nightmare with no way to wake up." She took a sip of the coffee, stalling. Noah would know everything and she would have to accept whatever he did with that information. "He taught me how to steal, how to wait for the right moment and slip my hand in a purse or lift a wallet. I stole shopping bags while people posed for pictures and sold whatever was inside. We lived off the money we made selling the things we stole until it wasn't enough. Until Lincoln wanted more. He always wanted more."

Shame wrapped itself around her heart until she thought she'd die from it. There would be no going back from this. It wasn't just Noah she might lose. Her job, her friendship with Lily, everything could be gone, burned away by the ugly truth she carried within her.

But now that she'd decided to say it, it was like a tidal wave beating against a wall, an irresistible force that couldn't be stopped. She whispered a prayer in her heart, knowing God was there, praying for His strength to carry her through, trusting that He would be with her no matter what happened next.

"When the stealing wasn't enough for him, he took me to this club. He told me I had to earn more money, to . . . dance." She tripped over the word, confessing it, freeing it from the vault of her soul, acknowledging the depth of her shame, the scars of her mistakes. "I didn't want to, but I didn't have anywhere else to go. And he made it sound like it was no big deal, like it was easy."

Tears flowed unchecked as the memory of that first night washed over her. She'd stood on the stage under the spotlights, exposed and vulnerable, naked and alone. There had been no end to the hatred she'd felt, for herself, for Lincoln, for everyone who had left her, for the God she had despised. Men leered at her, they mocked her, they demanded more from her, laughing as she stumbled her way through that first clumsy dance, tossing wrinkled and stained dollar bills at her feet, their hands trying to touch her, grab her, claim her.

When the song ended she'd run from the stage, holding the clothes she'd peeled away against her chest as if she could take back what she'd done, wish it away and pretend it had all been a bad dream. The money she had sold herself for was forgotten on the stage.

She'd run to Lincoln, thinking he would comfort her, that he'd take her away from the smoke-filled club, away from the hungry looks of the men and the apathetic glances of the other girls.

But he hadn't. He'd grabbed her shoulders and shaken her until her head whipped back and lights danced in her vision. It wasn't over. She was going back up there. She would do it again and again, selling bits of her soul to anyone who would pay for it, surrendering the last part of her body because he demanded it, because if she didn't do what he said, he'd make her pay in other ways.

The horror of it, the helpless horror hadn't diminished. It was as fresh and as real as it had been that night. The stench of stale cigarettes and cheap cologne, the endless thump of music and the empty laughter, it all followed her, seared into her memory.

Noah was still as she spoke, immobile as if he was worried that moving even a little bit would spook her and she'd stop.

"I hated myself. I hated what I had become. The night you found me . . . I couldn't take it anymore. I wanted to disappear. I wanted to die. So I tried. And then you—" He knew the rest. He'd seen her broken and bruised, running into the arms of death. "I should have told you all of this from the start. I don't deserve your forgiveness, Noah. I've done horrible things and I hurt you. I put you in danger. Your whole family is in danger because of me. I wanted to leave last night to protect you, but I couldn't. You're my family and the thought of never seeing you again . . . " She sniffed and wiped her nose with her sleeve. "I should have said goodbye. I should have said a lot of things. I'm sorry. For everything."

For the first time since she started down the path of her past, she looked at him, expecting to see shock and revulsion, expecting him to shrink back, to avoid the taint of her sins, expecting him to get up and leave, to distance himself from her. It was what she deserved.

Through her tears, she searched his face and what she saw there broke her heart wide open. Not disgust or condemnation, but something else, something she hadn't dared to hope for, a glimmer, a reflection of something she had hidden in her heart for so long. Without a word, he got up from the table and knelt in front of her. Gathering her into his arms, he held her against him like a precious treasure. Then he began to speak.

No, not speak. Pray. He was praying over her.

"Mighty God, thank You. Thank You for saving Hannah, for bringing her to this moment. For bringing her to our church and to our family. Thank You, Lord, for bringing my Hannah back to me."

Chapter Twenty-Nine

NOAH SAT NEXT TO HANNAH on the sofa, his arm around her shoulders as Detective Sullivan paced the living room floor. Kate's dad hadn't hesitated when they'd called him. He'd shown up and immediately taken charge of the situation. Noah had to admit it was a relief knowing he was on their side. Joe Sullivan had over twenty years on the police force and he was one of his dad's closest friends.

His dad was in his recliner, his usually-calm and peaceful demeanor tense and worried. When Hannah had shown them the letter from Lincoln, white hot rage had filled Noah. That this man had put her through so much, used her so badly and then thought he could come back and threaten her, put his hands on her. The more he thought about it, the more his fists itched to hit something, preferably Lincoln's face.

So, he kept his arm around her instead, keeping her against his side as if the force of his will could keep her safe.

Looking at the letter, his dad's face had hardened in a way Noah had never seen. He'd pulled Hannah into a fierce hug and whispered, "You're safe here." Then he went to call Detective Sullivan.

At first, Hannah had balked at involving the police. Whether it was from embarrassment or the years she'd spent avoiding the cops, he couldn't tell, but both he and his dad had insisted. This wasn't something they could handle on their own. It was beyond their control, and they needed help.

The barrel-chested detective stopped his pacing and looked at Hannah. "Sasha?"

"It was the name he gave me." She blushed and dropped her gaze, staring at the scuffed toes of her tennis shoes. Noah tightened his arm around her, reminding her with his body that he was with her, that he wasn't going anywhere. He noticed the long look his dad gave him, his perceptive gaze sliding from his face to his arm curled protectively around Hannah, but they'd save that conversation for a later time. The only thing that mattered now was keeping Hannah safe.

"And you said he came by the church yesterday?" When she nodded, Detective Sullivan resumed his pacing. Back and forth across the rug he went while Noah waited, anxious to do something, anything.

"Okay," the detective said, as if he'd come to a decision. He sat on the love seat, his attention focused on Hannah. "We're going to file an official report and arrange for some extra protection for you at the church. I can schedule a few drive-bys with the local patrol and we'll make sure we have a plain clothes officer there on Sunday mornings to keep an eye on things. If he comes around again, we'll be there."

Hannah seemed to shrink as she huddled closer to Noah. Listening to Detective Sullivan lay out the options, seeing the letter, and knowing the threats Lincoln had made against Hannah, Ben, and the church, feeling the oppressive worry in the room, the fear of what might be waiting, lurking in the shadows, he was starting to understand why her first instinct had been to run. The fact that she'd come back, that she'd been willing to face all of this, proved she was braver than she knew. He made up his mind to tell her that, he would remind her of that fact over and over until she finally believed him.

In the midst of all of it, she found her voice. "Yes," she said and his heart swelled with pride at her courage. "I can do that."

Detective Sullivan went into the kitchen to make the phone calls that would set everything into motion. His deep voice rumbled down the hallway, the words *stalker*, *threat*, and *danger* causing Hannah to grow more and more tense with each passing second.

"Let's get some air," Noah said and took her hand, leading her to the front door.

They stepped into the late morning light, the lingering chill already giving way to the warmth of a fall day in Los Angeles. They walked to the steps and sat side by side on the top step, watching the empty street, lost in their own thoughts.

"It's going to be okay." Did she remember him saying those same words to her the night he found her at the church? It was the same hollow promise he had no power to keep then and certainly not now. It was a platitude that filled the empty space when the truth was too ugly to speak, a hope and a prayer that someday everything would be all right, that the future would bring something better.

"I'm sorry I got you involved in this," she whispered as she stared at their still-intertwined hands, weariness and regret spilling into the morning.

Shifting on the step, he turned to face her. "I'm not."

She lifted her eyes to meet his and he could see the indecision, as if she was still debating whether she should stay, or if she should take the bag that remained unpacked in their kitchen and go. To save them, to spare them . . . to spare him from whatever was coming. It was all there, written in the sadness building in the brown depths of her eyes.

He wouldn't lose her again. Not now.

Cupping her cheek with his hand, the softness of her skin was cool and smooth against his palm, and he tilted her face to his. "The night I found you, that was the worst night of my life." When she started to pull away, he held fast. "But it was also the best. I didn't know it then, but I do now. Before I met you, I was confused and paralyzed. I didn't know what to do with my life, what I wanted. Then you showed up." Gently, he threaded his hand through her hair, letting it drift through his fingers like waves of the sea, his thumb caressing the side of her cheek, catching the tear that slipped from her lashes. "Now I know."

Uncertainty sparkled in her eyes. "And what is it?" she asked.

"You. I want you, Hannah. By my side, my partner, my helpmate, the person who calls me out when I'm being stupid and tells me when I'm doing something right. I have never wanted anything more than to see you smile, knowing it's for me."

She wiped away the tears that rolled freely down her face. "But everything I've done . . . how could you possibly forget that? How could you ever look at me and not see me like that, not think about me in that club?" Shaking her head, her shoulders slumped, weighed down by the burdens of her past. "I was a stripper, Noah." She snapped the word with a harsh finality, as if that was the end, the deciding factor that had branded her guilty and sentenced her to a lifetime of condemnation. "And you're going to be a pastor. It could never work between us."

"Says who?" His knees bumped against hers on the small step as a black car drove slowly past, scattering the birds that had gathered in the street. The background sounds of the city went on all around them, but Noah didn't pay any attention to them. His focus was on the woman in front of him, the woman who was, as far as he was concerned, still a flight risk. He had this one moment, this one chance to convince her to stay, to let him fight with her, fight for her, to let him be the man she deserved.

"Hannah, I'm not perfect. I never will be. I will mess up. I will make you mad. I will forget things and I might make you crazy sometimes, but I will never leave you. There is nothing anyone can say that will change my mind. I know you."

The conviction in his words drew her eyes, swimming with silver tears, to his. "I know you're brave and strong and smart. And you got that way because of everything you've been through. Hannah or Sasha or whatever you want to call yourself, I know who you are and I love you."

The words slipped out but he didn't regret them. She was the other half of his heart, the woman God had been leading him to his entire life. There was no reason to deny what had been in front of him this whole time. It was her, it had always been her, and if he had to spend the rest of his life convincing her that he loved her and would love her forever, then he would do it.

A tentative smile crossed her lips and she gripped his hand tightly. "My name is Hannah," she whispered. "And I love you, too."

Joy ignited in his chest, a brilliant flash of excitement and relief that flooded his limbs and made him glad he was already sitting down. Pulling her close, he wrapped his arm around her shoulders, pressing her against his side, recognizing how perfectly she fit. They were two broken pieces that made a whole. Resting his head on hers, he said a silent prayer of thanksgiving for the woman God had brought him and asked for protection in the days to come.

Chapter Thirty

THE NEXT FEW DAYS WERE a whirlwind of confusion for Hannah. She swung wildly from happiness to terror, tossed back and forth from minute to minute. She jumped at every sound, expecting to see Lincoln lurking around every corner, constantly waiting for him to show up, and half hoping he would just so the whole thing would be over. But he'd vanished. Instead of making her feel better, not knowing where he was made her feel worse, as if he was nowhere and everywhere at the same time.

The patrol cars that rolled past the church were both a comfort and a reminder. When she started to relax, when she could take a deep breath, she'd see the police car drive slowly past and the reality of the situation would come rushing back. If Lincoln was watching her, he would know that she was fighting back. She'd broken the cardinal rule of their relationship. She'd talked. She'd involved the police. So even with the police protection, she was more nervous, more on edge. Lincoln wasn't a man who took rejection well. She couldn't believe he would quietly go away, accept her decision, and move on.

But in spite of the worry and anxiety that followed her every move, she had Noah. Noah who loved her, Noah who wanted her to stay. Noah who promised to never leave her. Even knowing what she was and what she'd done, he had chosen her. She didn't bother to hide her smile or the tingle of happiness that leapt to life when he walked into the office. They talked on the phone long into the night, and a spark of excitement raced through her when she heard his voice. They talked about everything and nothing, and she went to sleep with the memory of his voice echoing in her dreams.

Noah picked her up from Ben's house every morning. He worked his way through all of Ben's cars, giving each one a test drive to the church. Then he drove her home at night. At first, she protested the extra time it took him to drive her back and forth to the church, saying it was unnecessary, but Noah had given her an option, either he would drive her or he'd ask Detective Sullivan to have a cop pick her up every morning to make sure she got to the church safely. Hannah had happily chosen Noah.

After hearing about the letter and Lincoln's threats, Kate found a heavy, wooden baseball bat in the garage and stationed it in the kitchen. With the high-tech security system in the movie star's house and the frequent police patrols, Hannah didn't think they'd need the baseball bat, but it gave her a welcome sense of security anyway.

Noah hadn't been able to convince her to go out with him in public, not while the police were still trying to find Lincoln, so they settled for take-out at the Shaw house or movies on the big screen TV at Ben's place. They were making the best of a tense situation and she didn't know how she would have made it through without Noah's strong, steady presence. He made her laugh when the worry became too much. He held her hand and whispered words of love until Kate made gagging sounds and threatened to use the baseball bat on them.

Sitting at her desk in the church office, neglecting the work that sat in neat piles all around her, she watched Noah prepare another sermon. Evan had been more than thrilled when Noah told him that he would like to come on staff as an Associate Pastor, if the offer was still available. And of course it was. Evan was ecstatic. He gave Hannah all the credit for it and Noah didn't disagree. Now, watching him study and prepare, a swell of wonder filled her heart. This man loved her.

A silly grin spread across her face, just in time for Noah to look up and see it. She didn't care. Let him see how much she loved him. She wouldn't be ashamed, not again.

"What's got you so happy," he asked.

She shrugged, ignoring the heat that crept up her cheeks. "Nothing. Just thinking."

A uniquely male smirk crossed his face. "Thinking about anyone in particular?"

"Yes actually," she said and he leaned forward, a rakish twinkle in his blue eyes. "Ben and Lily."

The smirk on his face vanished and his crestfallen expression made her giggle. "They're coming back tonight," she continued. "And I'm sure they would prefer it if I wasn't hanging around their house."

"They won't mind," he said. "Especially when they find out about everything that's happened."

Ben had been adamant that there would be no cell phones on their honeymoon. No distractions and no disruptions, so they didn't know about Lincoln, and they didn't know about her and Noah and whatever it was they were starting. It was going to be Noah's job to fill them in when he picked them up from the airport that night.

"Maybe," she said, "but I don't want to intrude. They're still a newly married couple and I'm sure they'll want their privacy."

"Why don't you and Kate come to our house for the night and we'll figure out something more permanent in the morning."

She wondered how much longer Kate would be staying. She hadn't said anything about Boston or going back to work, but she had also made herself conspicuously absent whenever Detective Sullivan showed up to talk about the investigation. It was as if she couldn't face her dad, as if she didn't know how to make conversation with the man who'd raised her. Family heartbreak was one thing they had in common, and, if anything, it gave Hannah a reason to like the high-stress lawyer.

Staying with Noah was a temporary solution, even with Evan there to chaperone. She wanted to do this right, to build a relationship based on God's principles and His will. Truthfully, she'd rather stay with Ben and Lily, but she needed to talk to them about it first. She also needed to figure out what exactly she and Noah were building and where they were heading.

But for tonight, they could make it work. Kate would be there, too, and she had proven to be an excellent third wheel. So, between Pastor Evan and a vaguely disapproving almost-friend, she supposed they'd be above reproach.

"That sounds good," she said, already planning to make Noah's favorite pancakes for breakfast the next morning as a surprise. "After work, we can head to Ben's house so I can pack up my stuff."

Noah grinned and her heart skipped a beat. They definitely needed to talk about what the future held.

*****

Hannah tapped her foot on the tile floor. Her one, sad bag was packed and ready to go. It had taken her less than thirty minutes to pack everything she owned into the borrowed bag, ready for another move to another temporary home. Although, if she were honest and let herself dream, she wondered if the little yellow house by the church could one day be more than a temporary home.

Waiting in the kitchen, she tried not to be impatient. Kate, who had been planning to stay in Los Angeles for only a week, had more stuff than she did, and judging by Noah's exasperated sigh most of it was probably still scattered around the guest room.

"You know," his voice echoed from the guest room and down the hallway, drifting into the kitchen to where she leaning against the counter, imagining how happy she was going to be waking up in the Shaw house the next morning. Ben's house was amazing, but it had never felt like home. "I do eventually have to pick Ben and Lily up from the airport, and they're coming back here to be alone." He teased Kate like a sister, and Hannah marveled that she'd ever been jealous of her.

"So, go drop Hannah off and come back for me. I'll be done by the time you get back." The disembodied voice shot back from the recess of the bedroom and Noah stomped to the kitchen.

"New plan," he said as he bent down to pick up Hannah's bag. "I'm taking you home first and then coming all the way back here." He shouted the words down the long hallway. "To get Kate. Then I'll go to the airport to get the newlyweds and drive back here . . . again." He yelled the final word, aiming it for the guest room Kate still occupied.

Stifling a laugh, Hannah nodded and followed him out the door. The sun was setting in the distance as they wound their way down the hills and headed back to his house. For so long she'd dreaded the sunset. Instead of the beautiful end of a day, it had signaled the coming of nights filled with shame. But not now. Beside Noah in his truck, the wind whipping through her hair, his hand holding hers, the sunset was once again a wondrous sight, once again a reminder of new beginnings, of the beauty all around her. Noah had given it back to her.

They pulled up to the Shaw house and he leapt out of the truck to open the passenger door for her. Standing on the sidewalk, she waited while he dug her bag out of the back. He turned to walk her up the steps, but she stopped him.

"I've got this." Taking her bag from his hands, she shooed him back to the truck. "You don't have a lot of time. Go get Kate so you won't be late to the airport. You don't want Ben and Lily to be stuck with a bunch of reporters."

Glancing at his watch, he blew out a breath in resignation. "I'll be back with Kate in about an hour . . . maybe a little less if traffic cooperates. Then I'll go get the newlyweds and save them from a paparazzi ambush."

Standing in the orange glow of the sunset, she squeezed his hand. "I love you." The words were like a hymn, like a poem written for the two of them, a promise made that the fading light would survive the night and rise again in the morning.

"I love you, too." His hand lingered on her face, the warmth filling her body and she wanted him to stay with her, to stay beside her forever.

But he couldn't. He hopped back in the truck, waving out the window as he drove off. She watched until the taillights faded from view, already calculating how long it would take for him to return, counting the minutes like a child on the last day of school.

Shaking her head at her own silly lovesickness and imagining how Lily would tease her, she turned to go up the steps to the door, her bag banging against her leg as she walked.

She never made it.

The shadows around her sprang to life, darkness taking on flesh as a man grabbed her. One hand clamped over her mouth while his arm wrapped around her chest with the strength of a chain snapping shut. The stench of alcohol, sweat, and dirt filled her nostrils as she fought for breath. Masculine fingers dug into her cheek, his palm pressing relentlessly against her lips as he dragged her backward, pulling her away from the house.

Her heart hammered, beating faster and faster as panic swam through her blood. She tasted it in her mouth as her teeth dug into her bottom lip. Her screams were muffled and useless beneath the heavy iron of his hand. The arm encircling her chest held her tight, trapping her between the tense muscles of his arm and the unforgiving wall of his body behind her. She kicked her feet, trying to find a foothold on the sidewalk, fighting for freedom, bucking and twisting, but it was no use.

"I can't believe you went to the cops." Lincoln's voice hissed like a snake, his fetid breath hot and moist against her ear even as her body turned to ice. "You're going to pay for this, Sasha."

He pulled her into the darkness, the yellow house and its porch light drifting farther and farther away. Her heels scraped against the broken concrete as she continued to fight, her hands reaching for the house that slipped from her grasp.

He tossed her into the backseat of a waiting car and leapt in beside her, barking an order to the man in driver's seat to drive. Tires squealed and the engine roared as they raced into the night. The last thing she saw was her bag, the paltry remains of the life she had created, forgotten and abandoned on the sidewalk.

Chapter Thirty-One

NOAH STIFLED A SARCASTIC COMMENT as his house finally came into view, nearly two hours after he'd dropped off Hannah and headed back for Kate. Kate who, when he arrived, still wasn't done packing. Kate who had more bags than any one person needed. Kate who sat unruffled and unbothered beside him, like they were out for a drive through the countryside instead of on a tight time schedule. Glancing at the clock on the dashboard he debated not stopping and unceremoniously shoving her out of the truck.

The sun had set, taking the last spark of daylight with it. Above the neon lights, a crescent moon was rising. Another minute ticked by and he gripped the wheel in frustration. He should have already been at the airport. If Ben and Lily were on schedule, their jet had just landed at a local private airfield and he had to get over there before the paparazzi found them. He calculated the time it would take to get to the church to fetch the limo and race to the airport. Fortunately, Ben had chosen a close airfield, but even with that in his favor he doubted he'd be following the speed limit and there was no time for the fancy chauffeur clothes. They'd have to take him as he was in his jeans, t-shirt, and the warm, blue flannel Lily had given him for his birthday almost four years ago. It was a good thing he'd decided to become a pastor because he was turning into a lousy limo driver.

He tried and failed to take a deep breath as the truck lurched to a stop. He hated being late. Hopefully Ben and Lily would understand, especially when he blamed the whole thing on his sister's best friend. Lily would be thrilled to find out Kate was still in town, but he needed to tell her about Hannah before she saw Kate and jumped to the wrong conclusion. Lily may have been hoping for things to work out between he and Kate even more than he had been. Now he hoped she'd be just as happy when she found out about Hannah and their new relationship.

And what exactly was their relationship? They hadn't defined it, they'd barely had time to figure it out. He loved her, that was the one thing he was sure of. Looking up at the lights shining in the windows of the house, he thought of her sitting in the living room, probably watching a superhero movie with his dad. Smiling to himself, he remembered the day he'd discovered her weakness for superhero movies. She didn't go for the sappy, romantic movies like his sister. Not his Hannah, she went for action and adventure and good conquering evil.

His Hannah.

The words had stuck with him ever since his dad first said them. She was his Hannah.

Certainty wrapped itself around his heart. They belonged together. They belonged to each other. After he dropped off Ben and Lily, he would come back here and the two of them would talk. Knowing she was in the house, waiting for him, spurred him into action.

He slammed the truck into park, but didn't bother to turn off the engine. He wasn't staying long. He jumped out and started grabbing bags from the back. Kate was being far too leisurely for his taste as she slowly got out of the car, slinging her overnight bag over her shoulder, a picture of someone blissfully unaware of the minutes slipping away and the paparazzi closing in on her best friend and her husband, and she certainly wasn't aware of the monumental, potentially life-changing decisions Noah was considering as he stared at the house and dreamt of the woman waiting inside.

"You're far too tense, Noah," she teased. "You should relax." He scowled at her but she only giggled. "Oh, for Heaven's sake, if you're that worried just go already. I can take it from here."

But he couldn't leave her on the sidewalk with all of those bags, those ridiculous, over packed, way too much stuff for one person bags. So, he stalked towards the house without a word. He could at least drop them on the porch for her. Or maybe he'd bring them into the house and say a quick *hello* to Hannah before heading for the church. The thought of seeing her face quickened his pace across the sidewalk.

He stopped suddenly, dread knocking the air from his lungs like a sledgehammer toppling a wall.

Hannah's bag was sitting on the ground, knocked onto its side less than a foot from the concrete stairs.

Taking the steps two at a time, he raced to the front door and threw it open. "Hannah!" he yelled, his fear growing with every second she didn't reply. Dropping Kate's bags, he untangled himself from the straps and darted down the hallway. "Hannah!"

His dad poked his head into the hallway from the living room. "She's not here. I thought you were going to pick the girls up and drive them over here."

Hannah wasn't there. She'd never made it into the house.

"God, help her." It was the only prayer he could muster as reality crashed into him like a rockslide breaking free and he staggered under the weight of it. He'd left her alone and Lincoln had found her. He must have been waiting here, waiting for his chance to grab her and Noah had given it to him.

"Son, where is she?" His dad's hand was on his arm, but he couldn't feel it. He couldn't think past the raging storm of terror and anger and desperation building within him. He said he'd protect her. He'd been the one to encourage her to go to the police. He told her he would be there for her, and the one time it mattered most, he'd failed. This was his fault.

He had to find her.

"Lincoln," he rasped. "Lincoln has her." Purpose filled his steps as he strode to the door.

"Where are you going?" Kate called, but he didn't stop. He wouldn't stop. Not until he'd found her. Not until she was back in his arms.

Digging into his pocket, he found the keys to the church gate and the limo and tossed them to Kate. "Go to the airport and get Ben and Lily. All the information you need is in the glove compartment." Turning to his dad, he felt the hardness of his own face, heard the cool resolve in his voice. "Call Detective Sullivan, tell him what happened."

"So you're just going to go racing off into the night?" Kate clutched the keys in her hand, genuine fear shining in her eyes. "You don't even know where she is. Please, wait for my dad to get here. He'll know what to do."

She was right. The words echoed in his brain. Kate was right. He didn't know where to start. There was no point in randomly driving around the streets of Hollywood hoping to spot her somewhere. The police had spent two weeks trying to find Lincoln and failed. He didn't have their resources or their leads. The chances of him finding her on his own were miniscule. There were too many places Lincoln could have taken her, he'd never be able to search the city on his own, he wouldn't even be able to search Hollywood Boulevard on his own. Kate's advice was logical, smart, and it was exactly what he should do. He should wait at the house and let someone else handle it.

He hesitated for a second. One second before walking out the front door to his waiting truck.

Kate's high heels skittered on the sidewalk behind him as he slammed the door. Breathless, she ran to the truck window. "NJ's," she stammered. "There's some club called NJ's. I don't know where it is but this guy at the movie studio thought he recognized Hannah and said he saw her there."

Her hand trembled on the door and he knew she wanted him to stay, to wait for Detective Sullivan and let the police take charge. But he couldn't. He couldn't sit by and do nothing, not while Hannah was in danger, not when he was the one who'd left her alone.

"Thank you," he said and managed a weak smile.

She stepped away and he hit the gas, heading toward the bright lights in the distance. Hannah was out there somewhere, and he was going to find her.

Chapter Thirty-Two

NAUSEA THREATENED TO CRIPPLE HER. She was shaking, suffocating in the too-warm room, paralyzed by terror, smothered by her nightmares come to life.

The room was exactly as she remembered it, exactly how it appeared in her dreams. Nothing had changed. Nothing except her.

The cloying scent of countless cheap perfumes was saturated into the walls. Frayed and stained costumes, if the thin scraps of clothing could be called costumes, hung on hooks and crooked metal hangers. Gauzy, sequined strips of fabric filled the spaces between large mirrors that were rimmed with dull yellow lights, wrapping the room in a kaleidoscope of clashing colors. No matter where she turned, her reflection stared back at her.

The dressing room had been both her sanctuary and her prison, the beginning of her downward spiral and the place where she thought she was going to die. Now, after months of freedom, after a taste of life far away from all of this, she was back. Back to where it all began. Trapped again, captured by the chains she had tried to escape. She wanted to scream, to beat her fists against the walls until they collapsed and she could run away, run away from all of it. But it wouldn't do any good. There was no way out, not this time.

Wrapping her arms around her knees, she winced as she brushed against the bruises that were starting to form. They had sped away from Noah's house, Lincoln's arms holding her like a snake constricting its prey. When they'd turned into the alley behind the club, she'd known. She'd known exactly where he brought her.

He dragged her from the car, through the backdoor, and threw her in the dressing room. Cruelty laced his smile as he twisted the thick gold rings on his fingers. "You and I are getting a fresh start tonight. I'm getting my stuff together and then we're leaving. We'll be on the road before anyone knows you're gone."

Her stomach roiled, and she hated that her hands shook as he stepped closer, hated that her back pressed further against the wall behind her even though there was nowhere to go.

Clenching her teeth to keep from screaming, she said nothing. Scattered fragments of prayers rushed through her head. There was nothing cohesive, nothing intelligent or thought out, just a jumble of words that sprang from the depths of her soul, winging their way to God, carried on the scattered remains of her faith.

Lincoln smirked and sauntered out of the room, the loud click of the door echoing behind him.

As soon as the door closed, she leapt up, twisting the handle and yanking it open again, only to see the hard, unsympathetic face of a man she didn't recognize staring back at her. She took one step into the doorway and his body shifted, his muscular chest blocking the only way out. He didn't need to say the words for her to know she wasn't getting out of this room.

She slammed the door in his face, panic bubbling in her chest, and retreated to a far corner. Huddled amidst the synthetic feathers and fake fur, she listened to the relentless, pounding beat of the music, the scattered catcalls of the men sitting out in the club, their faces hidden behind the shield of the darkness, comfortable in their anonymity.

Time crept by, measured only by the women who came and went, barely sparing her a glance in the mirrors as they touched up their lipstick, fluffed their hair or reapplied mascara to already blackened lashes. She recognized a few of them, women she had once considered her friends, or what passed for friendship in the chaos that she had been living in. She had robbed a few of them of the pills she thought would end her life.

In the end, none of it had mattered. Whether she stayed, whether she left, whether she lived or died, it didn't matter. She was right back where she started, sitting in the very room she'd been willing to die to escape. Her past was a leash that let her stray only so far before yanking her back, pulling her into the abyss, stripping her of hope.

Despair filled her until she choked on her own tears. Whatever Lincoln had planned, whatever he was going to do, there was no way out. No one knew where she was.

No one will miss you.

The taunt hissed its way through her head, slithering through the tunnels of her mind. She didn't want to believe it, but the words coated her mind like an oil slick, oozing and seeping into every crevice of uncertainty.

Noah loved her. Noah would look for her.

But the words were hollow. Shame was too big and her hope was too small.

Noah will be glad to be rid of you. After all the trouble you caused, none of them will want you back.

Doubt mingled with despair in a whirlpool of loneliness, dragging her deeper and deeper into the churning black water, into the well of fear that had never gone away, the self-loathing that had been waiting, biding its time, ready to strike. There had been no second chance, no clean slate, all this time she'd been lying to herself, daring to believe she could be more than this, that she could make a new life.

She had no idea how much time had gone by since Lincoln grabbed her and threw her in the car. Did Noah even know she was gone? Was he still at Ben's house tapping his foot impatiently and shouting for Kate to hurry up? Had it been hours or only minutes?

The realization that she might never see him again, never hear his voice or feel the warmth of his hand on hers nearly broke her. Her heart shattered. It was a physical sensation, a pain that started in her chest and spread throughout her body until her entire being felt the loss as pieces of her heart were ripped away. There would be no happy ending, no forever, not for them.

She cried until she had nothing left, until she was drained and empty. She would sit there in her self-pity and sorrow, waiting for whatever misery Lincoln was going to visit on her. What was the point in fighting if it all ended back here anyway? Why bother?

Rubbing her nose on her sleeve, she stared into nothing, willing herself to become nothing.

The door opened, and one of the dancers walked in. She sat in front of the mirror and began applying make-up. Their eyes met in the mirror, but Hannah didn't say anything. There was no point in asking for help.

Drawing a thick black line under her eye, the woman looked at her. "Are you new?"

Hannah shook her head, watching the movement in the reflection, but disconnected from it, as if every minute that passed she floated further away from her body, drifting into an abyss that would swallow her whole.

The woman painted her face, her gaze flickering to hers. After applying bright red lipstick, the dancer slipped her hands behind her neck and removed a thin gold necklace. She hung it over one of the round lightbulbs beside the mirror and walked out.

A simple gold cross caught the light as it lay against the chipped white frame, dangling in the space between the shadows. Hannah stared at it, a reminder, a promise. God was here. In the midst of the sorrow and shame, in the midst of the debauchery and the evils plans, He was here, a light shining in the darkness. No matter what came next, God had not left her. He was with her.

Words that had been written on her heart years before, words that had been spoken over her, words her mother had whispered to her came flooding back, seeds long dormant sprouting to life. *Be strong and courageous, do not be afraid or terrified because of them, for the Lord your God goes with you; He will never leave you or forsake you.*

As she looked at the cross, a flicker, an ember came to life. She prayed, stoking the small fire of courage that struggled to live, whispering words of Scripture, and holding on to the hope they gave her.

Had it really been just a few hours ago that she'd been in Ben's house, packing for her brief stay with Evan and Noah? She'd been laughing about Kate's procrastination and planning a future with Noah. That last ride in his truck seemed like years ago, like a dream she had conjured to escape the reality of this dressing room and everything that went with it. But it wasn't a dream. It was real. Noah loved her. God was with her. Over and over she repeated those truths to herself, refusing to let the circumstances around her shake her faith again.

Fresh strength filled her, a new conviction that this would not be the end. She belonged to God and no one else. Lincoln would not steal that from her, and she would not surrender it. She was not alone. She would never be alone again.

Chapter Thirty-Three

NOAH BANGED HIS FIST ON the steering wheel. Pain radiated up his wrist, but he didn't care. Time was running out. There was no club called NJ's in Hollywood or anywhere in Los Angeles. He couldn't believe Lincoln would be in Santa Monica or out in the Valley. The night he'd found Hannah, Lincoln had dumped her at the church. He wouldn't have driven far. He would have wanted to get rid of her as quickly as possible. That meant the club had to be close . . . but where?

His GPS was no help, and there was nothing listed in the online yellow pages. He'd called his dad once to see if Detective Sullivan was there and if he had any idea where NJ's was, but neither man had anything new to offer. Detective Sullivan tried to convince him to come back, to take a break and let the cops handle it, but he couldn't. Hannah was out there somewhere and he wouldn't go home without her.

He drove up and down Hollywood Boulevard, down the smaller roads behind it, and the dimly lit alleys. He stalked The Sunset Strip and drove past tourist spots and local hangouts, past trendy restaurants and homeless encampments, trying to remember everything Hannah had said about her time in Hollywood, any detail that could point him in the right direction, but none of the pieces fit. She'd been so reluctant to share her past, so afraid to talk about it, that he didn't have a starting place.

Guilt grew with every passing minute, building brick by brick as he blamed himself. He'd left her alone. He hadn't asked about her past. He hadn't made her feel like she could talk to him about it. Over and over the voice of regret pointed out his mistakes while images of what might happen to her taunted him in agonizing clarity.

So he kept driving.

Clouds covered the waning moon and the sky turned black as the neon lights of Hollywood burst to life. Flashing signs beckoned, and the sidewalks grew even more crowded, like the blinking lights and dancing shadows were a playground for the people who walked by, oblivious to what lurked beneath the colorful facade.

Traffic was heavy, the roads clogged and busy. As he was forced to slow to a stop in the congested street, he was keenly aware of time slipping by. Time that Hannah could be taken farther away, whisked off to a place he would never find, a place she might never escape. It had taken attempted suicide for her to get away the last time. He doubted Lincoln would let her go again.

Frustration built as he sat in the truck, trapped by cars on every side, but even if they all disappeared, he still wouldn't know where to look. He scanned the business signs he'd passed twice already, looking for something new, a clue, something he might have missed.

While the stoplight glowed red in front of him, he glanced to his left. A square, black and white photo of Marilyn Monroe blazed above a plain brown door. Hanging beneath the photo in bright red letters the name of the club flashed on and off. Norma Jean's.

The traffic light turned green but he didn't move. He stared at the sign, transfixed by the rhythmic flashing. Behind him a driver honked.

Norma Jean's.

NJ's.

Stomping on the gas, he sped to the intersection and flipped a U-turn. It was worth a shot.

Chapter Thirty-Four

THE DOOR TO THE DRESSING room flew open, bouncing into the wall with a loud crack. It recoiled back, ricocheting off the wall and Lincoln stopped it with his hand. Murderous rage simmered in his eyes as he stared at her. "Time to go."

Her legs were weak, shaking from both adrenaline and cold, but she forced herself to stand. She would face Lincoln on her feet. She would not cower, not again. "Where?"

"Vegas. Florida. Somewhere no one can find you." His voice dropped to an ominous growl as he paced towards her, his hands balled into tight fists, the gold of his rings winking in the gloomy half-light of the dressing room. "There's always a market for your type of talents."

Her gaze drifted to the cross that hung on the mirror. *Be strong and courageous. I am not alone. God is with me.*

Standing straight, she rolled her shoulders back and met his gaze without flinching. "I'm not going with you."

He stopped. Whether it was because of her simple answer or the way she refused to shrink and grovel before him she didn't know. It was a brief respite, a pause in the war, a breath before the end. His eyes narrowed, their dangerous focus trained on her.

"You don't have a choice." He resumed his path towards her. "You can come with me or you can die."

He grabbed her arm, his grip like a vice that went straight to the bone. She struggled to keep up as he pulled her through the dressing room, kicking stools and bags out of the way, knocking over hairspray canisters and lipstick tubes. She tripped and he yanked her upright, her shoulder twisting as she was forced to follow him.

He marched into the hallway, heedless of how she stumbled in his wake, and half-clothed women scattered, vanishing like paper butterflies in the wind, stepping aside as he dragged her deeper into the darkness, silent witnesses to her plight. She resisted, trying to dig her feet into the slippery floor, but even the shadows fought her, blocking any hope of exit, funneling her down the long corridor behind him.

The backdoor loomed in front of her. If he got her out of the club, if he got her into a car, she would never escape. He'd spirit her away, drag her into an underworld she had only glimpsed, a depth of depravity she had suspected but never experienced. Past and present fused in her head. She couldn't breathe as panic threatened to consume her.

Be strong and courageous. The Lord your God goes with you.

She forced air into her lungs. God was with her.

Her head was spinning, pain pulsed in her arm, but she knew where she was. She knew this darkness, the black painted steps in front of her, the blinding light on the other side, the pounding music and the low rumble of voices. They were passing the stage.

Digging her heels into the ground, she spun to the left. His grip on her arm broke and she ran for the steps.

Lincoln cursed behind her, the hatred in the word shaking the walls. She had one foot on the first step when his hand closed on her elbow. She twisted and pulled away, her feet tripping on the stairs.

He did nothing when she fell, her hands and knees hitting the chipped wood. Somewhere behind her, a woman gasped, but no one stepped forward. No one helped her.

Blood pooled around a jagged splinter that pierced her palm. Looking up from the steps, she watched him advance on her, rage burning in his eyes. She scrambled backward, crawling up the steps, the thick curtain swaying behind her.

Lincoln's voice was dangerously close, the promise of violence echoing in every syllable. "No one is going to find your body this time."

His hand fisted in her hair, and he yanked her off the steps. Pain exploded in her scalp, and sparks danced in her eyes as he dragged her into the darkness. She lurched forward, pulling him off balance and his hand fell away. When the weight lifted, she ran up the stairs. She grabbed the curtain as his hand closed around her ankle.

Falling forward, she tumbled past the curtain and hit the polished black floor of the stage. She cried out as the splinter dug deeper into her hand. The white light of the spotlights blinded her and she felt the stares, the stunned silence that surrounded her.

Beyond the spotlights, hidden in the dark, a man laughed. Then another. It caught and carried like a wildfire, burning through the club, stripping her bare as she knelt in front of them, defenseless and alone.

But she wasn't alone. She knew it as certainly as she knew her name. God had not abandoned her. He was here. He was with her. He was right beside her, giving her the strength to stand, giving her the courage to face this.

She did not belong to these men. She did not belong to Lincoln. She belonged to God. She was His treasure, His daughter, His friend.

She was loved. With all her imperfections, with all of her mistakes, she was loved, unconditionally, perfectly, and extravagantly.

Determination surged through her. Pressing her hands against the floor, she stood. In the bright light she stood, her fear melting away as she faced the crowd. Silence stole the laughter as she peered into the darkness and met their eyes. They shifted uncomfortably in their seats, their entertainment daring to rise up against them, to stand as a witness to their cruelty.

She was not afraid.

She was immovable.

And she was not for sale.

*****

Noah walked into the dark club, the smell of cologne and spilled alcohol greeting him first. Scattered at small, round tables throughout the room, men sat in red vinyl chairs, wrapped in shadows, the table-tops cluttered with glasses and cash. Photos of a young red-haired girl named Norma Jean, who would one day be transformed into the iconic, platinum blonde superstar Marilyn Monroe, hung on the walls. The innocence and carefree expression of the girl in the photos clashed with the seedy bar that surrounded her.

Waitresses wearing little more than lingerie patrolled the floor, balancing trays of drinks and collecting empty glasses. Music pumped through the speakers, a pulsing, throbbing beat that vibrated through the room. The stage at the far end of the club was empty. Harsh, white spotlights continued to shine, no doubt a promise that something more was coming, a tease to keep the men from leaving.

The possibility that Hannah might be in there was enough to make his blood pound in his ears. That any woman would be brought there was sickening. He looked into every face, every girl who walked by, searching for Hannah, praying that she was there and at the same time hoping she wasn't.

He kept to the outskirts, walking the perimeter, squinting into the shadows, but he didn't see her. If she wasn't there, he was wasting time, letting her slip farther away while he searched the club in vain. Impatience told him to hurry, to keep moving, to try something else. The club had been a long shot anyway, a desperate gamble that hadn't paid off. He needed to get back on the streets, to keep looking.

Working his way around the bar, he headed for the exit. Once outside he would call Detective Sullivan again and see if he had any new leads. Even if this club hadn't been the right one, it gave him a new idea for what NJ's could mean. He'd search every club or bar that used a combination of those two letters.

The front door loomed before him as disappointment and relief warred within him. He was steps away from leaving, his hand reaching for the door handle, when a flurry of noise erupted behind him. Turning, he saw the thick curtain behind the stage waver and flap.

Excited whispers rose from the tables, anticipation filling the room like demonic whispers, contagious and destructive, and he hesitated. A heavy crash reverberated from somewhere behind the stage and then an eerie, portentous silence fell like mist over the room. Even the waitresses stopped and watched, waiting for whatever was going to come next.

The curtain flew open and a woman fell onto the stage, captured by the unforgiving spotlights, dissected by their blinding glow. She was fully clothed, her jeans and white shirt completely out of place for the scene she found herself in, the brown waves of her hair falling over her face. On her knees, she looked up, raising a hand to shield her eyes from the light.

Noah's breath caught and his heart plummeted.

Hannah.

Chapter Thirty-Five

A MAN IN THE BACK got up and walked out. Under the heat of the lights, she saw his silhouette rise and disappear into the street beyond. Another quickly followed. Still Hannah stood firm, claiming the stage as a battleground. She squinted into the darkness, unable to make out the faces that watched her, but defying their shadows, challenging them to step into the light, challenging them to face her. Let them see her. Let them know who she was. She was done being afraid.

She felt, rather than heard, Lincoln stomp onto the stage behind her. His heavy steps vibrated the wood boards beneath her feet. The force of his presence was like a wave that slammed against her, a violent rush that tried to knock her down, but she stood her ground. Grabbing her wrist, he yanked her towards him, wrenching her arm, twisting her away from the crowd until there was only his face staring down at her. Spittle bubbled at the corner of his mouth and anger leapt like an uncontrolled blaze in his eyes.

"You're going to pay for this, Sasha."

Startled gasps rose from the crowd, but she barely heard them. They echoed dimly in the back of her mind as she faced the man who ruined her life, who turned her into someone she didn't recognize, who would have done it again to countless others.

"My name is Hannah."

His teeth bared in a feral growl and from the corner of her eye she saw his fist clench. She tensed, anticipating the blow, but she would not go down easily, she would fight to her last breath.

With a curse, he raised his arm. Instinctually she lifted her hand to block him, but the blow never came. His eyes widened in shock and his grip on her wrist tightened and he pulled like a man falling from a cliff grasping for a rope. Glancing over his shoulder, Hannah froze, certain she was seeing things, her imagination making up something that couldn't be true, a desperate hallucination.

Noah held Lincoln's upraised arm, twisting it back, pulling him away from her. His nails scraped her skin as his grip on her wrist broke and he fell backward, hitting the ground with a brutal crash. He roared in outrage and leapt to his feet, squaring off against Noah, fury contorting his face into an ugly mask.

Noah shifted until he stood in front of her, his body a shield, his muscles taut and ready to fight, to defend her.

Lincoln smirked, and pulled a knife from his back pocket. The wicked blade flipped open, light catching and reflecting on the surface as he swung it towards them. "You made a big mistake, Preacher Boy. She isn't worth it."

Noah reached back, his arm searching for her and she grabbed it, wrapping her fingers in his sleeve. "Yes, she is."

Behind Lincoln, the big man who'd guarded the dressing room stepped on to the stage and stalked toward them. Chairs shifted, scraping against the floor and Hannah didn't need to turn around to know that more men were closing in behind them. Guiding her backward, Noah led her to the edge of the stage. They'd have to jump, try to make a run for it through the crowd.

Licking his lips, Lincoln's teeth flashed in warning as he prowled across the stage, closing in on them. "No one here is going to help you."

She slid back, unwilling to take her eyes off Lincoln, as her feet blindly searched for the edge, expecting the drop to the floor below. The heat of the spotlight burned into her back as she gripped Noah's arm. Sweat coated her hands, but she held on tight. They were cornered. The door was too far away. They'd never make it.

"That's not exactly true."

Hannah's head whipped around and her jaw dropped open. Ben stood at the foot of the stage, his eyes trained on Lincoln, the promise and certainty in his voice matching the hard set of his jaw. Beside him Lily, Kate, and Chris tensed like an army waiting for a call to battle.

Noah stepped back again, leading her to their friends, keeping his body between her and the knife, but Lincoln followed, unintimidated by the reinforcements. Crazed determination glittered in his gaze, his focus not on Noah, but on her. The black depths she saw there chilled her blood.

"I don't care what it takes, she's coming with me." Leveling his knife, he pointed it at her, the tip angled straight for her heart and took a step forward.

Without warning, Kate pulled herself onto the stage and marched in front of Noah, her red hair flying and her high heels clicking with every step. "You," she pointed a perfectly manicured finger at Lincoln, "are facing multiple charges. Kidnapping, false imprisonment, battery, assault with a deadly weapon. And that's just the start. Unless you want to see the inside of a jail cell, you better run. Now."

Her bravado, her boldness, shocked Hannah and she held her breath, waiting for Lincoln to strike. She reached for Kate, trying to pull her back, to draw her away from him, away from the knife that was still directed at her.

Lincoln looked at Kate and laughed, a brash, cackling sound, as he appraised her. "What are you? A cop?"

"No." Turning to Hannah, she met her gaze and for the first time, she saw something like friendship sparkling in the green depths. "I'm her lawyer." Kate jerked her head to the front door and the man striding purposefully through the crowd. "That's a cop."

Detective Sullivan, his gun drawn and pointed at Lincoln, stopped at the foot of the stage. "Drop your weapon, Son."

Chaos erupted as police officers poured from behind the curtain, spilling onto the stage, tackling Lincoln and the guard and throwing them to the ground. Men leapt from their chairs and rushed for the door, pushing and shoving as they fought for the exit only to find the way barred by more cops coming in from the front.

Lincoln cursed viciously as he was handcuffed and hauled up between two police officers. Threats tumbled from his lips but Hannah ignored them as Noah pulled her into the shelter of his arms, wrapping her in an embrace she hoped would never end. Trembling, she clung to him, inhaling the comfort of his presence, whispering incoherent prayers as his arms tightened around her.

He had come for her.

Stepping away, he took off his flannel shirt and wrapped it around her shoulders. Soap and spice surrounded her, and she buried her face in the soft fabric as he gathered her into his arms again, holding her like he could absorb her into his own skin.

"Are you all right?" His voice rumbled against her head as his heart thundered against her own, two hearts racing and beating as one, calling to each other. He had found her. In spite of everything, Noah had found her.

Tipping her head back, she looked into his eyes, falling into the blue depths and happy to stay there forever. "I am now."

Combing his hands through her hair, he shook his head. "When I saw you standing up there, my heart stopped." He paused and she dropped her head, but he cupped her chin gently, not letting her hide, not giving shame a chance to start its ugly whispers again. "That was the bravest thing I've ever seen."

His gaze met hers and what she saw there took her breath away. Love. Love reflected there, shining brighter than the spotlights that surrounded them, stronger than the evil that tried to keep them apart. Love that had searched for her and fought for her.

She wanted to speak, to tell him everything that was in her heart, but she couldn't, the words wouldn't come, there weren't any words for what she felt. Tears built, spilling over with all the words she couldn't say, so she buried her face against his chest, seeking the island of safety for a bit longer.

His hands rubbed her back, holding her close, enveloping her in the shelter of his love. She heard the mumble of his voice over her head, talking to someone, but she closed her eyes until there was only Noah. For the rest of her life, there would be only Noah.

Chapter Thirty-Six

"I CAN'T BELIEVE YOU BROUGHT my sister to a strip club." Noah shook his head at Ben, his arm still wrapped around Hannah's shoulders. He hadn't been lying when he told her that what she had done was brave, but it had also terrified him. The few seconds it had taken him to push through the crowd and reach the stage had felt like hours. He'd run across the club, but it had taken too long. He was moving in slow motion while Lincoln and Hannah had been speeding up. In those few seconds he had imagined losing her, certain he wouldn't make it in time, that he was going to be forced to watch as Lincoln hurt her, unable to help, too late to save her.

He wasn't fond of fighting, but he had never been so happy to throw a man to the ground before, not even when he'd tossed Ben out of his limo all those months ago. When he thought about what could have happened, how close it had been, his fists ached to find Lincoln to beat him bloody.

His hand tensed and Hannah looked at him. Taking a deep breath, he reminded himself that she was okay, that Lincoln couldn't hurt her again. Detective Sullivan assured them that he would never hurt anyone again.

"Hey," the movie star who was now his brother said, "you try stopping your sister when her mind is made up."

Lily smacked his arm, but there was a smile on her face and she didn't deny it.

Hannah shifted under his arm, snuggling closer to him and he squeezed her shoulder in return. "How did you know where I was?" she asked.

Kate cleared her throat. "Well, while Lancelot here raced off to rescue you . . ." She winked at him. " . . . the rest of us used logic and common sense. I called Chris and told him to get to the airport to fetch these two." She pointed to Ben and Lily. "While I waited at the house for my dad so we could try to piece together what NJ's might be and organize a search. After Chris returned with the very confused newlyweds and we explained the situation, Ben made a few phone calls to his friends on the movie crew."

Ben shrugged. "It did not take too long to track down the club the grip mentioned. Apparently, it is quite popular among some of the crewmembers."

Sinking against his side again, Hannah sniffed. "Thank you. All of you."

Detective Sullivan approached their little group and snapped his notebook shut. "We're about done here. Hannah, you won't have to worry about Lincoln for a long time." He shook his head, the weight and worry of the evening settling on his shoulders. "There was a lot more going on here than we knew about. Prostitution, human trafficking, and Lincoln was neck deep in all of it."

Detective Sullivan reached for Hannah's arm, and patted it gently. "You helped stop some truly evil things tonight."

She smiled but stayed snuggled against Noah and he was happy to keep her there.

One of the officers across the club called to the detective and he nodded in acknowledgment before turning back to them. "If we need anything else, I'll call you. But for now, you can all go home."

Ben hopped off the stage, and, putting his hands around Lily's waist, helped her down.

"Hannah," Detective Sullivan continued. "It would help if you could come to the station tomorrow to give a more detailed statement. And I'm sure the prosecutor is going to want to talk to you, too."

Noah felt her exhaustion and he was about to object, but Kate beat him to it.

"As her lawyer, I think my client could use a day to recover. She'll be there on Friday."

Father and daughter stared hard at each other until Detective Sullivan sighed and gave in. "Friday will be fine." Then he kissed Kate on the head. "But I want to see you for dinner this weekend, young lady."

Kate rolled her eyes as he walked away, but she didn't say no. She dangled her legs off the edge of the stage, banging her feet against the wooden side.

Hannah pulled away from him and turned to the lawyer. "Thank you, Kate. For everything."

Kicking her feet again, she shrugged, playing at a nonchalance Noah knew was fake. "It's what family does. I—"

She stopped, cut off in mid-sentence, the color draining from her face as she stared at something in the distance.

"Kate?" he asked, but she didn't answer, her attention captivated and distracted. "What is it?"

Following the direction of her gaze he looked at the front of the club, but all he saw was the back of a man in a gray suit disappearing into the night. The door closed, and Kate shook her head as if trying to find her way through a thick patch of fog.

"I—I know that man." She didn't say it to anyone in particular and Noah doubted she even remembered he and Hannah were there as she leapt from the stage and went to her father.

"What was that about?" Hannah asked as they watched Kate argue with the hardened police detective.

He shook his head. "I have no idea."

The clean up continued around them. Police officers were coming and going as Ben and Lily stood together by the door, clearly ready to leave, while Chris hovered near where Kate and her dad continued to argue.

He knew they should go. There was no reason to stay here, no reason to linger, but he couldn't bring himself to get up, not when Hannah was leaning against him, so close he could smell the lavender in her hair and feel the warmth of her body. So he held her, willing to let the whole world go on without them.

But when Lily held up her cell phone and shouted across the room, he knew their time was up. "I'm pretty sure we're all grounded." She waved her phone at him. "Dad is freaking out."

He laughed and felt Hannah smile against his shoulder. "What do we do now?" she whispered.

Leaning back so he could look at her, memorizing every curve of her face, the black of her lashes and the soft pink scar that tracked across her forehead, he brushed a lock of hair behind her ear. "Now we go home."

He jumped from the stage and opened his arms to her. As he set her down beside him, he threaded his hand through hers then together they walked into the night and turned toward home.

Chapter Thirty-Seven

HANNAH LAY ON THE BED, staring at the ceiling. She was back in the guest room at the Shaw house, the room she had come to know so well, the room that felt like home. As tired as she was, she couldn't sleep. Every time she closed her eyes, images from the last twenty-four hours played through her memory. The good and the bad, the fear and the joy. How could she sleep when it felt like she had lived an entire lifetime in less than a day?

As the first light of dawn brightened the window, she tiptoed out of the room. Walking as quietly as she could, she passed the living room that had been turned into a bunkroom. Noah slept on the sofa while Chris was curled up on the too-small loveseat.

After they returned last night and shared their stories, no one had the energy to go home. Spare blankets and pillows were found and distributed and everyone crashed wherever there was an open space. Lily and Ben shared her room while Kate was in Noah's room. Hannah once again took the guest room.

She slipped silently past the living room and the sleeping men and headed for the kitchen, surprised by the smell of coffee already brewing.

Lily sat at the small kitchen table, a cup of coffee and a bowl of cereal in front of her. Her hair was lighter, bleached by days spent in the Mediterranean sun, and though dark circles lingered under her eyes, she was tan and wide awake.

"Can't sleep?" Hannah asked as she found another mug and poured herself a cup of coffee.

"My sleep schedule is all messed up. Too many time zones. My body has no idea what time it is." Lily blew on the still-steaming drink before taking a sip. "Plus, I think I have an adrenaline hangover from last night. That was a lot of information to process all at once."

Hannah sat across from her friend, wondering what she thought about everything she had seen and heard. Noah hadn't said anything about their relationship, but Hannah guessed he didn't need to say anything. She was pretty sure they made it obvious to anyone within a one-mile radius that they had fallen for each other.

They drank their coffee as the sun rose, its golden light filling the room. "Are you upset?" Hannah asked. "About me and Noah? I'm sure it wasn't what you expected."

Cocking her head to the side, Lily stared at her. "Upset? Why?"

"Well, I know you thought that he and Kate . . . that things would work out between them." Worry had stayed awake with her and it snapped to attention, sending flights of anxious butterflies flying in her stomach. She didn't want Lily to be disappointed, to disapprove of her and Noah being together.

Lily set down her coffee cup and looked at her. "I want Noah to be happy. That's the only thing I've ever wanted for him. And to be honest, I've never seen him happier than he was last night. I didn't think he was ever going to let you go." She snickered as she added more cereal to her bowl and scooped up the sugary flakes.

Hannah blushed, remembering the weight of his arm on her shoulders, the feel of his hand in hers. Throughout the night he had stayed by her side, as if he was worried that if he looked away for even a second she might disappear again. She loved him. She wanted to be with him, but she didn't want to hurt Lily. "It's just . . ." She stumbled, stuck on the words. "Kate's your friend."

Leaving the spoon in the cereal bowl, Lily reached across the table, and placed her hand on hers. "You're my friend, too. Noah loves you, and so do I." She squeezed her fingers, gripping them tightly. "I'm thrilled for both of you. God knew exactly what He was doing when He brought you to our church."

Relief and joy welled within her as Lily spoke. God had always been in control. He had always been with her. He had never given up on her. His hand had been making a path through the sea of her life even when she couldn't see it.

"Besides," Lily said with a giggle and a conspiratorial wink, "after last night, I think you might be more than just my friend pretty soon."

As morning light spread through the kitchen and a chorus of snores drifted in from the living room, Hannah embraced the simple wonder of the moment.

"You know," Lily said. "With all these people in the house, there's only one thing to do."

As she crossed to the cupboard above the stove, Hannah was already reaching for the baking mix. "Pancakes?"

Lily grinned. "Pancakes."

*****

They ran out of pancake mix before they ran out of hungry people. Chris made an emergency run to the store for additional supplies, and Lily kept the griddle hot. In the lull between batches, Hannah stepped out onto the front porch, embracing the quiet and letting the crisp morning air cool her face.

The door opened and closed behind her, but she didn't need to turn around to know who it was.

"Waiting for the pancake delivery guy?" Noah's arm encircled her shoulders with practiced ease, as if they had both been searching for this exact fit their entire lives.

"Just enjoying the moment," she replied and snuggled closer to him. "This is one packed house." Wind blew through the trees and russet colored leaves drifted to the sidewalk. Autumn had finally arrived in Hollywood. The long days and heat of summer had passed. Fall was here, and winter was close on its heels.

"I can't remember the last time the house was this full." His hand traced circles on her shoulder, a light touch that went straight to her heart.

"Probably around the holidays," she said, knowing how full her own parents' house would get during Thanksgiving and Christmas. While flipping pancakes that morning, Lily had already started making plans for the upcoming holidays. Hannah was willing to bet there would be a to-do list and a color-coded notebook in the works before the day was over.

Noah cleared his throat and stepped away, letting his arm drift from her shoulder and down her arm until he clasped her fingers delicately in his.

"Well that's as good of a segue as I'm ever going to get." His right hand was tucked behind his back, hiding something from her view. "Hannah," he began, his voice suddenly serious. "I know we just started . . . dating." The word didn't break free easily. It wasn't big enough, wasn't strong enough, to encompass what they felt for each other, what they meant to each other.

Nervous anticipation bloomed in her toes and worked its way up her body. When he dropped to one knee in front of her, she wobbled like she might faint. She tried to speak, but before she could get a single word out, his hand whipped out from behind his back and she blinked.

A Christmas stocking dangled in front of her. Plush red velvet with her name embroidered in gold lettering across the fuzzy white cuff.

Looking up at her from his bended knee, his blue eyes twinkled with mischief. "Will you spend Christmas with me?"

She couldn't stop the laugh that burst from her mouth. It was the most ridiculous thing she'd ever seen, Noah on the ground with a Christmas stocking. But it was also the most romantic. After everything that had happened and where they had been only twelve hours earlier, he could still make her laugh, and that laugh felt incredible.

She hadn't been broken. She could stand on the porch of a little yellow house on a sunny autumn day with the man she loved and laugh. If that wasn't a miracle she didn't know what was.

"Christmas is still over a month away," she said primly, even though there was no place she would rather be for Christmas. She wanted to spend every Christmas here, every Thanksgiving, every New Year's, with Noah by her side.

"You should be impressed, I'm planning ahead." He shrugged and shook the stocking, the oversized toe swinging towards her. "So, what do you say? Spend Christmas with me? And every day until then?"

"I would love that." Reaching down she took the stocking from his hand and held it against her chest. "But—"

Noah stood and rested his hand on her cheek, worry flickered in his eyes. "But what?"

She leaned into his touch, craving the warmth and the certainty it brought. Holding the stocking close, her fingers brushed the soft white fuzz, as she tried to find the right words. "I need to go back. I need to see my parents."

She knew it. It had settled in her heart during the long hours of the night, the gentle whisper that told her over and over that it was time to go home.

"Then let's go." He gripped her hand, a smile on his face, as if he was ready to leave that moment.

"You make it sound so simple." Hannah sighed and stared into the distance, as if she could see their house. If she tried hard enough, she might see what she was looking for. She didn't expect them to welcome her back with open arms. She didn't deserve their forgiveness, but she owed them an apology. "It's just . . . hard. I don't know how to start. What am I going to say? After everything I've done, how badly I hurt them, what can I possibly say that will make it okay?" She tried to picture her parents' faces, to remember the sound of their voices. The deepest fear she carried rose to the surface, something long buried finding its way to the top of her mind. "What if they don't want to see me?"

Noah pulled her close, his arms linking behind her back as she leaned against him, the Christmas stocking squished between them. "We'll figure it out," he said. "Together."

They stood in the shade of the porch, the morning light glowing golden and bright around them. They stood as one, their hearts turned towards the future that waited for them.

"So, what are we celebrating?" Chris climbed up the steps, a reusable grocery bag swinging from each hand. She giggled as the director arched an eyebrow at them, his expression full of mischief.

"Christmas," she said and waved her brand new stocking at him.

"Already? Can't we get through Pancake Day first?"

With an exaggerated sigh he walked past them. As he disappeared into the house a cheer echoed from the open door. "Pancakes!" the voices inside shouted.

Laughter and teasing drifted from the kitchen, out the door, and carried into the day. The sounds of friendship and family, of loved ones who stood by each other, forgave each other, and made each other better. Noah took her hand and led her to the door, to the people waiting for them inside. They crossed the scuffed wooden planks and together they went home.

Chapter Thirty-Eight

NOAH'S TRUCK RUMBLED UP THE long, empty miles of the I-5 corridor. They'd left Los Angeles almost six hours ago and with every mile they drove north, Hannah grew more anxious. Endless rows of almond trees and citrus orchards flew by along the sides of the road. They passed caravans of long-haul trucks and mini-vans filled with families. Small towns popped up every hundred miles or so to cater to weary travelers. They stopped for snacks and restroom breaks, but they always turned north again, bringing her closer and closer to the life she left behind.

Vague memories of her last trip on that same freeway flashed through her mind. Images of the innocent girl she'd been racing headlong into the arms of destruction. If she'd only known, if she'd only listened, but it was too late to change it now. The only thing left to do was face the consequences of her choices and try to repair the damage she had caused.

When they turned inland, away from the crowds of the Bay Area, her stomach twisted into knots. The dry brown of the inland valley gave way to mountains and trees. They climbed steadily upward until even the smell of the air became familiar. Noah tried to keep the mood light, making jokes and teasing her, but the closer they got to her hometown, the harder it was for her to concentrate on anything except the conversation to come.

"They might not even be there," she blurted out, the twisting train of her thoughts landing on the only excuse she had left. "What if they moved? What if they don't even live there anymore?"

Noah reached over and squeezed her hand. "They're still there. I checked before we left."

She blinked, staring at the side of his face as he drove. "How? How did you find them?"

Balancing his wrist on the steering wheel, he counted off the reasons on his fingers. "A pastor's daughter from Northern California named Hannah Smith." He grinned as he emphasized her last name and she laughed. She'd told him the truth. Not even the doctor in the hospital had believed her, but Noah had. "A few phone calls, a lot of Google, and presto."

As they left the freeway and turned into her hometown, she thought she might be sick. Every street, every store brought back a wash of memories. The trees were bare, their empty branches swaying in the chill breeze. They'd left the mild weather of Hollywood and stepped into the early winter of Northern California. Christmas decorations dotted the shop windows and the same red and green garlands she remembered from her childhood covered the lampposts.

They passed the bookstore her parents had taken her and her sister to when they got good report cards and the coffee shop where she and her friends had hung out trying to act like adults. It was so real, so much a part of her memories and suddenly she was in the midst of it, surrounded by everything that she had thought was a burden, unable to find her way back into the world she had taken for granted.

She was glad he had entered the address into his phone because she didn't have the strength to tell him the directions. He navigated them flawlessly through the town and onto the quiet road that passed her parents' house. Mailboxes lined the road, each one they passed a marker signaling that they were getting closer, each number sending a spear of nervous energy through her body. She wanted to run, to beg Noah to turn the car around, to promise they'd come back another time.

She prayed for strength instead. No matter what happened, God would be with her. She would apologize. She would ask for their forgiveness and if they wanted her to leave, she would leave.

As they turned into the grave driveway of her parents' home, she gripped her hands into tight fists. The last time she had seen the house she was looking in the rearview mirror of her boyfriend's car, laughing as they raced across the rocks, heedless of the pain she was leaving in her wake.

Noah pulled the truck to a stop near the detached garage. He turned to her and cupped her chin in his hand. "No matter what happens, I love you."

She tried to respond, but the words were stuck in her throat, trapped by the lump that lodged there as she stared at the front porch. She used to sit in those weathered rocking chairs. When she was five, she'd leapt from the top step when she thought her mother wasn't looking and scraped her knee on the gravel below. As a teenager, she'd watered the flowers in the window boxes, grumbling about being forced to do it.

Noah got out of the truck and opened her door for her. She stepped onto the pebbles below her feet, the crunch of the rocks like a lullaby she'd forgotten. She stared at the house across the distance like it was an island she couldn't reach.

One step, she told herself. She just had to take one step.

The gravel shifted under her shoe, the sound too loud, too familiar. She was only a few hundred feet from the door, but it had never felt so far away.

The air around her stopped moving, the sounds of the birds and breeze evaporated as the front door opened. Blood pounded in her head, she couldn't breathe. Her vision swam with tears but she saw enough. Her dad was running to her, his arms open wide, crossing the distance between them. He pulled her into his arms, swinging her off the ground, lifting her into the air like she was his little girl again, like the years they had lost were blowing away, vanishing in wild, reckless joy.

Setting her on her feet, he crushed her against him, his voice rumbling against her hair. "Thank You, God. Thank You for bringing my daughter home."

Held in her father's arms, sobs broke free from the well of her soul and she wept. Apologizing for what she'd done, begging for his forgiveness, telling him how much she missed him, she cried until she thought her heart would burst, tears and words she had kept locked inside for too long burst forth.

Her dad pulled away, his strong hands framing her face, tears tracking down his cheeks. "You're my daughter. I love you. I will always love you."

A gentle hand touched her arm and Hannah turned to her mother. There were no words to speak as she took her daughter in her arms, her tears falling into Hannah's hair. Her father's hand was warm and strong on her back as they stood there, the three of them bound together, the family that had been broken and torn apart finally restored and whole.

They laughed and cried and hugged until Hannah thought she might have accidentally driven to Heaven itself. All her life she had run from the people who loved her most, yet they hadn't given up on her. When she was on the streets of Hollywood she thought she was alone and forgotten, but the whole time she had been loved, and she had been prayed for. The night she almost died, the night she ended up at the church, minutes away from death, the night Noah found her and the Shaws took her in, that very night her parents had been praying for her. God's grace surrounded them, she felt it in every breath, in every heartbeat.

Overwhelmed. That was the only word she could think of. She was overwhelmed.

Overwhelmed by joy.

Overwhelmed by love.

Overwhelmed by grace.

Epilogue

ON CHRISTMAS MORNING THEY CROWDED into the Shaws' living room. Ben sat beside Lily at the foot of the tree, a Santa hat perched on her head as her eyes twinkled at all the gifts waiting to be opened. Evan was in his recliner, a cup of cocoa in his hand. Chris and Kate and Detective Sullivan squeezed together on the sofa. No one had been more surprised than her dad when Kate announced that she was going to stay in Los Angeles for a while. She hadn't given a reason for her sudden decision, but no one complained.

Hannah and Noah sat together on the loveseat, snuggled as close as they could get while he stalled and teased. He told jokes, questioned Ben about his career, and asked his dad to define obscure theological terms, all meant to drive Lily crazy until she couldn't take it anymore and she started passing out gifts, shoving a square box into his hands just to shut him up.

Christmas carols filled the air as the scent of pies cooling in the kitchen drifted down the hallway. A fire burned brightly, snapping and cracking as it warmed the room. There was laughter and joy, cocoa and cookies. It was Hollywood so there wasn't any snow, but the house was filled with everything Christmas should be.

Noah looked at the friends and family that surrounded him. Hannah laughed beside him, her smile brightening every inch of the room. They were heading up to visit her parents the next day, and he couldn't wait to see them again. After he'd driven Hannah up there last month, they'd asked her to stay with them until Thanksgiving. He had been thrilled for her, knowing they needed that time together, but he'd missed her terribly. The days he spent without her, not seeing her across the desk in the office, not taking her to dinner, had been lonely. Even with his new responsibilities as an Associate Pastor at the church, he had missed her, and thought of her constantly. He'd literally counted the days until she came home and Lily had teased him mercilessly for it.

Now that she was here, beside him, celebrating with his family, he knew it was where she was meant to be. For the hundredth time that morning, he glanced at the newest stockings that had been hung on the mantel. His mother's stocking still hung next to his dad's. Ben and Lily's stockings were to one side and his and Hannah's were on the other. They'd added stockings for Kate and Chris as well. If their little family kept growing, they were going to need a bigger fireplace.

Smiling as Kate opened a gift, his eyes drifted back to Hannah's stocking. If he looked hard enough, he could just make out the shape he was looking for. There, hidden at the very bottom, a small, velvet box with his mother's engagement ring inside.

Hannah leaned against him and he tightened his arm around her shoulder. The years of uncertainty and indecision faded away. Today and every day, this was where he was meant to be.

Acknowledgments

This story is so special to me, and I am profoundly grateful to all of the people who made this book possible. I couldn't wait to share Noah and Hannah's love story, because it's really a story of God's amazing grace. He finds us when we're lost and brings us home.

Thank you to Ambassador International for continuing to believe in this series and for your enthusiastic support. Special thanks to my editor, Daphne, for once again sharing her keen eye and encouraging words with me.

Huge thanks, hugs, and cookies to my critique partners; Kellie, Christa, and Emily. I cannot thank you each enough for once again sharing your time and brilliance with me. Hannah got this ending because of you!

A simple "thank you" isn't big enough for my husband, Paul, and my children, Emily and Brett. Your love and support brought this book to life. Thank you for standing by me, for your constant encouragement, and for the coffee, chocolate, and hugs when I needed them.

My heart is humbled before God and His unfailing love. Thank You, Lord, for giving me the chance to share this story.

And finally, thank you to all of you . . . my reader friends. There are millions of books in the world and I am so blessed that you chose to read this one. Thank you for being a part of the Shaw family, for cheering for them, crying with them, and loving them. None of this would be possible without you and I am deeply grateful for you. I hope you'll be back for book three and Kate's story.

Soli Deo Gloria

"Michelle Keener's novel could be classified as rom-com, however, there is a depth to her characters that goes beyond quirky and cute . . . to illustrate the patience of God when He seeks us . . . I highly recommend this novel."

—SUZY PARISH
Author of *Flowers from Afghanistan*, Awarded a Bronze Medal by the Military Writers Society of America

Mission Hollywood

a Red Carpet Romance
Book One

MICHELLE KEENER

Read Lily and Ben's Story . . .

A Hollywood bad boy. A pastor's daughter.
What could possibly go wrong?

Movie star Ben Prescott arrives back in Hollywood after causing a scandal with his ex-girlfriend in Rome. Chased through the airport by paparazzi, he jumps into a limo hoping for a quick getaway. Instead he finds Lily Shaw, a pastor's daughter and preschool teacher. When the paparazzi capture a photo of the two of them together, Ben's agent demands that he do whatever it takes to keep the story from hitting the gossip pages . . . even volunteer to work at Lily's church.

Sparks fly as the movie star and the pastor's daughter work side by side. When Lily accompanies Ben to the premiere of his latest movie, Hollywood takes notice. Under intense media scrutiny and pressure from the movie industry, Ben must risk his career to follow his heart, but Lily wants the one thing he doesn't have, faith.

Mission Hollywood is an inspirational story about love, faith, and second chances.

For more information about
Michelle Keener
&
Made in Hollywood
please visit:

www.michellekeener.com
www.facebook.com/mkeenerwrites
@MKeenerWrites
www.instagram.com/mkeenerwrites

For more information about
AMBASSADOR INTERNATIONAL
please visit:

www.ambassador-international.com
@AmbassadorIntl
www.facebook.com/AmbassadorIntl

If you enjoyed this book, please consider leaving us a review on
Amazon, Goodreads, or our website.